DYLAN

D.L. Gardner

Dylan
D.L. Gardner
Copyright © 2018 by D.L. Gardner

D.L. Gardner
Port Orchard WA
http://gardnersart.com

Dylan/ D.L. Gardner. -- 1st ed.

This book is dedicated to all the people of the world who
struggle to find themselves.
May you realize the pearls within.

*We all have hopes and fears. We all make mistakes. We all doubt
ourselves. You're no different.*

-Liona

Contents

C Chapter 1

A Touch of the Uncommon

Uncle Jim rolled his wheelchair all over Windy Point looking to buy a suit I could wear to graduation. I jogged behind him trying to keep up. What a sight we made! Two fellas shopping; one an old bearded Rumpelstiltskin-looking guy; long gray beard, curly hair sticking out from under his wool cap—while it was too warm to wear a wool cap—spinning his wheels like some sort of speed-demon at a special Olympics game. And me in my blue jeans tagging behind, my flannel shirt too short for my long arms, the cuffs flopping like beagle's ears, my shirt tail flapping in the breeze. I followed because that's what you do with Uncle Jim. You follow. Follow and listen cause he's full of wisdom. He says things that touch you inside and make you think–and make you feel.

We came to the thrift shop at the corner of Maple and Oak. Uncle Jim stopped for a minute, giving me time to peer into the glass window. There was a grandfather clock with a clapper missing, a wooden high chair that looked like an antique, and a mannequin wearing a pleated skirt, a white blouse and a vest. Someone had draped a backpack over one of her shoulders and I think they meant for her to look like a schoolgirl. I chuckled a little because she was too old to wear those kinds of clothes. Just like I was too old to go to school anymore.

"Let's go to Ame's Hardware," Uncle Jim said, without going into the store.

"But—" I thought to argue, but the words didn't come right away.

7

"You're starting a new life, now Dylan. You don't need clothes people wore and left behind. It's time someone bought you something new."

The local hardware store carries everything. So much that you can't even find the hardware. Candy, home décor, barbecues, sports items, shoes. The store carries clothes too, but not many, and no sizes for boys my height. I don't fit into the men's sizes because I'm too skinny.

"Guess your slacks we bought you last Christmas will do for pants. They still fit?" Uncle Jim made another turn around the T-shirt aisle, rustling through racks of sale items until he came up with a nice white dress shirt. "Try it on."

I pulled my flannel off without unbuttoning it— my sweaty chest now bared—and slipped on the shirt, worried about the smell I might leave behind if we didn't buy it. As soon as I buttoned the top button a grimace came over his wrinkled face.

"Sleeves are short," he said.

"I can roll them up. See?" I folded the cuff of one sleeve over and over until it rolled neatly on my elbow.

Uncle Jim nodded, and his smile returned. "Works for me if it works for you," he said. "Give it here."

Later that night while driving back home from the school, Aunt Agnes let us know she didn't like that I rolled my sleeves up for something as ritzy as a graduation. Said it wasn't appropriate. I didn't see the problem because I wore my gown over it anyway.

"Stop your bellyaching," Uncle Jim told her. He was in the back of the van looking out the rear window. He could have sat on the seat next to me, but Aunt Agnes was always rough moving him, so instead of causing a fight, he just stayed in his wheel chair. "It's the best we could do. He's at that awkward age when nothing fits."

"It's his own fault he can't find clothes to fit. Other tall boys have clothes that fit nicely."

8

"He's too skinny," Uncle Jim argued.

"He should be working out, then. Getting into sports or something. He's lazy."

Aunt Agnes was never low on insults. It bothered Uncle Jim more than it bothered me.

"He doesn't connect the dots right," I heard Aunt Agnes complain to my cousin Shirley.

My cousin rode shotgun anytime we went anywhere together. She looked over her shoulder at me with eyes so blue you'd think they were going to jump out past those thick pasty eyelashes like a fish in a pond chasing a rooster tail. She scoffed while Aunt Agnes kept talking. "Did you hear him tonight stuttering and slobbering on his own spittle? He can't carry on a civil conversation. An embarrassment, that boy. Twenty years old and he's just now graduating. I doubt he can read past the third-grade level. Frankly, I'm surprised he graduated unless the school district just wanted to get rid of him." She shook her head as she made a right-hand turn into our driveway. "Really! Now what?"

I rolled my eyes. But Uncle Jim growled, and then went into a coughing fit. He didn't say anything though. Once we came to a stop, Aunt Agnes lowered the lift, and Uncle Jim steam-rolled into the house. I followed him inside with Aunt Agnes at my heels. Uncle Jim threw his baseball cap on the couch, and grumbled something fierce, maneuvering his chair through the litter in our living room. I could see a fight coming. Aunt Agnes and Uncle Jim fought a lot. Usually about me. I appreciated his support, but I didn't like him yelling. I didn't like seeing him upset because he'd always go into a coughing fit or run up a fever. Besides, the shrill screaming Aunt Agnes did remind me of my mother and how she sounded when she hit me with a belt. I dodged into my room and waited for Aunt Agnes to leave, holding my hands over my ears until the front door slammed.

After a few moments of silence, the TV came on and I peeked out of my room.

"News is on," Uncle Jim said.

I joined him on the couch next to his wheel chair and watched the news with him, but I mostly watched him. His face lost some of the redness he had when he was arguing with Aunt Agnes, but there were tears in his eyes. He patted me on the knee.

"It'll be okay. You'll be fine."

There was nothing I wouldn't do for Uncle Jim. He was always there for me. If he hadn't been, I'd be in a foster home with strangers somewhere. Uncle Jim fought for custody. Said that I was family and family needed to stick together.

"You'll get that grant for culinary school that you wanted," he whispered to me during the commercials. "You'll get in and you'll be a famous chef. I just know it!"

I smiled at the thought of being a famous chef. I loved to cook, and I was good at it. I cooked all of Uncle Jim's meals.

"We'll talk tomorrow. Got some forms to fill out. When I get home from the hospital. Okay?" He turned to me and smiled through his tears. I nodded.

Even after the excitement died down, I still didn't feel very good. I crawled in my bed with my clothes on and buried myself under the covers like I usually do when I get that sick feeling inside, like something's wrong. We'd had a long day; sleep came quickly.

The morning was grey and foggy so only a little light passed through my window, but enough to wake me up. We didn't use the heat this time of year, so I put on my hoody. I heard Uncle Jim in the bathroom. I yawned, stretched, then trooped into the kitchen and filled the tea kettle for coffee. Uncle Jim didn't say anything when he rolled into the living room and turned on the TV. I figured he still mulled over the words he and Aunt Agnes had exchanged.

Once his coffee was done, I took it out to him. "Is Aunt Agnes coming for you again this morning?" I asked. The less I saw of Aunt Agnes the better.

"Yes. I have an early appointment."

"Then I'm going for a walk."

I didn't want to leave. I'd rather spend the morning with him. We used to watch the news together and talk about what was going on in the world. Since his kidneys started acting up we didn't have those times anymore.

"I understand," Uncle Jim said. "We'll spend time together this evening."

"I'd like that." I gave him a smile, hoping it would cheer him up. "I'll do some beach combing. I'll bring some oysters back for tonight's stew." I grabbed my pail from the porch steps.

I might be slow, but I have something no one else has. Magic. I can make a dinner out of thin air, but I like using real ingredients too. I usually mix and match, collecting fresh food off the beach and then preparing a meal with a snap of my fingers.

"You be careful and don't bust your knuckles shucking them oysters," Uncle Jim shouted as he rolled his wheelchair to the front door.

"I'll try," I called back to him and waved. Little chance I wouldn't bust my knuckles, or bruise my fingers, or scrape my knees, but no sense worrying Uncle Jim. I walked briskly to the beach, which was pretty much our backyard. Uncle Jim didn't want a fence. Not having a fence gave the appearance that we had a lot more property than Uncle Jim paid for. I could walk past the sand dunes in our yard and keep going until I reached the sea.

My magic came from the ocean. I didn't even have to be there to get empowerment. All I had to do was close my eyes and imagine the foamy surf splashing over the oyster beds, and visualize the water gliding gracefully down the beach, leaving imprints of its ripples in the sand. If I meditated long enough, the power flowed into me and tingled the left side of my body. If I wanted to use the energy, I had to use my left hand, or left foot, or whatever was on the left side of me to wield it.

Sometimes the magic came on its own and wasn't as pleasant. When that happened, my body felt as if I stuck a butter knife in a toaster. I would freeze up as if I were electrocuted, even if I had no desire to wield any magic. I had no control over what I did with all the extra power. Such events happened twice in my childhood and both times were in the presence of my mother when she was angry with me.

I shook my head. I had to stop thinking about the past. The sun beat down on my back, and a flock of seagulls called.

Anyway, Uncle Jim didn't like me dwelling on the dark days. He told me to keep control of my thoughts.

So, I trudged on through the sand, hoping I'd run into my friend Tim Lan. Tim Lan used to live in Vietnam and spoke with a funny accent that kept me on my toes trying to understand. He was a little guy. Skinny like me. His skin was darker than mine though, kind of like what my coffee looks like when I put cream in it. He smiled a lot. I mean a lot! And his grin was almost too big for his face, but he had white teeth and sparkling eyes. I learned all my oyster picking skills from watching Tim Lan shuck. He'd flop open oysters faster than me, and he never seemed to scrape his knuckles like I did.

I had my quota of oysters before my wristwatch read ten o'clock. I didn't feel like going home right away as Uncle Jim never came back from his appointments before three. So, I figured I had time to do my magic. I performed this simple trick a lot in secret when I was a younger. I considered it just a silly pastime, but I had to hide from mother because I never knew what would set her off. If she saw me use magic and got mad, then I'd have to stop, and playing with magic was one of the few enjoyments I ever had. Not so with Uncle Jim. He even watched me once and thought it was cool.

I set an opened oyster shell in front of me and with my left hand, flicked my fingers to get the magic moving. Once the energy tingled and made even my fingernails twitch, I made a tiny circle in the air about a quarter of an inch above the shell. Repeatedly I'd spin, drumming up more and more power inside of me and directing it into my hands. Soon the pretty colors in the oyster shells adhered to my rotating finger so that they looked like lasers. I twirled and twisted and rolled those colors into little balls. There were enough colors in one large shell to make three or four of these marbles. There were seven shells on the beach in front of me, so I would have twenty some marbles when I finished. So, entranced with the magic swirling before my eyes, I failed to notice a man watching me until his shadow darken the sand. I looked over my shoulder and there was Tim Lan wide-eyed with his usual friendly grin. He didn't say anything, he just stood there looking at the shells, the twirling colors, and the marbles.

"What?" I asked. His staring made me uncomfortable.

"Watching." he mumbled and pointed to my venture.

At first, I was self-conscious and considered stopping, but he encouraged me by nodding. "Go, go ahead, Em." he said. He liked to call me "Em". Means 'friend' in Vietnamese.

Once I started up again I decided I liked his audience, so I took my time and demonstrated to Tim Lan how I made the oyster marbles. I knew he wouldn't be able to spin shells into little balls like I do, because Uncle Jim told me my magic was one-of-a-kind. I wasn't supposed to show anyone my tricks, but I had talked to Tim Lan before and he was a nice guy who taught me what he knew about sea life. I figured I owed him something. His grin grew wide and he stooped down next to me and picked one of the marbles up, revolving the iridescent ball in between his fingers as though he held a precious jewel. I nodded and smiled, proud of myself for making him happy.

"Where'd you learn?" he asked, his accent thick.

"Oh, nowhere really. I just do it."

"Hmm," he grunted. "Make the marble shine."

"Shine?"

He rolled up the sleeves to his thick denim jacket, pushing the cuffs to just below his elbows. His breath smelled like raw oysters, so I knew he'd been shucking and eating them. Sand speckled his coarse black hair like dandruff. His pants hugged to his muscular calves, showing off his sandals he told me once were hand made from hemp. The scent of ocean clung to him. A fragrance that adhered to me, too.

"Watch me," he said, and began rotating the marble in his hands. "Watch the pearl," Faster and faster he rubbed and soon the marble let out a faint light. "You see? Anything like this can shine. Good job!"

He held the glowing ball out for me to inspect. The pearl was cool, not warm like I thought something glowing like that should be. Amazed, I nodded. "How did you do that?"

"Magic. Like you." Wrinkles lined his eyes when he smiled, but age had not taken him captive. I would guess him to be a year or so older than Uncle Jim. "I can take one? Show my wife?"

"Sure," I said. "You can have them all." I plucked all the other marbles from their shells and put them in the palm of his calloused hand. I could make more anyway, so giving them away didn't much matter to me. He quickly shoved the marbles in his pocket and patted me on the back, nodding a thank you.

The mist had turned to rain, so I stood and brushed the wet sand off my pants. "I need to go home now and make coffee for Uncle Jim for when he gets home."

Tim Lan nodded, and as he did his whole body shook with happiness, which made me laugh. "Very good, I will see you again!" he said. "Maybe you'll make more? Maybe we can trade?"

"Yeah. Maybe." I watched him traipse across the oyster beds towards the woods beyond. He told me once he had a shanty on the beach near Reef Cove, but I'd never seen his house. Reef Cove was an all-day walk from our beach, but I guess Tim Lan didn't have much else to do except walk the shoreline. He turned and waved at me, his teeth glowing like the moon. I waved back and then headed toward our cul-de-sac and the small house Uncle Jim and I called home.

Right then the van pulled up. Aunt Agnes opened the back and lowered the platform for Uncle Jim's wheelchair. From where I was, he looked like Dr. Bones McCoy emerging out of the Starship Enterprise at the space station Yorktown, or somewhere like that. He took no time at all scooting off the ramp and up to the house. I hoped he'd be alone, but after Aunt Agnes folded the van up with her device and headed into the house too. I entered the house through the back door to the kitchen, so she wouldn't see me.

C Chapter 2

Annabella

"He can't stay here by himself for that long." I cringed at the sound of Aunt Agnes' voice. Why can't she just go away?

"Why not? He's an adult. He can keep watch over things." Uncle Jim contested.

"You think he's capable of keeping this place intact?"

"I'm coming home every night!" Uncle Jim's patient voice had already left him.

I peeked around the corner into the living room, just enough to see them but not enough so they'd know I was there. Uncle Jim's face flushed red, and he foamed at the mouth.

Aunt Agnes paced around the living room, picked a newspaper up off the floor, and tossed it on the couch.

Uncle Jim grabbed the same paper and slammed it on the coffee table. "He's never shown himself incapable. He's smart enough to finish high school, so don't you be talking him down." Uncle Jim threw his baseball cap on the couch and glowered at her something fierce.

"Someday that boy is going to be a major disappoint and you'll wish you had listened to me," Aunt Agnes went on.

"Listen to you to do what?"

"Put him in a home. You aren't well enough to take care of him and he's incapable of living a normal life." She took a deep breath. "I'll be coming to get you tomorrow, and every day after that until I can arrange for bus service."

Her high heels clicked brashly on the wood floor in the living room.

Uncle Jim glanced at me briefly as he passed by the kitchen and wheeled himself over to the hallway. There was a sadness in his eyes I hadn't seen before. "I guess that's what must happen, then," he said to Aunt Agnes.

"I don't care what you say, either," Aunt Agnes went on. "Tell Dylan we'll be finding him a place to live. I'm not going to have him in this house alone if you're going to be gone so much. Shirley's been calling boarding homes." She looked up at me, a startled gasp on her face. "Oh! Dylan! I didn't see you."

Of course, she didn't. She didn't look past her pug nose, and half the time she denied my existence anyway. I shrugged.

She always tried to dress proper, and today was no exception. A dull gray skirt, coat and gloves, she could blend into the fog easily enough. Younger than Uncle Jim, she looked older because she frowned all the time and had wrinkles and creases in her face like a dried-up plum.

"I'm not going anywhere," I said, a bit surprised at her talk about moving me out of my house. She had no right to say something like that. This house belonged to me and Uncle Jim.

"I'm not telling him any such thing," Uncle Jim defended me. He gave that funny smirk when he glanced my way, like we both knew Aunt Agnes didn't know what she was talking about. I smiled. He spun his wheelchair around to face her. "I'll take care of Dylan like I always have. And Dylan will take care of me, like he always does. I'll also get my own bus pass."

Aunt Agnes didn't like to be spoken to like that, she would rather boss people around, but there's no fighting Uncle Jim. So, she huffed a bit and slung her purse over her arm. "Have it your way, you always do," she muttered.

17

"Just don't blame me if he burns the house down!" She stepped outside and shut the door behind her.

I grunted the same time Uncle Jim puffed his cheeks and blew out a whistle.

"I'm sorry, Dylan," he whispered to me. He probably thought she hurt my feelings, but I didn't care about anything she said anymore. I was happy here with him and that's all that mattered.

He started to pull off his coat, which was wet from rain, so I rushed to help him and hooked the dripping jacket on the coat rack by the heater. "Your dinner will be ready in a jiffy," I said. "You're going to like this dish. Chicken Alfredo with a side of oyster stew and homemade bread."

I left Uncle Jim and went into the kitchen. I knew he was hungry and I wanted to pick up his spirits. I made real bread, well, almost real because I cheated, I tapped my thumbs together which created an electrical charge, which in turn suspended the dough in the air and worked the bread back and forth like sugar and cream in a taffy machine. I popped the loaf in the oven. For the main course, I closed my eyes and imagined Chicken Alfredo. The magic raced through my body and settled in my left hand which I then waved over a glass casserole dish. Soon juicy chunks of chicken manifested in a sauce. Another flip of the wrist speckled the concoction with paprika. I tossed the casserole in the oven and baked it until the meat fell apart and the sauce bubbled with an aroma so delicious I could sense the flavor just from the smell. Cooking didn't' take but a few minutes because a lot of power raced through my veins when I baked. Of course, the meal came out all juicy with spices and relishes and still the right texture for Uncle Jim who had trouble with his teeth. With the oyster chowder that bubbled on top of the stove I had prepared a feast.

When Uncle Jim rolled his chair down the hall to the bathroom I set the table for the both of us. I spooned out a bowl of oyster stew, and dished the casserole onto Uncle

Jim's plate, making sure he had the two biggest breasts of chicken. I sat down and waited for him.

"Coffee ready?" he asked as he rolled to the table.

"Yes sir," I poured coffee into his favorite mug, the white one with VFW in gold letters, and placed the mug in front of him.

"How was your day today?"

"I spent the day on the beach."

"Ah! Good."

"Tim Lan was there too."

"How is the old fart?" Uncle Jim met Tim Lan one time and they had a long conversation about Hanoi. He told me once that because Tim Lan was Vietnamese he had a soft spot in his heart for him. People like Tim Lan were the reason that Uncle Jim gave up the use of his legs and would have given up his life. Uncle Jim is a hero.

"Smiley as always," I said. "He watched me make marbles this morning."

"Did he? What did he say about your magical gems?"

"He liked them. He asked for some, so I gave him all that I made. I should bring one home for you. Tomorrow maybe."

"You're a very generous young man."

"Thank you," I straightened my back a little and smiled.

He sipped the coffee to taste. "Needs more sugar."

I'm forever forgetting where I put things so as I rose to look for the sugar bowl, he took my arm. "Sit down and just use your magic, Dylan. I've something important to tell you."

I only had to hold my finger over his mug for his brew to sweeten and when he hovered his hand over the cup I stopped. I looked up at him. His face was gray. I had never seen him so colorless before, and his eyes had a yellow to them that turned my stomach.

19

"I have to have dialysis every day from now on."

I'm no doctor and I don't understand medical terms much, but I gathered that was why Aunt Agnes was supposed to come and get him every day. My brow furrowed in response to his frown.

"Don't worry. I won't let Aunt Agnes send you to some other home. She gets some off-the-wall ideas sometimes." He looked at me with an eyebrow raised. "That is, if you don't want to go."

"I'm staying by you, Uncle Jim. You need me to be here."

He nodded. His hands trembled as he lifted the cup to his lips and some of the coffee spilled onto his lap, so I raced to the sink and got a rag. He didn't touch his dinner and there was a look on his face like he wanted to tell me something but instead he just shook his head. "I'm not ready to eat. Come sit with me in the living room." He placed his coffee mug between his knees and rolled out of the kitchen.

I followed him, turning off the light and looking back over my shoulder to make sure I shut off the stove because I forget to do that sometimes. Uncle Jim taught me to check everything before I leave a room. He told me that if I take my time, whatever I do will be done right.

I sat across from him on the couch and he rolled his wheelchair up to the coffee table and set his coffee cup down in front of him. I waited with my hands folded on my lap for a long time before he said anything. The setting sun shone brightly through the picture window, nearly blinding me because I was looking right at the glow. I closed the blinds. The room dimmed, and I stumbled over some newspapers on the floor, and bumped into the TV tray that had a puzzle partially put together. I switched on a lamp and then sat across from Uncle Jim again. He hadn't said anything to me, just sipped his coffee and made some faces like he was worried and frustrated and couldn't think of

20

how to say what he wanted. And then he looked at me square in my eyes and I knew something was wrong.

"Whatever happens…" he started and when I tilted my head and gave him a questioning look, he shook his head and started over. "Whatever happens, Dylan, you have to know what you want in life."

I nodded. I was a simple person. That made sense to me. "I just want to live here with you," I said.

He shook his head with a heavy frown. "That's not good enough. I'm not always going to be here." I didn't like the sound of that, so I was about to protest but he stopped me. "If I wasn't here. What would you want in life?"

I thought for a long moment, staring into his sad gray eyes. "To be a chef," I said quietly, certain that this was a trick question.

He shook his head. "That's what you want to do for a living, which is not the same thing. Ask yourself, what do you want out of life?"

I couldn't for the life of me think of anything other than what I just told him. I stuttered, starting a few sentences, I thought I could finish. "To be happy?" I finally said.

"And what does that mean for you?"

Well, being happy meant that I would be with him, but he made me take his presence out of the equation, so that was a stumper. I shrugged.

"What do you find about me that makes you happy when you're around me?" he asked quietly. I think he was trying to help me answer his question.

"You're good to me. You treat me like I'm a human being. You love me?"

"Ah! There is the answer, Dylan. Love."

"That's what I want out of life?"

"That's what you should be wanting out of life." Tears welled in his eyes. I didn't understand why. "You

21

find love by surrounding yourself with people who are good to you, just like you said. Don't settle for less, son."

I nodded not sure if I would be able to find anyone else who would be good to me. Certainly not Aunt Agnes, nor my cousin, Shirley. They were never good to me. While I was pondering who he might be talking about, he tapped me on the knee.

"In my room, under the bed there's a blue box with a lid. Go get it."

I jumped up, bumping the table so the coffee spilled again and veered for the kitchen to get a rag, but he waved me by and wiped the coffee with the cuff of his sleeve. I hurried to his room and turned on the light. I hacked out a cough from the dust under the bed. Uncle Jim and I clean sometimes but this was one place we hadn't even thought about since I can remember, if ever. I pulled out what must have been an old blue shoebox and wiped off the cobwebs with the corner of my coat.

"Be careful with that box," he called out to me, so I carried the package with two hands. He pushed his coffee cup out of the way and I laid the box down in front of him, kneeling by his wheelchair to get a close look as he opened it. I loved surprises. Even though he had big hands, he treated the crumbled old newspapers delicately, unwrapping the contents slower than I would have. When the last yellowed newsprint was removed, he held a porcelain figurine of a beautiful lady in a pink dress.

"This is a Royal Daulton." His voice was soft and gentle, and he handled the doll with the utmost care as he turned the statuette slowly, inspecting her. He held the bottom up toward me and pointed at the signature. "See that signature? She's old. She was your grandmother's."

"Your mom's?"

He nodded. "Annabella is her name. That was your grandmother's name. First issued in 1938. Your grandma had quite a collection, but your mother and Agnes took the other figurines and sold them. I managed to save this one. Worth lots of money now, but she's more a treasure to keep."

I sat awed at the delicate statue, her pale hands holding her skirt as she curtsied, a basket of tiny blue flowers on her arm and a friendly smile on her face. I immediately fell in love and wiped the drool from my face.

"She's yours, Dylan."

"No!" I said, afraid to touch her when he handed her to me. "I'll break her."

"No, you won't," he assured me. "You'll be careful. Go ahead. Take her."

The porcelain was cold to my touch, cold and smooth. I ran my finger over the indent of her skirt and touched her tiny hat, smiling up at Uncle Jim in gratitude. He pushed the box toward me.

"Put her away and don't let your mother or Agnes see her or she won't be yours for long. I don't have anything else left from my Mom or Dad to give you. I was overseas when they died. I found this packed away in an old dresser Agnes was going to throw out."

I wrapped the paper around the figurine just as carefully as Uncle Jim had unwrapped Annabella. "Where should I put her?"

He shrugged. "Someplace you know is going to stay with you."

I didn't own much. I had my own room, but it was empty except for my suitcase, my backpack and some dirty clothes I had thrown on the floor. Uncle Jim had me do laundry twice a week and today wasn't the day. I wanted to put Annabella on my shelf, but that didn't seem secret enough, not with Aunt Agnes coming over every day now, so I put the box in the bottom of my backpack and tucked a pair of sweatpants on top.

C Chapter 3

Changing Tide

Aunt Agnes said our cottage was a dump. She said since we were on the coast, the property was worth more than the house. She complained that our shack was hardly fit for two full grown men to live in, but Uncle Jim and I were happy. We didn't care how much room we had inside, because I would rather be outside on the beach, and he, well he was in a wheel chair and couldn't do a whole lot anyway. We played chess together sometimes, but mostly Uncle Jim would watch sports on TV, or read. That is, when he was home. Now that he was at the Kidney Center every day, we needed even less room. The yard was nothing to keep up. I had a push mower to mow the grass and dandelions, and Uncle Jim liked pruning the roses out front. We worked on the yard together in the summer time. Even though the outside needed painting, I think the house had a nice appearance. About as good as the other homes in the neighborhood. The inside was bad, but we didn't let our mess make it out the door. Even Uncle Jim admitted we were sloppy, but the only ones who saw our clutter were me and Uncle Jim and Aunt Agnes whenever she came around. We didn't care to clean up just for her. We knew where everything was, and the dishes were always washed, and food put away.

A white picket fence decorated the front yard, and honeysuckle draped over it. The backyard was sandy with a fire pit. We roasted hot dogs in the summer together. Everything was set up for Uncle Jim to get around easily in his wheelchair.

"You get outside this morning," Uncle Jim told me as Aunt Agnes pushed him out the door.

"I will. I'll get us some oysters. Maybe some razor clams today and make another stew– that is if you'll be hungry."

Uncle Jim nodded, but Aunt Agnes moved too quickly to carry on any more conversation with him. She rode up the lift with him, strapped in his chair and stepped out, slammed the back door and then got in the driver's seat. The van left with a puff of black smoke. Uncle Jim mentioned many times how he hated breathing all the carbon monoxide that collected in the back of the old van. He said the valves were shot and someone needed to replace them, but no one besides Uncle Jim knew how to work on cars, and Uncle Jim wasn't strong enough to lift the head. He suggested I do the lifting and I would have except Uncle Jim never had the money to replace the gaskets, so fixing the van was only something we talked about doing. Maybe someday we can save up some money and buy a new vehicle, or at least get a used van that doesn't smoke.

When Uncle Jim left that morning with Aunt Agnes, I took a bucket to the beach and started foraging. I found oysters, but razor clams are harder to locate especially on an oyster beach. I'd have to walk a mile or so, or else wait for low tide. I was still learning how to find them. Tim Lan taught me to dig in the sand whenever I saw water squirting up out of a hole. But clams are tricky and sometimes they're sneaky and can sense you digging for them. I don't know how seagulls survive unless they have an X-ray vision because they dig up clams all the time. Tim Lan also instructed me to leave the oyster shells on the beach because that was the law. He told me always to obey that law because the law was made to help the shellfish reseed, so we'll have something to eat next year.

I gathered my quota for the day early because the tide was out leaving lots of beds exposed. As hard as I tried to open the shells the way that Tim Lan's showed me, my knuckles still bled. I didn't care.

Ten o'clock was way too early to go home, so I set a few empty shells in front of me and then spun some marbles. Not many. I was distracted by the cold fog which settled low on the water, making the oyster beds, the ocean, and the clouds melt into one gray mass. Even my coat matched the weather. I found my spirits graying as well. I expected to see Tim Lan, but he never showed up.

Being alone that morning left an emptiness inside of me along with a strange feeling eating my insides. I thought not seeing Tim Lam was the reason that I sensed something wasn't right. I'd seen him every other day this week because Uncle Jim was at doctor appointments which gave me a lot of time alone on the beach. Bored with making marbles, I pocketed them and decided to go home.

I was surprised to see the van parked at our house so early. Seemed like Uncle Jim just left, and he's usually gone for at least four hours. Maybe they didn't need him to come in everyday after all. I hoped not. I miss him when he's gone.

Aunt Agnes jumped out of the driver's seat as I crossed the street. Instead of going around to the back to let Uncle Jim out of the van, she went running to our front door and started knocking so hard the big picture window rattled.

"Open up, Dylan!" She was bundled up in a black coat, her multicolored scarf wrapped tight around her neck and the fog had taken the curl out of her thinning hair. Aunt Agnes rarely looked unkempt, however today her mascara had formed dark masses under her eyes and she had no lipstick on.

"I'm not in there," I answered as I jogged up behind her and reached over to unlock the door. Her perfume gagged me as I brushed by. I put my hand over my nose and pretended I was about to sneeze.

"Get inside! I have something important to tell you."

I glanced at the van when I opened the door for her, wondering why Uncle Jim wasn't coming in. I didn't have time to ask, as she took me by the hem to my hoody and dragged me into the house. She made me sit on the couch and paced across the rug in front of me. The room darkened when she pulled the curtains closed. Three times she gave me an angry glance and I thought I had done something terrible. I held my hands on my lap and waited for the hammer. That's what Uncle Jim would say when he knew Aunt Agnes was mad. He called her temper a hammer. She tossed her coat on the armchair, and then rubbed her arms, and then wrung her hands in such a way I thought something was wrong with her. No longer did she look mad. Upset, yes.

"Do you need me to get Uncle Jim inside for you?" I asked.

"No," she snapped, pacing again.

"But he's…" I didn't like him being in the van by himself, and me being in the house alone with Aunt Agnes, especially when she was acting like this. I'd feel safer with him in the house. "He shouldn't be out there alone."

"No! she snapped.

I cowered back onto the couch. "Did I do something wrong?" My heart beat heavy not knowing what was coming. I felt bile coming up from my stomach too, and cold sweat on my forehead.

She breathed deep and looked me square in the face. Those gray eyes of hers made me want to crawl behind the pillows on the sofa, especially with all that make-up smeared around them. For the first time, I noticed the whites of her eyes were red, like she'd been crying. "Dylan, your Uncle passed."

27

I know I was supposed to understand her, but I didn't. "What do you mean?" I asked.

"He passed, Dylan. Oh god, how do I do this?" Rolling her eyes and her head at the same time made me feel slow. I didn't know what she was talking about. "Maybe you can't understand what that means." She looked at me again and moved closer so that I could smell the breath mint in her mouth. "Think about what I just said. Your uncle isn't coming back."

She kept on with her explaining and I just stared at her trying to comprehend all the words she was tossing at me so fast. Nothing she said made any sense. Of course, Uncle Jim is coming back. This is his house. He lives here. Where else would he go?

She finally sighed and rolled her eyes as if my 'slowness' exasperated her. "He's dead!" she said. "Can you understand that? Dead!"

At first, I couldn't move, I mean my arms just hung at my side, and a big lump formed in my throat. My head heated up. My mind went blank. She turned her back on me and walked to the window as though she had an interest in the garden, but the curtains were closed. My lips trembled. I had no idea what to do or what to say. I don't know if what happened to me is called blacking out, but I felt that my brain wasn't connected to my body right then. I wasn't there. I didn't hear her after that. I got up and walked past her, threw open the door and marched to the van. The back of the old green Dodge was locked, so trying to yank the door open did nothing. I peeked in the window but couldn't see in because dirt and fingerprints smeared the glass from the inside. I opened the passenger door and crawled in the front. I then looked over the seat at the back of the van where Uncle Jim should have been, but he wasn't there. His wheelchair was there, and I could smell him and there was a bit of his dandruff on the back of his seat. Not him though.

The lump in my throat grew larger, my heart beat hard and I thought I was going to faint, so I opened the window. I sat in the van for a long time thinking maybe I was having a bad dream and needed to wake up. But how do you make yourself wake up from a nightmare? Especially if you're already awake?

Sitting in the van didn't help. Uncle Jim didn't magically appear. Nothing changed. Nothing except the weather. The fog lifted and there was a touch of blue in the sky. The sunlight gave everything color, the hedge along the driveway, the grass with the dandelions peeking through. Even the clouds broke apart and became big powder puffs in the sky, white and cottony. I could see the ocean in the distance beyond our house, the fog lifting and floating away like steam out of a tea kettle. I wasn't cold, nor did I feel damp and from the sun beating on me through the window, I could see the day was going to be nice and sunny.

Good weather wasn't right either because it didn't fit the day. The weather should be stormy. Big thunderclouds should be letting loose with lightning and thunder and wind. Trees should be toppling over, and sirens should be screeching. How could the sun be out?

Today wasn't the day for Uncle Jim to go away. We had plans. We were going to talk about school. We might have played a game of checkers. I had plans for dinner, too. I would have cooked him a roast with mashed potatoes, gravy and candied carrots as a side. He loved roast beef. Just this morning he told me to have the coffee hot for him when he got home. I would have. He knows I would have.

Aunt Agnes stayed in the house while I sat in the van thinking all these thoughts and more. Maybe I scared her being out there. Or maybe she was glad, so she didn't have to try and explain anything else to me. She gets so frustrated with me. Maybe she didn't know what else to say.

29

The curtains to the house were open and I could see her through the picture window in the living room. She had the phone to her ear; her mouth was moving. She pushed back the curtains occasionally, to peek out at me. I should have gone back inside the house, I guess, and talked to her, or listened to her, but I didn't want to leave the van. Not without Uncle Jim.

C Chapter 4

Far Horizons

For three days, I stayed at my house by myself. I didn't go into Uncle Jim's room. I made him breakfast each day. Bacon and eggs over easy, and toast, just the way he liked it. I didn't even use magic to make the food but used my hands and grated the potatoes until the tips of my fingers were about to bleed. I set the table, and later I threw the food away because Uncle Jim didn't show up. After that I turned the TV on. The news. Uncle Jim's favorite station. I sat in front of the screen. When the news was over I switched to all of Uncle Jim's favorite programs and the sound nestled into an empty space inside of me and made me think maybe he was still here in his wheelchair, watching.

I didn't sleep at night. I tossed and turned and stared at the ceiling, listening to every sound the house made. The refrigerator, the heater. Sometimes a scratch of a mouse inside the walls gave the impression that maybe Uncle Jim was moving around in his bedroom.

Three days later around ten in the morning, I got a phone call.

"I'll be picking you up in an hour." Aunt Agnes said.

I paused, not sure if I heard right. "This is Dylan," I said.

"I know it's Dylan. I'm talking to you. The funeral is today and I'm coming to get you. Wear a suit and a tie if you have one and for Pete's sake change your underwear and your socks."

I hung up without saying anything. I didn't make breakfast that day. I had been sleepless and upset and I knew nothing would stay in my stomach even if I did eat. So why get more dishes dirty?

I didn't have a suit. All I had was the white shirt I wore at graduation and it was still dirty. I went to my room, locked the door tight because I didn't want Aunt Agnes coming into my bedroom when she got here. I had Annabella to take care of, after all. I looked at myself in the mirror. I hadn't had a haircut for three weeks. Uncle Jim and I were going to do that next Saturday when his VA check came. He needed some new undershirts and was going to buy me some socks because I had worn holes in all of mine.

I stood looking at my reflection, not critically, but not happy with myself. I was in my sweat pants and a ratty hoody. Kind of pathetic looking. My eyes had dark rings around them from not sleeping and not eating. I hadn't slept at all, thinking about Uncle Jim. Wishing he were still here. I didn't look all that healthy. I didn't feel good either.

Maybe I could get clean clothes with my magic. I closed my eyes and tried to get ahold of my thoughts, tried to calm myself so the magic could come. I visualized the beach like I normally do when I call on the superpowers; gentle waves rocking on shore, the sea foam and the oyster beds. Nothing happened, and I wondered if I had lost my touch. I shuddered and opened my eyes again. There were tears in me that I wouldn't let come out and that made concentrating hard. I stood still in front of the mirror for a long time, trying again and again to summons the magic. Maybe being sad complicated the matter. I breathed deeply and thought of what Uncle Jim would have offered as advice. Maybe he'd tell me to look toward the future. Maybe he'd remind me what a hard time I had breaking away from my Mom, but I did. And now look how much better life is for me. "Life isn't better without you, though

Uncle Jim," I said quietly, as if he were there in the mirror instead of my reflection.

I tried one more time and finally that warm sensation started trickling in. Almost comforting. I say almost because I pushed that feeling of comfort away. I didn't think feeling comfortable while Uncle Jim lay in a coffin at the church all alone was right. The comforting feeling turned into heat, which suddenly rushed to the whole left side of my body. The warmth pulsated as if waiting for instructions. I opened my eyes and looked at my reflection, my face red from the energy.

I had to verbally tell the magic what I wanted because, honestly, visualizing me in a suit and tie at this moment was near impossible. Lucky for me, the magic filled in all the blanks and dressed me properly.

Having clean clothes on made me feel better: a stiff white shirt with silver cufflinks, a royal blue tie, and a black pinstriped suit tailored to fit me perfectly. My dark eyes had somehow got their color back, my hair combed itself, and I even had a new pair of socks that was warm and wooly on my feet. Shiny loafers were at the foot of my bed, so I slipped them on.

I was ready, and no one knocked at my door, yet, so there was still time to unpack Annabella and hold her again. Funny but every time I took her out I could hear Uncle Jim's voice as plain as if he were sitting in the room with me, telling me about my grandma.

How delicate she felt in my hands, smooth and special, like a precious jewel. She made me think about gentle things, about how fine life was living here with Uncle Jim. I didn't need a future. I didn't need to go to culinary school. I could just stay home and take care of him forever if he'd let me. I'd be happy. He had told me I was more special than most folks because I had magic to call on.

33

And then I gasped because an odd thought came to me. My heart started racing. The magic still stirred, and I felt the blood and energy in my left hand pulsate as if there were a pair of bongo drums inside of me trying to beat their way out of my skin. Did I have that strong of magic to pull off what I was thinking? I mean, what would be the chances of bringing Uncle Jim back, again? The thought excited me!

Aunt Agnes pulled up in the driveway. I peeked out my bedroom window and saw her Buick, glad she hadn't driven the van. I don't think I could bear to see that big old Dodge ever again. When the car door slammed I quickly packed Annabella away into her newspaper and then the shoe box and then into my pack. By the time I stood at the mirror again brushing the creases out of my suit she knocked on my bedroom door. "Are you ready Dylan?"

"Yes, ma'am," I said.

"Well!" she huffed as I stepped out of the room and nearly bumped into her. "I hardly recognized you! Is that one of your uncle's old suits?"

I shrugged. I didn't want to lie but she didn't want to hear the answer anyway. Even though her clothes were pressed and clean, Aunt Agnes could have walked out of a horror movie. She wore a tight black skirt—I wondered how she could walk—and her jacket had shoulder pads that buffed her torso up like a football player. Her black veiled hat tipped to the side of her head seemed comical, as did the red lipstick on her wrinkled lips. I held back a laugh. The fresh air outside saved me from her perfume until I got into the back seat of the car.

Shirley was in the front also dressed in black, but she had a red scarf around her neck and didn't have the same vampire look as Aunt Agnes. Aside from her attitude I would have thought her pretty. Her blond hair curled in ringlets down her shoulders, her face touched up with powder, eyeliner framed her eyes and her lips were painted almost a purple color. She didn't smile when I got in the backseat of the car. Instead she snickered like she always does. "Why look at you, Dylan, you almost look normal."

"Hi Shirley," I said as blandly as I could. Uncle Jim knew how Shirley treated me. I remembered his advice when he told me to be nice to her no matter what she said. He told me ignoring her would be for my benefit, not hers. With much practice, I got pretty good at tuning her out.

She looked over her shoulder at me "You realize your mother will be there, don't you?"

A zap of electricity raced up my spine and my eyes popped wide open. No one told me my mother was coming to the funeral. Shirley grinned.

"Shirley why do you torture him?" Aunt Agnes whispered. "Don't worry, Dylan. Just stay with us and everything will be fine."

I sat in silence holding my hands together thinking about what might happen when I saw my mother. I hoped that the black magic didn't crawl through my veins at the sight of her, or that Shirley didn't hound me anymore about her. Shirley gave me one last, smug look as if something brewed in that demonic mind of hers.

Aunt Agnes turned the radio on, I think maybe to keep my cousin quiet. After we drove a while I relaxed and watched our little town crawl past the window. We stopped at the red light by the café where Uncle Jim and I used to go– he in his wheel chair and I strolling along next to him. He'd buy me cocoa in that coffee shop—cocoa with a cinnamon stick. I cracked my window a little bit to smell the aroma coming from the café.

"Shut your window, Dylan, I've got the heater on."

"Yes ma'am." I waited a few seconds until the scent drifted away before I rolled up the window.

We creeped past the store fronts, cars scrambling for parking places on the streets in front of them; the movie show flashing neon lights. Once we went through the last stoplight we picked up speed. One lane turned into two. We drove beyond our seaside town, through sandy hills and onto the freeway.

When we got to the chapel my heart skipped a beat. My mother stood by the front door to the funeral home holding hands with a dark-haired man with a beard. He wasn't dressed very well, but he had an overcoat that hid his dirty blue jeans. His shoes were as chewed up as my sneakers at home. My mother looked older than I remembered. I hadn't seen her for maybe two years. Thinner, and she still had that odd, jerk to her movements and kept her mouth open as if she didn't have the muscle strength to put her lips together. She wasn't dressed in proper funeral clothes either, but I doubt she had anything proper to wear. She wore jeans and a black frilly blouse that was cut low. Gray roots invaded the color of her dyed hair, like sea salt invading a muddy beach, straggled ends brushed her shoulders. She had to shake the loose hair out of her face so that she could see to wave at us. Shirley blew her a kiss gestured toward me with her thumb. I looked away. My mother forced a smile, her lips pale with lipstick. Powder covered her blemishes. "Dilly baby," she called out. Aunt Agnes drove on to park the car. I didn't want to get out, but Shirley opened the door for me, and my mother staggered down the sidewalk, arms out as if I would rush into them. I didn't. I took a step backward.

Any other time I had seen my mother after I was taken from her, Uncle Jim had been there. He could boss Mom, and his presence would give me courage to stick up for myself. There was no one now, only the snickering cousin whose flittering eyelashes and snarky smile hidden under her make-up added to my torment. The closer mother came, the more electrifying the heat in my body grew. The trembling began in my hands and I could feel the voltage crawling up my spine. I knew if she got too close I'd get a shock, so I took another step back. Aunt Agnes came in between the two of us.

"There's still a restraining order, Emma," she said.

My mother glared at Aunt Agnes and I thought those two would get in a fight right here at the chapel. Mother tossed her head, huffed, and glanced at her boyfriend. The look she gave my aunt gave me the chills. What a pair those two were with Aunt Agnes' hair pinned tight under a hat, old schoolmarm-looking, and mom bursting out of her clothing like she couldn't wait to get home and put her pajamas on. Mother's boyfriend pulled her away from Aunt Agnes just in time, and I sighed, relieved. I've seen Aunt Agnes and mother duke out their differences before. Not a pretty sight. I wonder sometimes how they survived growing up together. Uncle Jim was always the referee. He told me about some of their arguments. Not sure how those two women will settle things now that he's gone.

Before my mom took her boyfriend's hand she winked at me, and without saying another word after that, she followed him into the sanctuary swaying off balance. She had to hang on to him to walk, so I knew she was drunk.

"We'll wait a moment or two before we go in." Aunt Agnes picked up a program and fiddled with the trifold until the ends curled. I could tell she was heated by the way she rolled the brochure. Uncle Jim's photograph wound up in the shape of a cylinder, and then she slapped the tube against her dress, all the while keeping a keen eye on my mother. I made a note of where Mom sat, too. No way did I want to be near her.

"Dylan, your uncle's casket is in this other room, lying in state. Do you want to go pay your last respects?" Aunt Agnes asked me.

I did, but I didn't answer her.

"I do!" Shirley stepped toward the open door of the state room. I could see the flowers from the lobby; tall vases and wreaths of lilies and roses and forget-me-nots surrounding a black coffin. "Coming, Dylan?"

I didn't follow. I wanted to see him alone, so I waited with my hands in my pockets. Aunt Agnes smoothed out the program she had almost destroyed and read for a little bit. I guess she got tired of waiting because she looked up at me. "I'll be in the sanctuary in the back row. I'll save you and Shirley a seat. Come in quietly when you're done."

After Aunt Agnes left, Shirley stepped out of the state room dabbing at her eyes as if something was in them.

"Catching cold?" I asked. I know my question was mean, but this was Shirley and if those were real tears, and she had really cared about Uncle Jim she might have stopped by to see him while he was still alive. Not just in his coffin. Uncle Jim was good to all the family, to her too, but because he was old and in a wheel chair, Shirley never wanted to give him any time.

She brushed past me, bumping me a little on the way. I ignored her, slipped inside the state room and carefully closed the door.

The room was lit by the sun seeping through a large stained-glass window of red and gold design. A candle in a gold candelabra burned on the wooden platform above his coffin and an American flag was folded neatly on a table next to the altar. The atmosphere in there was heavy, creepy almost, but I wasn't going to let that bother me. This was Uncle Jim. I had nothing to be afraid of. The thick red carpet muted my footsteps as I walked up to the casket.

Man, I felt odd looking at him like that, like I was in a Steven King movie or something. So quiet, so still. Closed eyes. He wore a dark navy-blue suit too. I'd never seen him in that suit. He had a white carnation tucked in his pocket, and silver cufflinks on his cuffs, just like mine.

38

I ignored the sick in my stomach. I didn't like being around dead people. I'd never been to a funeral before. I shouldn't feel nauseous because this was Uncle Jim and I love Uncle Jim. I took his hand. Choking back tears, I started calling on my magic right away because I knew I would have to make this fast. I didn't want someone to walk in on us. The tingling came quickly. From experience, I found that the more I wanted something the faster the power came. Heat filled me, and soon my left hand throbbed, and there was even some iridescent color beaming out of my fingers.

"Uncle Jim," I said to him, and touched his face with the palm of my left hand. "You can get up now." I felt the magic travel from my fingers to his collar. I closed my eyes shut, wanting even harder than anything in the world to bring him back. I wanted so badly to have Uncle Jim here again that I thought I saw his chest rise when I opened my eyes.

"Uncle Jim!" I said.

He just lay there. The silence hit me like a bomb. It was so still in that room. I was acutely aware of the smell of roses from the flowers around his coffin. Another smell too coming from him, probably what they used to embalm him with and then that sick feeling returned. "Uncle Jim?" I said again and looked at his eyes. They were shut, not tight because that would have meant he was closing them himself. I thought I heard a voice in my head, so I listened. I swear the voice was Uncle Jim's.

"Dylan, everything is okay, now. I'm in a better place," he said, or so I thought. "I'm not coming home anymore."

That was all I heard. My heart sank, and reality hit me, after which the magic left, and I was touching the face of a cold corpse. I realized then this shell wasn't Uncle Jim. He was gone to that better place.

I wiped the wet from my eyes and swallowed the other tears that were trying to force their way out. My magic wasn't going to bring Uncle Jim back. Nothing was.

***

When the service was over Aunt Agnes, Shirley, and a few of my other cousins that I didn't know very well stood around outside in front of the chapel talking. I stood with them, but no one said anything to me. They all gossiped about how much they were going to miss Uncle Jim, and what a good man he was and that it was sad to see him die. They kind of argued over who knew him better, who was his favorite. I don't remember Uncle Jim mentioning any of them.

"Someone could give Dylan a ride back to the house while we go to the graveside," Aunt Agnes suggested.

"Not me, what about you Pete," Shirley chimed in.

"I'm parked behind everyone. Can't get out," Pete said.

"So, what do we do with Dylan?" Shirley whispered, and then glanced at me. I was used to this treatment, but today I felt I should say something.

"Why don't you ask me what I want to do?" I said right to Shirley's face. She gave me a dirty look and turned her back to me. I was used to people talking around me, still it would have been nice to be asked, being as I was the one who'd taken care of Uncle Jim for the last few years.

"What do you want to do?" Pete finally asked. Pete was Shirley's age, good looking and had bright blue eyes, brighter than Shirley's. His black suit was neatly pressed, and his hair combed back behind his big ears.

"I want to go to the cemetery," I told him, shocking the ladies out of their high heels. Funny no one argued with me, they just pointed me to a car and I got in. The smell of everyone's perfume and after-shave all mixed together in that limousine was difficult to handle. Thank goodness

Uncle Jim was getting buried outside where the air was fresh, and I could stand away from the crowd and not get sick.

I stood behind the crowd that encircled the grave, and the coffin with my uncle's casket hovering over it. Hard to think that my best and only friend was going into that hole and I would never see him again. I choked up but bit my lip to keep from making a scene. The preacher talked about loving people while we're here on earth. Uncle Jim had told me the same thing before he died. I should find someone to love, he said. I should surround myself with people who love me. And then he left me.

Uncle Jim should have been a preacher, I think. He would have made a good one.

Everyone said amen and then scattered to their cars. I stood there for a little bit waiting for the casket to be lowered into the hole, like they do in the movies. I guess they use heavy equipment these days, so nothing happened while I stood there. Shirley came back for me, tugging at me.

"Come on, Dylan. There's lots of work to do now."

I whispered one last goodbye to Uncle Jim.

C Chapter 5

The Crashing Surf

I might as well be one of those old oyster shells strewn across the beach on a foggy morning; shattered to pieces by crashing waves–my insides coarse and hollow because too many people had come by and pried me open with their knives, gobbling up my guts. I didn't know which was worse; the cracked and empty shells piled upon one another chipping at the mercy of the pounding breakers, or my hands bleeding and aching from cracking the shells, salt and sand being chafed into them, grinding itching pain.

That's me when Aunt Agnes and cousin Shirley came to the house and started taking all of Uncle Jim's things. I didn't care about some of the stuff. Uncle Jim and I talked about throwing a lot of our old junk away, like the newspapers piled up in the corner, or the clothes that the two of us went through and said we were going to give to the poor but never did. Uncle Jim had been collecting old war relics that only he could want. I didn't know what half of them were. But when Aunt Agnes and Shirley started packing the clothes he wore every day, I couldn't let that happen. I grabbed his Cammy coat from Shirley and she tugged back.

"Stop being so stubborn, Dylan," she said. "Unless you want to do all this work by yourself, which you should have been doing all along, let mom and I clean up. This place is disgusting."

"You can't take his coat. He needs his coat," I said, not really knowing what I was saying. I wasn't smart, but I knew that when someone dies that's the end of them. I'd been to the funeral and I saw his body and knew he was gone. He wasn't going to get cold again. But all his stuff didn't have to disappear, too. "I need his coat," I corrected myself, so I didn't sound like an idiot. "I don't mind having his stuff here. There's room in the closet for his belongings, none of his stuff would be in my way." I looked at Aunt Agnes, hoping she'd relent and stop putting everything in boxes.

"Dylan," she said in that condescending voice. "Everything has to go. Even your things. The house has to be empty."

I stood there with my mouth open and I felt wet welling in my eyes. "No." I said.

"Yes, Dylan. You have to go too." Shirley's voice resonated like an iron bell against my head. She bunched up the Cammy and stuffed the jacket in a box. I think she got some sort of satisfaction saying I had to go, too. Shirley never liked me. I could tell by the way she snickered whenever she saw me.

"No, I can stay here by myself," I argued. "I can take care of myself. I'm fine."

"Dylan, we're selling the house. You'll be living somewhere else."

No one gave me any warning about that. Uncle Jim's house never belonged to Aunt Agnes. We always talked about the property belonging to him and me. So, if he was gone, the house would be mine. I'd have a place to live for the rest of my life. "You don't want this house. It's just a shack. That's what you always said."

"A shack with ocean front property. Sorry Dylan. You'll get some of the inheritance, but the house must go! We'll find you a nicer place to live. I've been looking and have one scoped out. A place where you'll be well cared for. You won't even have to cook your meals."

"I like to cook."

"Come on Dylan, everyone knows if you were left in the kitchen alone you'd burn the house down," Shirley interjected. I wanted to punch her, but I knew better.

"Shirley!" Aunt Agnes shot a dagger eye at her. "No need to rile him." To me she spoke calmly, trying to patronize me. "It's true you'll get your meals, and someone will make sure you're well kept."

Well kept? I'm not a dog. I could only gape at the two, unable to defend myself because the words wouldn't come.

"With one phone call, we can get you there, tonight even!" Shirley took an empty crate into the kitchen and started packing my pots and pans. I ran in there after her. By now I was boiling inside. Those were my tools. Whatever she put in her wooden milk crate, I pulled out. She grabbed the muffin tin out of my hand and I yanked it back, slamming the end accidentally against her nose. "Mother!" She cried out and I ran to my room, muffin tin in hand. That's when I started shoving all my dirty clothes into my pack. Anything that would fit I rammed in there all balled up and wrinkled, like a crazy man. The muffin tin, too.

I heard them talking. "Don't get into a fight with him. Just let him be. You know how angry he gets when he's stressed. We'll get him to the counselor as soon as we're done here." Aunt Agnes said.

"Better get him there now or we'll never get done! I can't take any more of this," Shirley barked at her mother like a little kid even though she was a full-grown adult. Older than me.

I wanted to cry. I didn't. Uncle Jim once told me when I get that mad to count to ten, so I counted. Two or three times. I wiped my tears with my sleeve before they streamed down my face. I counted again. Uncle Jim wanted me to do things slow so that they got done right, so I took a deep breath and sat on my bed, put my pack on my lap and pulled everything out with the intent to arrange things neatly. I got to the blue box down at the bottom and carefully lifted the package up. Aunt Agnes barged into the room just then, and I barely had time to cover the box on my lap with some dirty clothes.

"Pack your things, Dylan. Shirley will take you to the park. There's no reason for you to be here right now."

"I don't want to go to the park," is all I could manage to say.

Her lips thinned, and I could see she didn't want an argument. "I'm not asking you Dylan. We're all as upset as you. Just pack your things and we'll take you to your new home."

She left before I could think of a response. I'd sworn never to use magic in front of Aunt Agnes, much less Shirley, but I wanted to. Not my good magic either. The black kind that would lock them out of the house and out of my life forever.

But I didn't. I kept my secret.

I thought about taking Annabella out of the box then, and just holding her because that would have been a comfort to me. She was the last thing Uncle Jim gave me and I could sense him speaking to me through her. I was afraid Aunt Agnes, or worse, cousin Shirley would burst into my room again if I did, though. They would take her from me, like Uncle Jim said they would, and I wouldn't be able to handle that. I put the blue box back into my pack, and folded my clothes neatly, one by one, and placed them on top.

C Chapter 6

Liona

I hated riding in the car with Shirley. She drove too fast, cut corners and passed everyone on the road. Besides, she snapped at me whenever I asked her a question, so I didn't talk. I just sat quietly and hung onto my seat all tense and held my breath when she raced through a yellow light. She was in a hurry to drop me off, I could tell. Frankly the feeling was mutual.

Elwood Estates wasn't too far from my uncle's house. We had to cross through two towns to get there by car, but if you walked up the beach and around the cliff they call Windy Point you'd come to Elwood Estates in an hour's time. I used to walk that way from Uncle Jim's house. The neighborhood was lush and green with big homes and big yards. Only rich people lived there, and old people who bought their houses a long time ago when property was cheap. Stone structures with brick chimneys that spouted little puffs of grey smoke and smelled like Christmas. Big trees guarded the yards. Every house had a porch. The city put in old fashioned streetlamps along the sidewalk so at night you'd think you were in a movie like It's a Wonderful Life. Ivy covered the yards where people didn't want to mow, and white picket fences held up honeysuckle vines. The homes were set far apart and some of the driveways disappeared into the forest, so you couldn't tell there was a residence except for the mailbox at the head of the drive, or a big iron gate. Shirley slowed down and stuck her head out the window.

"Let me know if you see a mailbox that reads 6773, Dylan. That's the address. You can read numbers, can't you?"

"I can read numbers," I said, growling under my breath. "I graduated high school, remember? I'm not completely stupid." I rolled down my window and squinted at the mailboxes but the ones I saw didn't have numbers on them.

"There it is." She made a sharp left-hand turn into a dirt driveway surrounded by all sorts of vegetation. Cedar and hemlock trees, wild rhododendrons and ivy grew along the lane. The car rumbled up over rocks and roots and into potholes. We twisted and turned and finally arrived at a very large gray, two-story house whose many trusses met at interesting points, with attic windows peeking curiously over the yard. Moss covered the roof in places and a red brick chimney confirmed there was a fireplace. That was one good thing. I liked fireplaces. Uncle Jim's house had a fireplace. We would roast hotdogs over the fire when it rained. When we came to a stop, Shirley jumped out, slammed the door and opened the trunk. "This is it. This is your new home."

I sat in the car and tried to collect my thoughts. I wasn't as anxious to step into this new world as much as Shirley was to have me out of hers. Aunt Agnes had told me I'd be going to a group home. To me, that meant a house full of strangers. I'm not good at making friends and socializing. I'm a private kind of person. The whole business of leaving my house by the sea, where I could have lived peacefully alone, in trade for living with a bunch of people I didn't know, repulsed me.

"Come on Dylan, get out of the car." Shirley had my suitcase in her hand and stood in-between me and the mansion, an impatient pout on her face. "What are you waiting for?"

That's when the door to the house opened and a middle-aged woman stepped out. She wore blue sweat pants and a sweat shirt that matched, had gray hair cut short, partially hidden under a baseball cap. She had a plump face and a cheerful smile. "You must be the van Pelens."

"Not me." Shirley was quick to detach herself from my name". I'm Shirley Barber. My cousin sitting in the car is Dylan van Pelen and he's your new resident." Shirley couldn't get my suitcase into the house quick enough. She rushed up the porch steps, her blond curls bouncing. I sat and watched until the woman came down the stairs and started walking toward me.

"Ah! Dylan, my name is Mrs. Wright! Good to have you."

I opened the car door, not wanting to look like a fool or a pouty child. I also didn't feel like smiling and being friendly, so I didn't say anything. I didn't take her hand either when she offered to shake mine. Why would I want to touch anyone? I wished I were a tortoise with a shell to crawl into.

"Oh, you're a shy one I see," she kept on. "That's okay. You aren't the first one we've had like that."

One what? Right away I knew I was going to hate living here.

She turned to Shirley as my cousin set my suitcase by the door and followed Mrs. Wright to the car.

"Sorry he's such a dunce," Shirley said, acting as though she were joking. I knew she wasn't.

Mrs. Wright waved the comment away. "Oh, he's no dunce. Just timid is all. He'll get used to being here. Everyone does sooner or later." She gave me a big smile and offered her hand again. "Come on, Dylan. Let's go inside. I'll show you your room."

My stomach rolled, and I fought back a gag. If Shirley hadn't taken my sleeve and dragged me out of the car, I probably would have run into the woods and thrown up. Nevertheless, if I didn't want to look like a wimp, I had to follow her. I pulled my pack from the front seat of the car and slung one strap over my shoulder. I freed my arm from my cousin and walked behind her and Mrs. Wright. They both chatted nonsense. The weather. The traffic. They talked about me, too, but I gave their gossip no mind. I was used to people talking as if I didn't exist. In a way, the invisibility made life easier because I could ignore them.

The porch had a pleasant smell. Potted plants lined the railing. Red geraniums and petunias draped from hanging baskets. A rustic, old, wooden swing hung by two chains near the entrance of the house. I paused for a moment and touched the chain, causing it to rock ever so slightly. I would like to sit on the swing someday, maybe, and rock back and forth. That is, if I must stay here. If I find no way out.

When Mrs. Wright opened the door and waited. My heart took a leap and that sick feeling returned. There were too many people in the room. I don't know how many, but they were everywhere. I looked over my shoulder for an escape. I wasn't quick enough. Shirley nudged me inside.

"Everybody, I want you to meet our new roommate, Dylan," Mrs. Wright said to all the faces staring at me. Vultures hungering after road kill is what I saw. "And this is his lovely cousin, Shirley Barber."

An energetic chorus of "Hi, Shirley" and a low tentative mumble of "Hi Dylan," sounded throughout the room. I had my hands in my pockets and kept my head bowed, not wanting to see any faces.

"Hey, everyone!" Shirley was filled with enthusiasm. I don't think she had ever been happier. "This is my dearest cousin Dylan," she put her arm around my shoulder. "You all be good to him. He means a lot to me!"

I glared at her from the corner of my eye and stood stiff as she hugged me. What a liar! She never hugged me before in her life. Never.

"We will," a man spoke up. "So long as you come around and check on us!" Laughter resonated against the unfamiliar walls. They were mocking me, siding with my cousin against me. For a moment I thought I heard my mother in their voices. I looked up for only a second and could see their teeth. They looked like a den of lions ready to pounce. Threatened by their jeering, I tightened my hold on my backpack, wondering if I shouldn't pull some magic from my pocket to terrify them. I could throw flames into the room to make them stop! But I decided against it because Shirley was there, and she didn't deserve to see my power.

Mrs. Wright took a stand next to me and pointed around the room at everyone, naming names. She had a strange smell to her and I decided that was the scent of her deodorant because it sure didn't smell like perfume. People nodded, but that was the extent of their greeting. I kept my head bowed and peeked up at each of them. I wouldn't remember names or faces. I didn't want to. I'd be gone in the morning.

"Mrs. Benson in the wheel chair over there," Mrs. Wright said. "Mr. Gravestone." He was a middle-aged man who didn't seem to have anything wrong with him except maybe his attitude. He didn't like me. I could tell by the sneer on his face. "Mr. Bromheimer,"

"Hello, Dylan." A gray haired and feeble man saluted me. His was the only voice that seemed warm and hospitable.

The last person Mrs. Wright introduced me to was Randy Hartman. Randy was about as young as I was, in a wheel chair, and sleeping. With the introductions over, I cleared my throat and stuttered in a low voice, "where is my room?"

"Oh yes, your room is upstairs. Shirley, we don't let guests upstairs, so he'll have to carry his things up there by himself. Dylan, once you unpack you can come down and have a conversation with everyone, Sort of break the ice, you know? And then have dinner with us. The house rules are posted on the wall over there," she pointed to a spot on the wall next to a wrought iron baker's rack where dishes, cups and saucers had been stacked. "We'll also give you a print-out of the rules. Mr. Gravestone oversees that."

I glanced at him. He gave a heavy nod and then lifted his chin as if telling me he had a job and was proud of it.

"That way you can become acquainted with our routine. We expect everyone to do chores, and we'll give you instructions on when and where. Your cousin and I will get your paperwork filled out." She called out to someone in the back room. "Liona, will you get the key to room 8 and show Dylan where he'll be staying?"

I stared at the girl named Liona as she emerged out of the shadows. She rummaged through a buffet looking for the key; chewing gum with her weight shifted to the side so one hand was on her hip and the other pushing things around in the drawer. Her hair caught my attention, too; brushed up and over to one side, streaked with purple and orange spikes which fell over her eyes. The bare side of her head was shaved in a pattern of triangles. Skillfully done. She wore one hoop earring and several more jewels in her ear that sparkled whenever they caught the light from the chandelier. She had as much black on as Aunt Agnes wore at Uncle Jim's funeral, only it looked good on her. Real good. She had on a leather jacket with a chain draping out of her pocket and a wide belt with silver grommets. Her skirt was short and tight, and she had black stockings and tall black boots. I'd never seen anyone dress like that before. Maybe because of the way her clothes fit is why I couldn't take my eyes off her. When the key was in her hand, she tossed the shiny object in the air, caught it, and at the same time, caught me staring. Her eyes were beautiful. Green and bright like a cat's eyes, lined with thick black lashes.

"Let's go." She had a raspy tone and tossed her head to the side for me to follow. My heart raced, but then when she snickered, my shoulders fell. She sounded too much like Shirley. My left-hand throbbed in my pocket and I hoped I wasn't drumming up uncontrollable black magic. I followed her up the stairs, suitcase in hand and backpack slung over my shoulder, glad to leave the voices of my cousin and the strangers behind.

The creamy colored hallway threatened to cave in on me, being so narrow. The floor creaked under my feet as we walked on the worn green carpet, past a row of rooms. She stopped at the end of the hall, turned the key and pushed a door open. When I took a step forward, her boot swung out in front of me and I tripped and fell flat on my face. I scrambled to stand up and jumped away from her.

"Oops," she said.

"What did you do that for?" I took a moment to catch my breath and straighten my clothes.

"Do what?"

"Trip me. You tripped me."

"You stumbled over my foot. Guess I have big feet."

Suddenly I was back with my Mom and she was reprimanding me for some dumb thing I did. I shuddered as a mild electric shock raced through my body. I glared at Liona, her big green eyes all innocent. I clenched the inside of my pocket with my left hand because power whirled through my body and I didn't want to do something stupid.

Her eyes grew wide and I swear she read my thoughts. "Magic, is it?"

"What?"

"I know what's happening to you."

How could she? I looked down at my jacket pocket. I didn't see anything, but I sure felt it.

"Listen here. I can cast a spell or two, too. So, don't think you're anything special. You do your work and be nice to people and we'll all get along. Otherwise I can make your stay here as black as Hades."

Her words were intimidating, but I didn't want her to think I was afraid. The magic in me subsided.

"My life's already black." Taking my hand out of my pocket, I set my suitcase down on the bed. I didn't take my pack off my back because I needed to protect Annabella from this witch.

"You think?"

"It is." I had forgotten all the advice Uncle Jim had given me about talking to a bully. I was supposed to turn around and walk away but here she was in my room. Where was I to go?

"So, you're a victim? And I suppose you plan on hiding away in your room and snubbing everyone here?"

"No. I'm not a victim." Uncle Jim would never let me position myself as a victim. He explained how bad my life would be if I thought people were picking on me all the time, even if they were, because that kind of attitude would keep me from doing things for myself. He told me to take each moment at a time and that there were moments when I could stand up tall, ready to defend myself. I was supposed to live for those moments. I straightened my back and lifted my chin, like Uncle Jim had me rehearse repeatedly, ever since I was little.

"Just so you know, I'm especially intolerant of people who hide inside of shells and who put up brick walls. First impression tells me you're one of those, so open up, buddy or you'll have nothing but enemies here."

"Not sure I want friends," I said.

"Oh yeah, you do."

She stood in the doorway, chewing her gum. I set my pack on the bed next to the suitcase, and then faced her empty handed, mustering all the bravery I could. Uncle Jim had told me to confront my enemies and not to back down. I took a breath, counted to ten and then looked her square in the eye. I didn't want to fight, not with a girl especially. Especially not with a pretty girl. "Look, I got bullied in high school, so I don't need this." I lowered my voice trying hard not to let the anger show.

We stared at each other. I know she was thinking of something snotty to say, I could tell by the way she looked at me and by the way she popped her gum. Pink gum, and she had to scrape the busted bubble off her lips with her teeth. She did so with no trouble and chewed the same gum over again, and then she popped it yet again.

"I can see why," she finally retorted.

Uncle Jim had also advised me that work was the best way to calm myself, so I turned away from her and ignored her. I started putting some of my clothes in the drawers, folding them up first because they had gotten wrinkled in the suitcase.

"Who's Uncle Jim?" Liona asked, still chewing.

Startled, I glanced up. How did she know my uncle? "Who wants to know?"

"I do."

I ignored her and folded up a shirt, tucking it in the top drawer. There had been no reason for her to pry into my private life, especially by reading my mind. I wasn't going to tell her anything.

"Why don't you just go live with him?'

"I did."

"So? What happened? What's wrong? Did he kick you out?"

That was enough! I set the stack of clothes down and turned to her, crushed inside. I didn't know who she was or what she was trying to do to me, but I had to stop her before I exploded. Uncle Jim told me to always be honest, to fight for the truth so that's what I did.

"Uncle Jim died," I began, trying to find words to explain without getting too personal. "We took care of each other, but he's gone now, and my Aunt is selling the house and doesn't know what to do with me, so she brought me here. So here I am. I can't help that you don't like me, but here I am. Now what?"

She stopped chewing. I think maybe I struck a chord with her and woke her up somehow. Maybe she isn't as mean as she wants to be.

I went on. "How did you know about my uncle? Did my aunt tell you? Did someone from my family come here and talk about me?"

"If they did I wasn't in on the conversation."

"How then?"

She chewed her gum at me, a snarky smile, the spitting image of Shirley. "Who's Shirley?"

I frowned.

She laughed. "I've got you puzzled. Say it."

I said nothing.

"Let me help you out. I read minds. You can't think anything without me knowing about it."

A heat rushed to my head. How was I going to stay private with this person around? "So, what do you want?" I asked. "Do you want me to crawl in a hole? Do you want me to hate you? What?"

"I don't want anything except for you to cooperate because trying to keep this place together is friggin hard enough as it is. We didn't need another tenant, especially someone who is going to demand more attention than we can give."

"I'm not here to cause trouble. And I could care less if I get any attention. I prefer not to! I didn't even ask to be here."

"Yeah? Well, that can be a problem too."

55

I realized she was blocking the doorway and suddenly I felt cramped. "No problem because I can skip out and let you have your stupid group home all to yourselves."

"Don't you dare! Mrs. Wright needs the money to keep this place going or she wouldn't have taken you on. Mess things up and you'll answer to me."

I wanted to make a face at her but that would have been juvenile. Uncle Jim always told me to act my age. Twenty years old! I didn't need to be making childish faces, so I held my tongue in my mouth. "Answer to you? Are you the warden?"

"Kinda."

"What would you do? Lock me in my room?" That didn't sound like a bad idea to me, so I cracked a smile. She glared in response to my grin. "Or would you beat me up?"

Her eyes narrowed even more, and then she shook her head real slow. "Forget I said anything. Just know that you'll have chores."

"So? I'm not afraid of work."

"Of course, you aren't." She made a move toward the hallway.

"I'm a good worker," I added, softly. That stopped her in her tracks and she opened her mouth to say something, but I guess she decided not to because she slipped all the way out of the room at that point. I shut the door, looking for a lock on the inside, but there was none.

The room was simple, not unlike my room at Uncle Jim's. I hadn't had a bedframe before, my mattresses at Uncle Jim's lay on the floor. The bed was firm, but I didn't mind. The clean sheets surprised me—that was a new luxury. A navy blue wool blanket looked cozy enough.

A dresser made of dark wood with a mirror twice as big as the one I had before. There was a closet and a few hangers. Mostly the room was comfortable. I opened the window to release the stuffy air. The scent of cedar from the woods filled the room and made it seem more spacious than it was. From the window I had a view of the front porch, the driveway, and the yard. For that I considered myself lucky. My room was also situated at the end of the hall, which meant I probably wouldn't hear a lot of foot traffic during the night. Plus, I could watch who came to the house, and who left. I might like my room, especially if I can hang out in it without being bothered by the other tenants.

If not, my only real hope would be to run away.

I sat on the bed for a long time thinking, wondering how I could use my magic to get out of here. I might have to wait until dark, but I've never been real fond of wandering around at night. My bedtime was 9:30. If I left in the day with my pack and suitcase, someone would get suspicious. Worse, Liona would read my mind and probably stop me or tell Mrs. Wright.

If I did get away, I could sneak back into Uncle Jim's and stay there after Aunt Agnes was done cleaning the house. Once I was at the house I would keep it from being sold. I'd just live there, and no one would be able to get rid of me. My magic would keep me well-fed. The idea seemed feasible.

I wanted out. I wanted my old life again. I wanted Uncle Jim, or at least the beach at Windy Point.

I pulled the shoe box out of my pack, unwrapped Annabella and held her in my hands, thinking about Uncle Jim and what he'd say if he knew where I was. He never liked establishments like this. When Aunt Agnes talked about putting him in a veteran's home he got downright mad at her. I think he'd be equally mad at seeing what she'd done to me. Wish I had the guts that Uncle Jim had.

A few minutes passed, and I found my mind wandering outside, thinking about the foamy sea again, and the oyster shells and how happy I had made Tim Lan with the little round balls I gave him. Already I missed the beach, though I knew I wasn't far from the ocean. The tingling began in my fingers at that moment. I touched Annabella with my left hand, swirling some of the colors in her dress so that they blended into each other. Soon enough, and with the right twist of my wrist, a little marble popped up and rolled around in the crease of her gown. I picked the ball up with my left hand and held the spun colors to my eyes. The power buzzed inside of me, a steady vibration like how the motor of an egg beater shakes your hand when you're mixing a cake batter. The energy grew stronger and stronger until my fingers trembled. Soon, light darted out of my hand into the marble that I held, and for the first time ever, I made something glow like how Tim Lan had made the pearl glow. The more I stared at the ball, the brighter the colors became until the marble shone and illuminated the entire room. I shut the overhead light off to get the full effect, and right away my spirits picked up. I could handle being here a little while, so long as I can practice magic in my room.

That's when there was a knock at the door. I could tell by her bubbly voice that the visitor was Mrs. Wright. "Dylan, dinner is ready. Wash up and come on down, now."

I stuck the marble in my coat pocket. My pocket lit up like a jack-o-lantern on Halloween. I looked around the room, searching for something to conceal the glow, because even though I wasn't feeling the power in me anymore, the marble was still radiant. I stuck it in the shoebox, wrapped Annabella up again and put everything back in my pack. The camouflage didn't work all that well because a dull glow could still be seen through my pack.

By this time, the smell of food lured me into facing the crowd downstairs. I hadn't eaten since the peanut butter sandwich Shirley made me before she rushed me out of the house that morning. I grabbed my backpack, hesitant to leave Annabella in the room by herself, and stepped into the hall. The door shut by itself and after trying the handle I realized the door also locked by itself too. Not sure I liked that, being as I didn't have a key.

C Chapter 7

Served à la Fantasia

The first person I encountered at the bottom of the stairwell after I set my backpack down was Mrs. Benson in her wheelchair. She was as thin as a toothpick. Her arms had all sorts of bruises on them and her skin was as pale as the powder blue dress she wore. Her hair was loosely pinned in a bun, with silver ringlets dangling over her ears. She might have been a pretty lady when she was younger, because she held her head up proud-like, and had a certain grace to her, even though she nodded her head a lot. She had a big smile on her face, but I don't think she even saw me because I smiled back, and she just kept staring. "Eddie?" she said to me and held out her hand. "What time is it?"

I looked at my watch. "A quarter to four, but I'm not Eddie."

She nodded some more. Mrs. Wright walked up behind her and took the handles to her wheelchair. "Dylan, Mrs. Benson's got dementia so she probably thinks you're someone else. No need to fuss over her, she's happy to see you whoever you are. Go on in the dining room and have a seat at the table."

I gave Mrs. Benson another nod and smile, and I think the twinkle in her eye was for me, but there's no telling. I approached the table cautiously mostly because everyone turned their heads my way when I walked in the room. Mr. Gravestone, sat upright, his eyes scoured over my person like I was diseased. He raised his napkin over his mouth and coughed, as though the sight of me made him gag. I had washed that morning, and combed my hair, so there was no reason to overreact. I sneered back at him.

Mr. Bromheimer blinked a few times and then gave me a friendly smile and I nodded. He tilted his head at Mr. Gravestone, rolling his eyes a bit. He had the same demeanor as Uncle Jim. He didn't seem to mind that he lived here, or that growing old and feeble posed a problem.

Awake now, Randy rocked stiffly in his wheelchair next to my seat. When he looked my way, he could barely turn his head as his whole body turned with it. He laughed and with a very forced attempt said, "Hi, Dy…Dy…Dylan."

"Hi Randy," I returned, and he laughed louder and said hi to me again.

My place at the table was directly across from Mr. Gravestone. His dark brown eyes bore a hole right through me, but his frown was more devilish than any I had ever seen; even on Aunt Agnes, even from what I remember of my Mom when she was tripping or coming off drugs. After I sat down, Mr. Bromheimer cracked a joke that made Mr. Gravestone turn and laugh. The two went into a giggle fit until Mrs. Wright interrupted them and asked them to pass the potatoes to me. Mr. Gravestone did with a left-over grin and watched me scoop the food onto my plate. I tried to avoid his stare.

Liona sat next to Mrs. Benson and fed her in-between her own bites. She glanced my way occasionally, not as often as I looked at her. She was the prettiest person in the room. Mrs. Wright was the only one talking and I don't think any of us paid much attention to what she said. Something about town and church service on Sunday and making our beds.

Out of the clear blue, while we were eating, with no cause for doing so, Mr. Gravestone said to me, "You ought to be ashamed of yourself."

I was the focus of everyone's attention then, and my face heated up like an electric blanket. The lettuce in my mouth went down whole. I dabbed my lips with the napkin to wipe dressing that spread over them while I choked.

"Pay him no mind," Mr. Bromheimer interrupted. "He's not himself."

"I'm completely myself, Ralph," Mr. Gravestone argued and threw his fork, which chipped his plate and bounced into my potatoes.

"Himself, himself," Randy ravened as he swayed back and forth, bumping the table with every thrust forward. His violent rocking caused my milk to spill all over my lap and on the floor. Liona jumped up and raced behind him, pulling Randy's wheel chair away from the table. He swung at her. I bounded to my feet in her defense.

"Don't get involved. We can handle it, Dylan. Finish your dinner," Mrs. Wright walked calmly to Randy and helped Liona strap him down. He wrestled like a pro, punching at the air with his fists and trying to head bump Liona while she knelt and strapped him in. "Get his helmet, Liona."

Liona was still buckling the lap belt while Mrs. Wright ran to the kitchen. I couldn't eat, and no way could I sit during this battle. Liona pointed to the living room. "On the couch. A blue bike helmet." I raced to retrieve the bike helmet while Liona and Mrs. Wright helped Randy swallow some meds. Five minutes went by before we were able to settle him. The other tenants watched intensely, except for Mrs. Benson who kept calling for Eddy.

When he was subdued, Mrs. Wright wheeled him to the living room and left him there alone. The dim light seeped through the curtains and cast the gold of sunset on his face, his head unnaturally bent backwards, snorting and drooling. I couldn't help but feel sorry for him. I know I had trouble functioning what with all my anxieties, but poor Randy had no control at all. I couldn't eat even though I was famished.

"Dylan! Pay attention to what you're doing," Mrs. Wright said.

I gave her an angry stare.

When Liona passed me on the way to her seat, she mumbled, "Chill out." I met her eyes. Her lips twitched into a quick smile which immediately turned into a sneer. I don't know if that short moment of grin was a thank you for getting Randy's bike helmet or what. I didn't ask. I sat and picked at my dinner, but I couldn't stop looking over my shoulder at Randy.

Later that evening, after Mrs. Wright had finished giving everyone their meds, she excused herself and went to her room.

Mr. Gravestone handed me my list of duties. "Here ya go kid." He chuckled as he walked out of the dining room into the living area.

The list had me working in the kitchen with Liona, probably because I was the only other person without a walker or a wheelchair. I was uneasy about being alone with her again, and if nighttime hadn't settled already I would have just grabbed my things and left. I wasn't used to wandering around in strange places at night, and sometimes the dark would bring on a panic attack. I didn't really know the neighborhood or how far away I was from Uncle Jim's house. So, I took my chances and cleared the dishes off the table.

Liona settled the tenants in the living room and turned on the TV for Mrs. Benson and Randy. Mr. Gravestone and Mr. Bromheimer sat at the chess board near the fireplace. I met her in the kitchen.

"Grab a towel." She didn't look at me and I got the feeling she didn't want to work with me any more than I wanted to work with her. I pulled a towel off a pile on the counter. She turned on the sink faucet and immersed the dishes in sudsy water.

"There's your key," she said and nodded at the microwave before she handed me a dish to dry.

I put the key in my pocket.

"Lock your door when you're out of your room so no one steals your things. You can't lock them from the inside because we don't want any self-haters here, if you know what I mean."

"I don't know what you mean."

"People that don't want to be people any more. Suicides. House policy is to have all tenants' rooms accessible by staff. In case they try to hurt themselves. It's happened before."

I couldn't imagine anyone trying to hurt themselves, much less killing themselves, but I guess it happens. That was a scary thought though. "I don't do that," I said.

She pulled the plug and we both watched the suds spiral down the drain.

"We aren't done," I said.

"The water's dirty. You might forget to take your meds or something who knows. So, we make sure you won't have a chance to do anything stupid like that."

"I don't take meds." I informed her, a little offended that she thought I was on drugs, or that I was stupid.

"Right."

"Why do you think I do?" Drugs was a big issue with me. Uncle Jim argued with the doctors when they tried to prescribe medications for me. He kept me safe from them all my life, even when the social workers wanted to give me pills for depression. Seeing my mom and the way drugs affected her made me hate what they do to people, and Uncle Jim respected that. He didn't take many himself, except he took meds for his cholesterol and his kidneys.

"They aren't mind altering drugs, though," he had explained to me.

"You've got problems. Even I take meds, sometimes." She didn't give me time to respond but kept on with her instructions. "Mrs. Wright and I both have a key to everyone's room and we'll be checking up on you. You have a key to get into yours but if you abuse that privilege, we take it away. If that happens, you'll have to ask us to let you into your room. That can get tedious for us as well as you, so do us all a favor and don't abuse your privileges. I honestly don't want to be playing door maid for you. I have enough work to do."

Again, I didn't know how I could abuse my privileges. Probably by running away but if I did that, I wouldn't need the key to my room anyway. "That shouldn't be so hard to handle," I mumbled. "So, are you in charge, here? While Mrs. Wright is away?"

"Did you just now figure that out?" She didn't seem to want to talk to me after that, so I didn't ask any more questions. Instead, I jiggled the key in my pocket as she filled the sink up again with hot water and bubbles.

"So, Dilly, ready to work?" She dropped a handful of silverware into the sink and started scrubbing, suds stuck to her arms like bubble bath.

"I'm used to working and Dilly's not my name."

"Yeah, you told me you've worked. Cool." She looked at me with a defiant eye. "You might have to get used to Dilly until I find a better name for you."

"Try Dylan. I like my name. Why change a good name?"

"What's in a name?" she asked, chuckling to herself.

"A person." I answered. She glimpsed at me and then submerged a dinner plate into the water.

If she was going to be snarky, I was an old hand at being on the receiving end. Shirley trained me well. "I didn't appreciate being tripped."

She grunted. "There's a lot of things I don't appreciate. Such as someone making more work for me, more stress, more problems."

"I didn't do anything to you."

"You're here."

"Not my fault."

"Maybe, maybe not. There's got to be a reason your auntie doesn't want you."

That stung. "Not a good one." I said wanting to blurt out everything that had happened to me ever since I was a kid, and how I had no control over how people had treated me. But I didn't know how to explain things, so I didn't. I just wiped the silverware pieces one by one, drying in-between the prongs of the forks, and the etching on the handles so that there were no water spots; so that they shone clean and ready for the next use. And then I placed them in their compartment in the drawer, stacking them neatly atop one another as if they were still in their boxes at the store.

I could have told her more. Like how my mother didn't want me around, or that the only person that ever wanted me around died, and that my aunt just wanted me out of her hair and I wouldn't want to live with her anyway. That I had a nice house and could have lived on my own, but they wanted to sell the property so now I'm homeless. But I couldn't say all those things because the pain I experienced would come back and hurt me again.

"I see," she mumbled softly, and looked at me. "Look, it's tough your Uncle died. I can tell he meant a lot to you."

She read my mind! All those things I just thought, she picked up on. Our eyes locked onto one another and all the bitterness was gone out of her. Just as astoundingly, the

swelling inside of me burst. I wiped my eyes with my
shirtsleeve, ashamed of my tears because Uncle Jim told
me to be strong no matter what. I'd been in plenty of
trouble at school for crying, so I knew better.

"Look Dylan, I have my reasons for being tough,
too, you know. I have problems too, okay? I've got a
history like you. Maybe worse, maybe better I don't know.
I get stressed out when there's too many people, too many
problems. And we're having a hard time right now
especially with Randy. He's too much for her to handle but
Mrs. Wright keeps bringing people in for the money and
she can barely take care of all of them. Lately, I've been
working my tailbone off."

"Why are you working? I thought you were like me,
like a patient?"

She grunted a laugh. "Patient? This isn't a hospital,
Not in so many words. This is a boarding house, a safe
place, sort of. Technically we're all tenants, even though
most of us need care of some sort. And in answer to your
question, I'm in charge when Mrs. Wright's gone because
she's kind of training me. She says she'll be paying me
once the business gets out of the red. That's why she keeps
taking on boarders. So she can pay her help."

That didn't make sense and I labored over the
puzzle in my mind.

She must have seen my frustration and laughed. "I
came here as a tenant."

"Why? What's wrong with you?"

"I don't fit into 'normal'."

"Why is that?"

"I have issues. Depression. Used to be manic
depressive. That talk about keeping doors unlocked because
people might hurt themselves? Well, Mrs. Wright made
that rule because of me. I was suicidal when I came here.
Tried a few times and drove everyone crazy. Scared my

parents. Couldn't hold a job. Couldn't manage money. Cut myself a lot."

"You cut yourself?" The thought of such a pretty girl trying to hurt herself upset me. "I don't understand."

"Didn't figure you would. My psychotic behavior is not something you should worry about. I've overcome a lot of my problems by having some stability here. I've learned not to run away. Working with the tenants here has been therapeutic for me, at least until Randy came. Still, my depression wasn't the only reason my folks sent me here. I don't think like normal people do, and…" she tapped her head and her voice trailed.

"And you have special powers?"

She nodded. "Kind of like you, I guess." She gave me an inquisitive look. She had no idea what my magic did.

I liked the idea that she thought we were alike. I found her attractive ever since I walked in the door. Maybe we could get along. "I've always been considered disabled." I said softly, "Aunt Agnes says I'm slow. Can't learn properly. I was never really ashamed of how I am, though, until Mr. Gravestone hinted that I should be."

"Screw Mr. Gravestone. Don't ever be ashamed of who you are."

When she brushed her purple locks from out of her eyes she gave me a smile sweeter than I'd ever seen. My knees suddenly felt weak. "Some things are fixable," she explained and then took her smile away as quickly as it had been offered.

"Your problem is fixed?"

"I wish! No, but I can live life on a day-to-day basis without sinking into a hell-hole."

"That's good. How'd you fix your life up?" I asked.

"Believe me, it's not fixed. But, like I said, hard work helps. I do ten times more than those high school students Mrs. Wright hires on the weekends. And the tenants trust me. I know everyone here and what they need.

When things are calm I'm okay. Just when people forget to take their meds, that's when hell breaks loose. I'll tell you something else, Dylan." She leaned toward me and whispered in my ear again. Her breath tickled. "After she leaves every night, I treat them with magic. I wouldn't normally. I don't like using magic, but you'd be surprised how well it works to keep things peaceful."

My eyes spread wide opened.

"I don't practice magic when Mrs. Wright is around. But when she leaves…well you'll see tonight. You could help me." She paused and studied me, her gaze intense. "I mean, depending on what exactly you can do with your magic."

I shook my head hard. "That's wrong," I said. "I don't do much with my power. Just silly things. Entertainment kind of things. I don't use it on people. I don't know if I could control it that well."

"Same here. I don't use it on them. I mean, I don't change them or anything. I just entertain them. You'll see. You can help me."

I still grimaced, not trusting the plan at all.

She didn't back down. "Just watch me, tonight."

I gave her a funny face, like I doubted my abilities. The idea had me spooked, too. What if I mess up?

"Take Mr. Gravestone," she said. "He's got dissociative identity disorder. Dual personalities. That's why one minute he can be laughing and the next minute say something like he did tonight. If you ask him what happened, or what he said, he'll deny having said anything. I try to catch him when he's the nice Mr. Gravestone, before he turns for the worse. Then I apply some magical power to keep him there longer."

"I don't know. That sounds manipulative," I said. "Counselors used to tell me my mom was manipulative." I shook my head again.

"It's not manipulative. It's healing and good for him. Believe me, if I were being manipulative, I'd do worse things to him. Sometimes I feel like tossing his cranky old body out to sea."

My mouth dropped.

She laughed. "Don't worry, I won't. I don't think. I hope not!"

I took a step back, wondering if she had that much power. She ran a dish under the faucet to rinse the suds off, and then handed the plate to me. "Don't be afraid of me, Dylan. I decided to like you. I think you're my people." She set the dish in the drainer and turned to face me. Her green eyes sparkled under the overhead light. She held out her fist. When I showed no sign of understanding, she took my free hand, curled my fingers together, and then bumped my fist with hers. "Friends?"

"Okay. Yeah, friends." I relaxed. Her grin made me smile. We stared at each other for a little while, the water still running in the sink. Suddenly I felt awkward. My face flushed, and I wanted to turn away, but I couldn't take my eyes off her.

"Good," she broke the gaucheness and turned off the water. After shaking the drips from the dish, she handed it to me and I wiped it with the towel.

"Mr. Gravestone is kind of scary," I said, thinking about the man's murky eyes that had ripped my gut out at the dinner table. "I bet he can be really mean."

"Mean? Pfft!" she said with a hiss. "He started a few fights here with some of the other tenants that have come and are since gone. Twice I had to interfere before things got out of hand. If he starts to pick up a plate while giving you the evil eye, duck!"

"Wow! What else do I need to know?" I was serious, but she just laughed.

"That's the worst, so far."

"Do you do any magic on the others?"

"I can help Mrs. Benson remember things and that makes her happy."

"Can you heal anyone? Like make Mr. Gravestone have only one personality instead of two permanently?"

"Nope." A quick and sharp response which I took as a sign not to press the matter, so I didn't. "Don't mess with nature. Not like that. I just comfort them. Mr. Bromheimer, he doesn't need much comfort. He's a pretty happy guy."

"What can you do for Randy?"

"Randy shouldn't be here." Her tone changed, and she grew solemn, like she didn't want to talk about Randy. She ran the rinse water over a pot she'd been scrubbing.

"What do you mean?"

She sighed heavily and shook her head. "Don't tell anyone, but Randy's supposed to have a personal caretaker. That means someone that takes care of him and him alone. I think Mrs. Wright is overstepping her license by keeping him. What she's doing could not possibly end well and I've warned her. Randy's way too much for me to handle. I hate when she leaves him here with me in charge."

I said nothing more. Liona's problems seemed to outweigh mine. "Maybe I can help you," I offered. She didn't answer, so I focused on drying the skillet.

"Good grief, Dylan, you're going to rub all the iron out of that thing," Liona commented. She handed me the oatmeal pan, so I put the skillet on the stove.

"Cast iron will rust if you don't dry it properly. Uncle Jim told me that."

"Yeah, didn't he tell you that you can put a cast iron skillet on the burner and cook it dry too, you know? You just need to rub a little oil in it. Tell me about your Uncle Jim. What was he like? Why were you so attached to him?"

"He's been like my dad. My real father disappeared when I was a baby. No one ever told me what happened to him, but I can guess. Mom didn't take care of me very well, so the social workers took me away from her. Uncle Jim asked for custody, so I lived with him." I whispered all this information because remembering those years was hard.

"What's with your mother? What do you mean she didn't take care of you very well? What did she do?"

"Drugs." I had no apologies for her. No defense and no feelings. "She had an accident when she was younger, hit by a car and had lots of surgeries and got addicted to pills. Never gave them up. She drinks too. Uncle Jim taking me in was the best thing that ever happened to me. He said her drugs would have killed us both."

"I'm sorry," she said with such a gentle voice it choked me up a bit. "So that's why no meds?"

"Yeah."

We worked quietly for a little while.

"Life is like that, you know? Stuff happens. You got to make the best of whatever, no matter what. Otherwise, where're you at?"

"I guess."

This is where I'm at. In a strange house with people unrelated to me and nothing to hope for. No future, no place else to go. Nothing.

"Cheer up, Dylan. Things will work out for you. I'm making something of my life. You can too."

We were done washing and drying the dishes, so she drained the sink and wiped it clean. "Well are you going to help me with the tenants, tonight?"

"I don't know," I mumbled.

Mrs. Wright had the tenants pretty content in the living area by the time Liona and I were done in the kitchen. She surprised me when she grabbed her purse, gave Liona a kiss on the cheek and then walked out the front door. Liona wasn't surprised so I didn't ask any questions.

I followed Liona as far as the dining room, fixed the chairs back under the table, put the linen away and avoided the living area because I was afraid of what Liona might ask me to do.

"Hey, Dylan, come on in here. Let's make these guys happy."

I stood by the door, unsure.

Mr. Gravestone and Mr. Bromheimer were still at their game of chess, each with two of the other's pawns in their cache, and Mr. Bromheimer had Mr. Gravestone's, queen. I knew how to play chess. Uncle Jim taught me. The two opponents had just started their game, so losing a queen so soon wasn't a good sign. Mr. Gravestone moved around on his seat nervously, obviously upset, while Mr. Bromheimer sat back on his chair with his arms crossed over his chest and a shameless smile spread across his face. He winked at me. I smiled but lost my grin when Mr. Gravestone scowled at me.

Liona walked behind Mr. Gravestone, put her hands on his shoulders and closed her eyes. Immediately the man's body relaxed. Her touch must be powerful. He reached up and patted Liona's hand.

"Depludag," Liona whispered. Sparks came from her fingertips and I jerked back. The flash only lasted for a second, enough to light up the table and Mr. Gravestone's face. His eyes were closed, so I don't think he noticed. The flicker scared me. I stepped back into the dining room and watched from there.

Soon enough, Mr. Gravestone laughed, reached over the game board and moved his bishop. "Check mate!" he said, brushing his hands together. "Got you this time Ralph!"

Mr. Bromheimer scratched the fuzz on his chin and studied the board for the longest time. He glanced up at Liona. There was a hurt look on his face, and then he laughed. "Next time you give me the massage," he told her. Liona winked at him, and then she winked at me. She walked over to Mrs. Benson and sat on the couch next to her wheel chair.

I moved back into the living room and became Liona's creeping shadow, there was so much more to learn. She held the old woman's hand for a long time and I could tell by the serene look on Mrs. Benson's face, Liona was helping her remember things from her past. The woman nodded and whispered names and places. Liona asked her questions but her voice was so low I couldn't understand.

That's when I noticed Randy in the corner by himself. Poor Randy, always alone. He reminded me of me. The outcast. I knew Randy was smart, he just couldn't communicate so people treated him like he didn't know anything. I knew because that's what people did to me. I walked over to him and pulled up a chair.

"Hi Randy," I said softly.

"Hi Dy...Dy...Dylan," he said eagerly and with a laugh. "How...how are you?"

"Hey, I'm good, I guess. How about you?"

"I...I'm fi....fi.... fine." Randy stared into space. I don't know if he was part blind, or couldn't focus, or if he just couldn't control his body well enough to look at me. Someone had combed his hair slick with oil. His large nose protruded like a proud Roman soldier, his lips were red from biting them.

The TV blared and made communication difficult. Since Gravestone and Bromheimer started another game of chess, and Liona tended to Mrs. Benson, I got up and turned off the television. Before I took my seat next to Randy again, I picked up my backpack by the stairs and brought it with me. "Hey, buddy I want to show you something," I said.

"Okay." Randy was quick to respond. He exhaled a peculiar laugh as I dug through my pack and pulled out the shoe box. Mr. Gravestone peered up from his game at me, sending a cold shiver of self-consciousness down my spine.

Hesitant to take Annabella out, I grabbed the lightning marble I had made earlier that evening and set the shoe box down by my feet.

With the marble tight in my fist, its light shone through my skin and made my whole hand glow. Liona glanced at me for a second. I turned my back to her. This was just between me and Randy. I took Randy's hand and held it for a little while. His palm was soft and warm, his hand large, fingers long. I put my left hand on top of his and started thinking about the ocean, the surf. I felt tingling and he laughed letting me know he felt the energy too.

"Randy, look here."

Randy strained his neck to look as I placed the marble in his hand, which was now glowing as bright as a headlight on a train.

"Wow!" he exclaimed and laughed excitedly. His whole body shook. "Wow!"

He called out loud enough that everyone raised their heads and looked at us. I quickly squeezed his hand shut, hiding the marble, but not the glow. "Shh," I said. "This is between you and me. We have some magic here, so don't say anything."

"I won't, Dy..Dylan," he stuttered. "That's our.... s...secret."

"Buddies," I affirmed and patted his hand. He grabbed both my hands with his other. I never felt a tighter grip, nor one so needy. He wanted a friend so bad I thought I was going to break in half.

He shook my hand and kept saying repeatedly, "Bud...buddies, Dy... Dylan!"

I agreed one more time and pulled my hand away leaving the marble in his. No sooner had I moved away from him, then he looked me in the eye and reached for my shirt. I tried to keep my distance because he scared me a little, he was so intense, so strong, so destitute. "Dy...Dylan. I lo... lo...love you!"

75

We had the attention of everyone in the room right then. "Me too, Randy," I whispered. "Love you too. Just between the two of us."

 Chapter 8

Crystal Shores

I didn't remember having an alarm clock, nor seeing one on the dresser the night before. I sure did spot it when the timer blared at six o'clock in the morning. My heart thumped against my chest and I jerked upright in bed thinking maybe the house was burning down. Who wakes up at six in the morning? It took a good minute-and-a-half for me to catch my breath before I pulled back the covers and reached the Tasmania Devil Timepiece—another minute to figure out how to shut the thing off. Someone tapped on the door. Liona.

"Rise and shine, van Dough. We're on breakfast duty today."

"Van Dough?" I grumbled without letting her in.

"You're a cook, aren't you? Thought I'd drop the name Dilly and use this one for a while. See how this name suits you."

"What's wrong with Dylan?" I called out through the closed door, but her footsteps scurrying down the hall told me she hadn't heard.

I pulled my pants up quickly and threw one of my t-shirts on. I wiped my hair back with my hands because I didn't remember where my comb might be. After I used the restroom and washed up, I bounced down the carpeted stairs now lit with gold nightlights along the railing. Morning had not yet peaked through the window. I found Liona in the kitchen peeling potatoes. Right away, she handed me a knife.

"Coffee?" she asked and nodded toward the pot. I took a deep breath because the aroma was so pleasant. Her attitude was more pleasant than mine.

"Don't drink coffee. Just smell it," I said.

Was she mocking me when she laughed? "How did you know I was a cook?" I set a potato on the cutting board and began chopping.

"Magic," she answered.

"But I hadn't even thought about being a cook, and this morning you knew. How?'

"I read people." She turned to face me, a glint in her eye that made me stop what I was doing. "So, like right now I'm reading that you don't want to cut potatoes."

"That's crazy. I like being in the kitchen at six-thirty in the morning with the prettiest girl in the world," I muttered. It was early, and my guard was down. I would never had said that if I were awake.

She raised her eyebrows in surprise. "Oh? Well, even so, you don't want to cut potatoes."

I grunted because she was right. I didn't want to cut potatoes. I wanted to flick my wrist and have them magically divide into neat little cubicles ready for the pan. I also wanted to show off how cool I was because I was able to do that. She raised her eyebrows.

"Are you daring me?"

She didn't answer but stood there with that beaming grin of hers.

"Watch me!" I closed my eyes and envisioned the foamy sea, which helped me to call my magic. Being around Liona was like being hooked up to a battery charger. No sooner had the rumbling surf popped into my mind then my body started buzzing. I made a grand display, using both of my hands just for show, spinning them around my head, wrists flipping back and forth and then 'voilà' there they were, a huge pile of potatoes in a big glass bowl all cut up and ready for cooking. Best thing was, not a spud from the bag had been used. Liona shut the kitchen door quickly before I had finished my grand display.

"I'm impressed!" she whispered, "but…"

Never had anyone beside Uncle Jim been impressed with my enchanted accomplishments. Then again, no one besides Tim Lan had seen them. I hadn't ever cooked for anyone else either. I laughed, not out loud because that would have made me look arrogant. A surge of pride took over for one quick moment and then I let it go. I knew better than to hang on to vanity. "But what?" I asked.

"Next you'll want to cook them without lifting a finger."

How could I argue? I was about to heat my fantasy oven when she took my hand. "Don't! Not if Mrs. Wright is in the house. No more magic. Not now," she cautioned. "Let's go for a walk."

"A walk?"

"You like the beach. Let's go to the beach."

"But breakfast?"

"We have time." She moved behind me, untied my apron and tossed it on the counter. I was a little tongue-tied, surprised that she wanted to walk with me.

We slipped out of the dark house into the chilly night air. I shivered.

"Walking will warm you up. Come on," she urged, taking my hand.

Not a lot of fog shielded the sunrise and would probably burn off once the sun came up. She coaxed me along. Her touch thrilled me more than even getting tickets to a ball game. Once we hit the beach, she ran, and I jogged alongside. When we got to the wet sand, we stopped and took our shoes off. I couldn't help but look out over the sea. So many colors were in the sky, the radiance mirrored as golds and oranges and turquoise blue glistening on the water. I breathed the salty air. Life was good, after all.

79

"So, this is where your magic comes from?"

"Yes." I said, still amazed at what she knew about me when I hadn't told her hardly anything. "There's a lot of power in the sea. Just thinking about it makes me tingle inside. And where does yours come from?"

"The air I guess. My heart. Curiosity and wanting to know about people. I don't know, the magic just happens."

"You can read my mind? I mean you can see right through me? As a person."

"Yep."

"All the time? So, no matter what I'm thinking you can tap into my thoughts?"

"Pretty much."

"That's powerful."

She turned to me, squinting. "Too powerful. I don't like being able to read minds all that much. I can't help it, but I don't like it."

"Why?"

"It can be scary sometimes. I have power to manipulate, like you suggested, and I don't want to be that kind of person, like your Aunt Agnes, for instance."

"Oh," I said. "You know my Aunt Agnes?"

"I met her. She came to the house to pay for your room and board."

I looked away, at the sea. The thought of Aunt Agnes taking my house away and putting me in the group home shamed me. "Maybe I could have used my magic to stop her." I mumbled.

"You think you could have?"

I shrugged, not knowing how spinning marbles or cooking would have stopped Aunt Agnes.

"It was pretty obvious by her conversation with Mrs. Wright, that your Aunt Agnes manipulates you. Probably other people do the same thing, too."

"Why do you say that?"

"I don't know. I don't want to offend you, but you seem to be naïve. There are some things you don't understand."

I couldn't argue, and the conversation didn't need to go any further. "You used a spell on Mr. Gravestone?"

"The spell kept him in his real self instead of flying off into the grumpy Mr. Gravestone. I just made that part of his personality stronger. Besides, the magic was for his own good, and everyone else's."

"So, you get to decide what's good for people?"

"Why so many questions? Are you wanting to know about spells?"

"No!" The thought frightened me. "I'd like to know about you, though."

She tilted her head curiously and studied my eyes. We stood almost the same height, me being a little taller than her but not by much. I saw the wheels spinning, that she was working magic trying to read me. "See anything?" I asked, a curt smile slipping out of my frown.

"Yes, I do."

I raised a brow because I had no idea what she was seeing. I didn't even know what I was thinking. "Tell me."

"You're teasing me. I can see that. I'm trying to find out why."

My smile disappeared and then I shut down. "Don't," I said and looked away. I started walking again and she followed.

"And why not?"

"Because why should you know so much about me when I don't know anything about you. I'd rather talk. That would be..." I searched for a word that I couldn't grab hold of, so I settled for, "more equal."

"Okay. Then let's talk."

We walked slowly toward the water, the sand cool between our toes, passing shallow dunes with ice plants draped over them and broad-leafed grasses that bent in the breeze. I tried to think of something to say but now that I wanted to talk, my mind went blank.

"Tell me about yourself, Dylan?"

"Not much to tell," I said, suddenly self-conscious of all the things about me I could tell her, but that I didn't want anyone to know, especially Liona.

"Why is that?"

"Not much here, I guess," I tapped my head, feeling dumb. "Only half a brain, if that."

"I see."

I glanced at her. I didn't mean for her to agree with me. She winked and that made me smile. "That's what my Aunt Agnes says about me."

"I don't think I care for your Aunt Agnes. She shouldn't degrade you like that."

"She's okay. She just doesn't like me a whole lot."

"I suppose your mom does the same thing?" She pushed a strand of her hair away from her face. Sun rays sparkled like glitter on her purple hair, and on her eyelashes.

I didn't answer. If I did she'd start asking a lot more questions that I didn't want to answer. "What about your folks?"

"They live in Glenwood. Inland about seventy-five miles. Fancy neighborhood. Fancier than this one. I grew up sheltered with everything I could possibly want. Two-parent family. Both mom and dad worked and made good money. We lived in a nice neighborhood, nice home, nice school."

"What happened?"

"I don't know. Too polished a life, I guess. Everything fit together like a perfect puzzle. I should have been happy. I guess I ruined it for myself, and..." her voice trailed into the sound of the breakers.

"Did your parents love you?"

"Yes, they did. Very much. They gave me all the material goods I ever asked for."

"I don't think that's what I mean."

She took my hand. "That's what I like about you Dylan. Your innocence. Like you, I could have used a hug occasionally, but they were too career-minded and never had the time. Or else they just didn't know any other way to show their love."

"What happened? I mean how did you end up here?"

She let out a long breath, her eyes focused where mine had been, on the shoreline, the seagulls. Out there, somewhere as if out there could bring those years back and we could change them. "I did something really stupid."

"With magic?" It was a guess.

"Yeah. With magic. After that I fell apart. I ran away more than once, trying to get attention, or to hide, or make someone feel sorry for me, or whatever. The counselor just diagnosed my issues as manic depressive and gave me meds. I never told them the real reason. The meds took the memories away. Like you, I hated meds, but when I didn't take them I couldn't stand myself."

I wanted to ask her what she did to cause all that misery, but there seemed to be a wall around her preventing me from prying any further.

"Did you drink?"

"No. I never drank. I'd probably be dead if I did. Never got into alcohol or partying either. I was a loner though, kind of like you."

Our eyes met briefly.

"Worst, though, is I always hurt myself. On purpose. After I graduated from high school, my parents were afraid to let me live by myself, so they worked things out with Mrs. Wright to send me here."

"Do you like living here?"

"Kept my mind occupied; kept me busy. Probably saved my life."

"But do you like living here?"

She didn't answer right away. Instead she lifted her head to the breeze that blew in from the surf and took a deep breath. I watched her, she was so fine to look at. When she caught me staring at her, I faced the ocean too.

"But I'm not sure what I want. I don't want to live in a boarding home forever. I know that." She peered at me. "What do you want, Dylan?"

Those kinds of questions were hard for me, so I'm glad Uncle Jim helped me figure it out before he died. "Love," I said. "I'm supposed to find people that are kind to me and then live around them. That's what Uncle Jim told me to do." I heard a little grunt come from her and I wasn't sure what to make of it. "Seems to me you like living at the boarding house," I suggested.

"I liked it better before Randy came."

"I like Randy."

"He's a lot of work. When Mrs. Wright is gone, Randy's my responsibility, and that's a tough job. I warned her about taking him on, but she needs the money."

"I see. Why does she leave the house so much?"

"She has a crippled grandchild she's helping to raise. Has to babysit so her daughter can work nights."

"Oh."

"That makes things hard for me, you know? In a way, the boarding house is good for me, but Randy..." she shook her head. "He's too much like how my brother was," she whispered.

I don't think she meant for me to hear that. She took a deep breath. "I'm wanting to get off on my own someday. Have my own house, maybe a family if I can ever get my head straight. Then sometimes I think maybe I'll never be that healthy and it freaks me out. Frankly, I'm scared of my magic. Sometimes it makes life easier, but sometimes it makes life worse. A lot worse."

"I think you're healthy."

She laughed and shook her head but didn't argue. "Don't say anything to Mrs. Wright about what I said concerning Randy."

"I won't."

"We should head back and make breakfast now."

C Chapter 9

Summer Tide

Worried that Liona would become too stressed because of so much responsibility, I helped her with her chores, giving extra attention to Randy. When it didn't rain, I spent time in the yard taking care of the flower garden pulling weeds. There were some iris bulbs to separate, and grass would grow in between the cracks on the walkway to the house so I used a hoe to dig up the roots. One day I climbed on the roof and sprinkled laundry soap to kill the moss. That was Uncle Jim's remedy and it worked. Mr. Bromheimer called me a hero when I was done.

After a couple of weeks, Mrs. Wright saw I could be trusted with the clippers, so I pruned roses and the hedge along the driveway. I might have liked living in the group home, except there were rules that made me angry, such as not being allowed on the beach by myself.

"It's not fair," I whispered to Liona one evening after dinner when we were cleaning up.

"What's not fair?"

"Not being able to go to the beach by myself. I used to always go to the beach. I lived on the beach, pretty much. All the time Uncle Jim was away at the hospital I spent time there, gathering oysters and clams. I could bring shellfish back for us to eat!"

"But if you could go to the beach alone, then by rights all the tenants would be allowed to go. Think of what would happen if Mr. Gravestone went to the beach by himself."

At first, I rejected her reasoning, but then I thought a little harder. "He'd get lost," I said.

"Or get in a fight with one of the neighbors on the way there," she added.

"Then isn't it cheating that we sneak out before breakfast and go for walks?"

"No. We aren't alone. Besides, no one knows."

One day, when we were at the breakfast table I decided I was going to air my thoughts again to Mrs. Wright.

"I have something to say," I said, as I wiped my mouth with my napkin and set my fork down. "I think the tenants need fresh air."

Mrs. Wright set her fork down, too, and looked me straight in the eyes. "Dylan. You tell me this every morning at breakfast and I explain to you every morning that we have a lovely porch and a big swing for the tenants to sit on. You can get plenty of fresh air on the porch."

"No disrespect meant, Mrs. Wright, but just sitting on the porch isn't enough. There's more in the world to see."

She chuckled quietly and took a sip of her tea. The other tenants looked at both of us but kept eating. Liona looked as if she were holding her breath.

"Dylan, I happen to know you have a history of taking very long walks on the beach. Your aunt told me about your habits. She said sometimes you would be gone for hours. So, I must ask you, are you requesting this annuity for yourself? Or are you really concerned about the other tenants? I cannot have you wandering up and down the Pacific Coast shoreline by yourself with no supervision. There would be no way to guarantee your safety. I might add, that your safety is covered in our contract with your aunt."

I wasn't sure how to respond. This was the first time she ever mentioned my walks on the beach, or Aunt Agnes, or my habits. I didn't expect an answer like that.

Liona interrupted us and came to my defense. "Dylan cares a lot about all the tenants, Mrs. Wright. He wants to see them happy. And I think he's correct. I think we all need to get out in the sunshine and get some exercise. We could all go together. We wouldn't have to go far. I'd be more than willing to help."

Mrs. Wright didn't respond to our request right away, but later that afternoon she told Liona and I that we could take everyone for a walk if we stayed on the cul-de-sac off Elm Street, and only walked on the sidewalk. After that day, Liona and I were granted the privilege of helping everybody get some fresh air.

Saturday morning Liona and I took the tenants for their first outing. Mrs. Wright hired a team of teenagers from the local high school to clean the house that day, so she was glad to get us all out of the way.

I pushed Randy in his wheel chair on the sidewalk and Liona pushed Mrs. Benson behind me. Mr. Gravestone and Mr. Bromheimer followed with their walkers after us. We had to travel slow because all Mr. Gravestone could do was shuffle his feet. He said his back hurt and he refused to change out of his slippers. The day was warm and pleasant, so I didn't really mind going slow. They all loved going outside. Mrs. Benson couldn't stop talking about the flowers in the neighbor's garden and Randy was fascinated by the mailboxes. He wanted me to open them, so he could see what was in them, but I told him that wasn't allowed. I stopped at the empty corner lot that adjacent to the beach so that Randy could see the ocean.

"Look at those big white birds, Randy! Those are seagulls."

"See.... gulls," he said and laughed. He always laughed when I talked to him.

"You see how they pluck at the sand? And then fly into the sky? Watch!" I pointed to one gull. Randy was laughing and watching. "He has something in his mouth. Do you know what that is?"

"No."

"A clam. He's going to drop it. Look! And now he flies down…" I narrated the gull's food journey as the bird dove on the sand to retrieve its clam. "He cracked the shell and now he can get at the meat."

Randy had listened to every word, followed the bird's flight by moving his head up and down, and then laughed as the seagull pecked at the shellfish on the ground. "Ew," he finally moaned. "Raw clam."

I patted him on the shoulder. "Yeah, but they eat all their food raw, so they don't care."

Randy got a kick out of that and went off into a laughing frenzy. "I sh…sh…should crack cl…clams like that too," he said.

"Then you'd have to eat them raw, Randy," I teased.

He made a grunting noise and then laughed again. "No way."

After lunch, Mrs. Wright put Randy and Mrs. Benson down for a nap and the two older gentlemen amused themselves with a game of chess.

"Liona," I said when we were back in the kitchen cleaning up. We hadn't talked to each other the whole time we were doing the dishes mostly because we were busy and lost in our own thoughts.

"What?"

She seemed disinterested in having a conversation. I gathered up courage before I spoke. "Do you want to sit outside on the swing with me?"

"Why?"

"Because I've been wanting to sit there ever since I came here."

"Then you should sit there."

"But do you want to sit with me?"

"You need me to sit there with you?"

"No," I said, thinking about whether my request came from a need. "I guess I could sit there by myself."

She turned around and looked at me, wiping her hands on her apron. Our eyes made a pleasant connection. We both liked looking at each other, I think. At least, I liked looking at her. Not just because she was pretty, but because I felt strong when our eyes met. Strong and powerful. Powerful the same as my magic made me feel, except this power went through my whole body, not just my left side.

"Okay. I can sit with you. That sounds like fun."

The day was warm and overcast. Birds sang and swarmed in the tall poplar tree next to the house. Honeysuckle was in bloom. I could smell its sweet fragrance from the porch.

Liona rocked the swing gently as I sat quiet with my hands folded on my lap. Uncle Jim and I never talked much, so I was glad that Liona didn't always expect a conversation. Instead I enjoyed the warm air on my face. I could taste the ocean too. I thought about Uncle Jim, pictured his face and imagined him watching me. I think he'd be happy for me, sitting here next to a girl. Even though there wasn't anything between me and Liona, Uncle Jim would probably think there was.

She peered at me from the corner of her eye when that thought about Uncle Jim came to mind, so I focused on the hibiscus in bloom by the porch, and the pretty pink of the flowers. They reminded me of Annabella's dress. We sat there and rocked, me in my blue jeans and sweatshirt. She wore jeans like mine today, only hers were tight and showed off her shape and she wore a green-colored hoodie that matched her eyes. Her purple and orange hair shone brazen against the gray of the day.

She smelled sweet too, not like perfume but like a subtle wisp of rose petals across your fingers tips. A fragrance that only comes once every few whiffs, and when it does you breathe in long and hard so as not to miss a moment of its flavor.

"Would you like to see something special? Something my Uncle Jim gave me?" I asked.

"Okay. Sure."

"Wait here," I stood up slowly so as not to rock the swing too hard. "Please?" I added so she didn't think I was bossing her.

"Okay."

I rushed up the stairs two at a time and unlocked my door, snatched my pack, raced back down the stairs, and leapt through the living room, nodding cordially to Mr. Gravestone and Mr. Bromheimer who stopped their chess playing to gawk at me. I then jogged back outside.

"I want to show you this." I panted after all that running. "My Uncle Jim gave this figurine to me before he died." Liona scooted closer to me as I unwrapped Annabella the same precise way Uncle Jim had the first day he showed her to me. Careful so the paper wouldn't tear, or Annabella wouldn't drop. When she was completely uncovered, I held her in front of both of us, turning her gently.

Liona's eyes opened wide when I handed the figurine to her. Annabella looked good in Liona's slender fingers, as if she belonged there, for Liona's skin was nearly as pale as Annabella's, and just as smooth.

"She's beautiful, Dylan," Liona said.

"I know. She was my grandma's. Only relic Uncle Jim had that belonged to my family. Everything else got sold while he was in Vietnam."

"What a special gift. You must be very proud to have her, then."

91

I nodded. I hadn't expected to get choked up. "I wish I could keep her somewhere on display. Like on the mantel or something so everyone could see her."

"Yeah, that's not a good idea. Too many people come and go. You could put her on your dresser in your room though."

I could, but I didn't. I wrapped the figurine in newspaper again, put her back in her box, and then I put the box in my pack again.

Life at the boarding home was peaceful for a week after that. Even though I hadn't gotten to a point where I could call Mrs. Wright's boarding house home, the place wasn't hostile either. With the greenery around the porch, birds singing and occasional sunshine, the home felt more like a retreat. My bedroom was comfortable, and I enjoyed the hot shower. I wasn't a recluse, but when we weren't eating or cleaning up, or working outside, I stayed to myself unless Liona wanted to sit on the swing. I hadn't healed from Uncle Jim's death, and I still missed the oyster beds at Windy Point.

Some things never heal.

I became accustomed to taking Randy outside with the others. He wanted to see the sea gulls whenever we went for our walk, so I'd stop at the end of the street overlooking the water every day. Some days he would argue with me to stay longer. He didn't want to leave. I didn't either. I think if he weren't in a wheel chair I would have taken him to the tide pools at Windy Point, or to shuck oysters. He would have liked that. I bet he would have loved to see me spinning pearls.

Sometimes on our walks, Randy and I would stay at the corner watching the surf, the seagulls, and an occasional sandpiper while Liona took the other tenants down the block and back. She didn't mind.

"I'm happy that Randy is getting some enjoyment in life," she whispered to me as she wheeled Mrs. Benson by.

I looked at Randy. He smiled up at the sky. At me. At the seagulls.

"Me too," I told Liona. "He's got a hard life."

"It's…s pretty here," Randy said.

"The scenery is beautiful," I agreed, happy that Randy felt the same way about the ocean as I did. We stood there quiet, breathing the salty air, Randy in his wheel chair and I behind him. My thoughts wandered. When the breeze picked up, I wrapped his blanket around his shoulders.

"You ready to go home?"

"No," he said, even though he shivered.

We waited until the others returned.

Dinner after our walks were more pleasant because everyone came home tired. By this time, I had learned what everyone liked to eat so I would whip up a little treat for each of them. Even Mr. Gravestone kept his dirty looks to himself. It could be that Liona worked some magic on him in secret, and that's why we saw only the congenial side him. I didn't know, but I liked to think the reason was my cooking.

I brought the glow-marble to Randy's room every night when I took him to bed, making sure the marble was on his dresser where he could see the lovely colors and soft illumination. I was half-tempted to show him Annabella, but I didn't. The time wasn't right. Someday I will tell him about my grandma and Uncle Jim, and the story behind Annabella.

C Chapter 10

Typhoon

My alarm went off Monday morning, and just like every morning I jumped out of bed with my heart pounding. I shut the ringer off quickly. After I washed, I looked for my pack and remembered I had left it in the living room when we came home from our walk. I trusted everyone in the house now and was certain no one would hurt Annabella. People here had proven to be trustworthy, even Mr. Gravestone, since we all had gotten to know each other during our walks. Besides, no one in the boarding house seemed particularly interested in my stuff.

I thought I'd find Liona busy in the kitchen, but instead when I stepped out of my room, she buzzed through the hall, slammed doors and cursed like I'd never heard her swear before. She nearly bumped into me from behind when I reached the bottom stair, and that's when I saw Randy in the living room.

He swayed back and forth in his chair like he was upset over something, moaning and making strange noises with his tongue. I strode over to him to see what was wrong, thinking maybe I could quiet him. He stopped rocking but didn't pay me any mind. He stared at the ceiling. Drool ran down his mouth.

"Don't get too close, Dylan, I'm warning you." I had never heard Liona speak in such a stressful tone of voice. "He's restrained, not enough, but that was the best I could do without getting hit in the head. He's got a long reach so be careful!"

I put my hands in my hoodie pockets and strolled up to him, talking low. "You wouldn't hit your old buddy Dylan now, would you Randy?" I asked him.

"Watch out!" Liona warned me again.

Randy didn't seem to hear me, at least he didn't respond to my voice. He was strapped down in his chair by a lap belt at the waist, and had his helmet buckled securely, yet his arms were free. When I started talking to him, he perked up. With his fists clenched tight grasping the arms to his wheelchair, he groaned, rolled his eyes and bit his tongue. The closer I got, the more animate he became.

"He's miserable," I said, my stomach turning sour at the sight. He ground his teeth and tears rolled down his cheeks. "Where is Mrs. Wright?" I could feel Randy's pain, though I had no idea what ailed him.

"Not here!" Liona answered with bitterness. She moved about the house rummaging through every drawer she could find. The buffet, the desk, the night table. She picked up a stack of papers piled on top of several magazines and slammed them down again. "And from what I can tell, he's out of his meds. I can't find them anywhere. He hasn't had any since yesterday afternoon. Maybe Mrs. Wright took them with her last night. What a dumb thing to do!" She threw her hands up in disgust. "I don't know why she would do something like that. She knows what happens when Randy doesn't take his meds!"

At that moment, Mr. Gravestone appeared from the downstairs hall, leaning heavily on his walker and mumbling profanities. He stood next to the grandfather clock. The pose he struck could have been used for a monster in an old Hitchcock movie. His thin hair stuck out in spikes. His robe draped open revealed his skeletal frame and saggy sweatpants. The scowl on his face might have killed a flock of crows. Liona rolled her eyes. "Go back to bed Mr. Gravestone. Breakfast is nowhere near being ready, yet."

"How can I sleep with all this ghastly commotion?" he snarled. "Give the kid a sedative or knock him upside the head with a two-by-four. One or the other. Shut him up!"

At that moment, Randy let out a scream. He nearly tipped his wheel chair over he rocked so hard.

"What can I do?" I asked, nearing panic. I exchanged glances with Mr. Gravestone, his angry, mine wide eyed.

"Cook breakfast, okay? I'm going to see if there are any sedatives upstairs, and call Mrs. Wright's cell phone. I have no idea where she's at, but she needs to be here!"

Relieved that Liona gave me something to do, I retreated to the kitchen, while she ran upstairs. When I saw that she ran upstairs and left Randy howling at the top of his lungs in the living room, I called out to her.

"Liona?" I wanted to ask her if maybe she could use her magic to calm him down, but she was gone before I could get her attention. I decided at that moment that if Liona wouldn't attempt to use her magical powers to ease his pain, then I would.

I'd never used my magic on anyone before, so it might be worth a try. Randy and I had become close friends and because I cared for him, I don't think I could cause him any harm. I took a deep breath, walked cautiously into the living room and knelt next to his chair. I had to dodge away when he swung, but he was slow, and I was fast. He missed me. "Randy, listen," I said.

He moaned. His eyes were glazy, and he had a faraway look. I don't even know if he could sense me near him, much less hear me. I kept talking though because there was always the chance I'd get through. "Listen to me I'm going to give you something to make you feel better. Remember that glow marble? I'm going to give you some magic like the glow marble. You'll feel better inside when I do, okay?"

"Oh god," Mr. Gravestone grumbled and then took his walker back down the hall to his bedroom. I ignored the old man.

Randy had stopped swinging his arms, so I stood up and touched his hand, which was grasping his wheel chair. His knuckles turned white he was so strong, and tense.

"You're hurting inside, aren't you?" I asked him quietly, my heart going out to him. Of course, he didn't answer. Too much pain ran through him. I wanted badly to take that pain away so that he didn't hurt so much. He was too good of a person. He deserved to be smiling and laughing.

"Listen Randy, I'm going to help you." I rested my hand on his. My fingertips began to tingle. Conjuring magic on Randy's behalf was easy because I had a lot of desire for him to feel better. The magic to pulsated in the palm of my hand like a locomotive. The energy then sped through my fingers into his. The light raced up his arm. He relaxed for a second. A thin smile parted from his lips and he sighed. Thrilled that the magic was working, I sent more energy into him. I watched the glow of light travel into his arm like a Star Wars laser beam filling his body with electricity, only these were good waves of heat filling him.

Suddenly, an odd stinging sensation burned my fingers. The light rays were doubling back into my hand again. My fingers cramped and then contorted. Pain shot through my arm. The left side of my body stiffened. My shoulder ached, and then my chest throbbed, and I thought I was having a heart attack. I doubled over, every muscle inside of me tightened in spasm. I cried out. I had never felt anything so horrible. My knees gave out and I shrank to the floor, still touching Randy's hand. I couldn't let go. My cries sounded like Randy's. I shook in anguish. There was no let up. I couldn't breathe.

"No!" Liona screamed and ran from the dining room to the two of us. She pried my hand off Randy's and pulled me away from him. If only for a second, I caught him staring at me in disbelief, free from pain, from seizure. And then he squinted and doubled over again, moaning. She dragged me to the couch and scolded me, her voice a whisper. "You can't practice magic on him, fool!" she said, her hands a cool relief as she patted my cheeks and wiped my tears away with her thumbs.

Randy cried out again, loud enough to wake up the other tenants. I couldn't bear to watch him. Still cramped and aching from my muscles having been so tight, I leaned on Liona's shoulder and balanced myself enough to stand. Waiting for the dizziness to subside, I held the back of a chair. Liona was all over me, holding me up, stroking my face.

"Are you okay?" she kept whispering. When most of my senses returned, and my body no longer seized, I peeled myself away from her and hurried to the kitchen. I grabbed a sack of potatoes and heaved them onto the table. Alone again I breathed deeply and tried to compose myself. My body shook.

"Are you all right?" Liona asked from the doorway.

"I think so."

She walked up to me and grabbed my arms, her grip firm and strong. I hadn't been grabbed like that since I was a kid. At first, her touch startled me, but when she looked deep into my eyes I knew she had a genuine concern for me. "Don't ever attempt to use your magic to take someone's pain away. Ever! Do you understand? There's no place for the pain to go but in your body. Don't mess with nature! Just don't!"

"Okay," I said, having learned my lesson. "I won't!" Her anger showed in the color of her face. "You're mad." I didn't ask her, I told her.

"Damn right I'm mad. You scared the crap out of me. I don't want anything crazy like that to happen to you.

Who knows where that might have gone? You could have died!"

She left me–as shook up as I was–alone in the kitchen. Confused. I took some more deep breaths and then remembered I was supposed to make breakfast. While washing my hands, I thought about calling on my powers to get the food cooked. I closed my eyes shut, but I was too upset to visualize the ocean, or oysters, or anything peaceful. What with Randy still crying out, and Mr. Gravestone yelling at him to shut up and Liona slamming doors, nothing was going right. I sliced my finger chopping the potatoes and hot grease splattered on my wrist when I dropped them in the pan.

Liona dashed in the kitchen once and left immediately when the front door opened. I saw Mrs. Wright came into the house, just as upset as Liona. She walked right past Randy and pulled Liona aside.

"I need to talk with you," she said.

"Where have you been?" Liona shouted.

Mrs. Wright answered with a hushed voice. I get that she didn't want the tenants to be alarmed but I don't see how anyone in the house wasn't scared out of their gourds, already. I sucked on my bleeding finger as I watched the two.

"I got a call from a social worker yesterday just before her office closed. The matter needed to be discussed this morning so meeting her today was very important. I was downtown at first light, trying to straighten things out."

"Where are Randy's pills?" Liona demanded. She didn't show any signs of being interested in social workers or appointments or Mrs. Wright's problems. I secretly rooted for her, because I was as angry at Mrs. Wright as much as Liona was.

"Here. In my purse. I had to get his prescription filled." She delved through her handback and pulled out a bottle of pills. "I'm sorry. I thought the trip would be a short one."

"Look at him!" Liona responded. She swore unmentionable words as she grabbed the pill bottle from Mrs. Wright's hands. I jumped aside as she flew past me to the sink, filled a cup with water, and raced toward Randy.

That's when I noticed Mr. Gravestone sitting on the couch with my blue shoebox on his lap. I wanted to go get it from him but if I left the food, the potatoes would burn. Maybe Liona would notice and take my box from him. I flipped the potatoes and pulled a carton of eggs from the fridge, turning my head often whenever I passed by the doorway, keeping an eye on Mr. Gravestone and Annabella.

Once I had cracked the last egg, and scrambled and cooked them, I brought the food to the table. Mr. Bromheimer came alone into the dining room. He didn't sit down right away. Liona wheeled Mrs. Benson in for breakfast, but that was as far as we got with our meal because we were interrupted again.

Two cars pulled up in the driveway. One of them was a police car. The other van looked like the one Aunt Agnes drove Uncle Jim to the doctors in. People got out of the vehicles and came knocking on the front door—two women and a law officer. The knock was loud and brought back memories of when I lived with my mother because police were always showing up at our house for one thing or another.

Mrs. Wright hurried to let them in as if she was expecting company. Liona followed her.

I stayed in the dining room with Mrs. Benson and Mr. Bromheimer. Mr. Bromheimer pulled his chair out and sat down, but he didn't pick up his fork even though his breakfast was steaming hot in front of him. He leaned back on his chair.

Mr. Gravestone sat in the living room on the couch with my box, and Randy, much calmer than before because his meds were taking effect, rocked back and forth in his wheel chair in front of the fireplace. He had his helmet on, and his lap belt strapped across his waist, which kept him snug in his wheelchair. I felt bad for him, but I would never use magic to help him, again. The pain had been too much for me. I guess I'm a weakling. No one gave Randy tribute for his courage. To me, he was as brave as Uncle Jim had been in Vietnam.

Mr. Gravestone finally set my box down on the couch. I took that as a cue to rescue Annabella, so I sprung into the living room. When I had ahold of the shoebox, he tried to grab it back and grumbled and spat at me. "What are you doing?" he asked. "You're just as much a maniac as the rest of these morons."

Still holding the shoebox, I pushed his hands off the other end, and carefully stepped away.

As Mrs. Wright let the strangers into the house, I went about looking for a safe place for Annabella. I cradled the box in my arms as I walked across the room and sat next to Randy on the rocking chair. I scooted so close to him that our knees touched. I put the shoe box on my lap, opened it, found the glow marble, and slipped the ball into my hands, closing the lid securely. I spoke Randy's name softly.

"Randy?" I tried to get his attention. However, the conversation between Mrs. Wright and the social workers was impossible to ignore. They stood by the door. Two women in dark wool coats and high heels. One had short dark hair and bright red lipstick. The other's blond hair was tied back in a ponytail. She was much younger than the first and someone called her Lynn. The police officer stood behind them with his arms crossed. Mrs. Wright disappeared down the hall for a moment, and the women moved farther into the living room. Their eyes scanned us all like vultures checking out road kill, scrutinizing the house with critical frowns. I shuffled in my seat. Nervous. I'd seen too many social workers when I was a little boy. Always too eager to pounce, they took me away from what had been familiar. My house, my bedroom that had been a kind of refuge. My school. I didn't have many friends, but Mrs. Dall, my sixth-grade teacher in my old school liked me. The social workers pulled me out of that school and put me in a new one. Even Uncle Jim had to fight them off at one point or they would have taken me away from him.

Mrs. Wright returned from her den with a pile of papers in her hands. She held them out to the women to read. The social workers shook their heads.

"This is all true. It's all evidence that I've been taking good care of Randy.?" Mrs. Wright said.

Randy made a grunting sound just then.

"You can take these to the hearing and show the judge, but to us they mean nothing."

"He's been here for three months," Mrs. Wright argued. "We've had no problem. He's healthy, eats well, even gets fresh air daily. We're perfectly capable of taking care of him."

"Not according to our records. This facility is unacceptable for someone in Randy's condition." The dark haired social worker made a sour face and handed the papers back to Mrs. Wright.

Randy moaned again. "No…n. n.no"

"Three months in this facility should never have happened. He should never have been here in the first place. We're taking him away. Now. Today." She nodded to Lynn and then to the police officer who glanced this way with a perplexed look on his face. I could feel Randy tremble since our knees were still touching.

"I can't let him go!" Mrs. Wright protested.

"You don't have a choice. Where are his belongings?"

Liona turned her back on all of them and went down the hall to Randy's room.

"What are you going to do with him?" Mrs. Wright's face paled. She looked terrified.

"That information is confidential. He's no longer a concern of yours. You'll be getting a bill from the state for the misappropriation of funds."

"Misappropriation? What? You're going to make me pay you back? The money was used for his care."

The older social worker lifted her briefcase onto the table and pulled a bundle of papers out. She handed them to Mrs. Wright. "Which you provided illegally. I'm sorry, Mrs. Wright. If you would like to contest the decision, you're entitled to a hearing. I doubt you'll have any luck getting Randy back, but with a lawyer you may be able to waiver the fee. Be thankful we aren't closing this place down entirely."

When Mrs. Wright looked at me, I was no help. What could I say? I took Randy's hand, and he squeezed mine so hard it hurt.

When Liona came back with Randy's luggage, she handed them to Lynn, who quickly dodged out the door with them. The other social worker spoke to the policeman, pointed at us, and said something I didn't hear. He nodded.

I felt a fever come on. This couldn't be happening. They were taking Randy away.

"Randy?" I slid the glowing ball to him. He stared at it for a moment, then with his long white fingers he clenched it tight. The light bled through his flesh so that his fist looked like a cannon ball. Instead of laughing like before, he leaned toward me, contorted his face in a ghastly way, furrowed his brow, and barred his teeth. He looked so much like a pit bull I thought he would snap at me and tear me to pieces.

He shoved me away from him with both his fists, pushing his glowing knuckles into my chest. His chair rolled backward from the force. "No! N…no," he said. "I'm no…ot going with them. You ca…nt…make me, Dyl.an."

I heard furniture move behind me. The lamp. The coffee table. They were clearing a path to get Randy through.

"Randy, look at me," I caught his attention for a moment. "I'm with you, buddy. I'm not going to make you do anything you don't want to!" I meant it with all my heart, but even though I swore an oath I had no control over the matter.

Randy tried to focus on me, but he was full of emotion. I knew because Randy was a lot like me in ways. Like a dam holding back unmeasurable amounts of water and having no release, no faucet to let the words flow, or the tears. Randy was bottled up right now. His face burned red, his lips were almost bleeding from clamping his teeth on them.

They surrounded us like a pack of wolves. The social worker came around the back of the couch to get at him from his right, and the police officer moved in on his left. The closer they got, the more violent Randy became. He stopped glaring at me and pushed the wheels on his chair back and forth to avoid being seized, running over my toes. At that point Lynn came back into the house and moved swiftly toward us as well.

"Nooo," Randy moaned. "I'm staying with my bud….bud…dy." His eyes grew wide with fear. He really didn't want to go.

"Can't you let him stay?" I asked when I looked up at the policeman. No one responded to me. Mrs. Wright pleaded with them, but her cause was more to keep her boarding house and her reputation. I don't think she had that much love for Randy.

I had to stop this madness. I tried standing up, but both women hovered over me. They were behind my chair, coming to the end of the couch. If I had stood, I'd have bumped heads with one.

"I…. I'm not leaving," Randy repeated, rolling even further backward so that his chair was now flat against the wall. "Dy…Dylan! Stop them, Dylan." He sounded like a wild animal dying in the woods, and he was crying out my name to save him.

A split moment's time was not enough for me to think. I wanted to come to his rescue and protect him. Maybe grab his chair and wheel him out the back door but it was too late and then things got crazy. When the dark haired social worker squeezed in behind him, she took hold of his wheelchair. Randy dropped the marble. As I reached down to pick it up and put it back in the shoe box, Randy started swinging his arms at the women. I didn't have time to dodge. I got in the way and he popped me in the eye. It was an accident, but it hurt. I saw stars! The pain was so great I couldn't think at all. I stood up holding my eye. My shoe box slid off my lap. Randy screamed so loud I had to plug my ears. The policeman jumped over the couch to get behind Randy.

Everyone yelled and gave orders, but no one could get close enough to Randy because he was swinging something fierce. They tried to contain him. Randy's a strong guy though, and he swung back and forth, grabbing anything that got in his way. If I wasn't holding my eye, I might have been able to stop him.

What happened then, happened too fast. And yet I saw everything in slow motion. One moment my box was on the floor at his feet and the next moment it was upside down on his lap, and then Annabella was air born, flying across the room and slamming into the brick fireplace.

The crash split my heart in two.

Pieces of her flew into the air as she shattered. Bit by bit she fell, her delicate, white porcelain body splintered into thousands of tiny shards and spewed out across the hearth, into the rug, and on the end tables.

I paid no attention to what went on around me after that. I plummeted into a black void. I saw shapes moving, which could have been the social workers pushing Randy out of the house, and Mrs. Wright who followed them outside, or maybe Mr. Gravestone who drove his walker into the dining room and down the hall. I don't know. I heard voices. I even heard my name once.

Fire burned inside of me, flames roared out of control like the wild fire Uncle Jim and I witnessed last summer in the mountains. Raging hot and fierce, and I wished then that the flames consumed me, ate me up like a charcoal falling into a barbecue pit. The sounds around me deadened until I couldn't hear anything. Not a thing. Only silence. A death sonata for my beautiful Annabella who lay in unrecognizable bits; tiny white and pink chips scattered across the floor; fragments of my grandma's keepsake.

My last gift from Uncle Jim.

"Dylan," the voice said. I blinked, squeezed my eyes tight and blinked again. "Dylan." It was Liona. She stood by the couch, one hand resting on its arm, the other twisting a stray lock that had fallen on the wrong side of her head. Her earring dangled and caught the sunlight from the window. Her eyes sparkled, not in gladness. No, I think there was a tear. No one else was in the room.

"I'm sorry," she said.

What could she be sorry for? She didn't destroy Annabella. She didn't give it to Randy. She didn't tell those people to come over and take my friend away or lose his medicine. She had nothing to do with any of this.

Next to Liona on the floor was my pack. I moved toward her to pick it up. That's when the shock came. That terrifying electricity that I hated so much. Lasting only a minute, I froze and took a deep breath. I knew I couldn't control it and that's why I hoped beyond hope it would go away before I did something to hurt someone. Liona's eyes were wide open. She didn't say anything though. I don't know what I looked like, probably a monster because she took a step back as if she was afraid of me. I resented that as soon as the tingling subsided. I glared at her, but I doubt she understood. She probably thought I hated her. I slowly got control of my arms and reached out for my pack, slipped it on my back and stood up straight. I looked into those pretty green eyes again. Eyes that I didn't deserve to look at because I'm leaving them. For good. I'm leaving all of this for good. I didn't even want my clothes up in my room anymore. I just wanted out. I just wanted to smell the sea air. Calm myself on the beach. Conjure some good magic maybe. Forget all of this. Forget this home, these people. Maybe even forget Annabella ever existed.

"Dylan." She followed me to the door. I ignored her and pushed her arm off mine as I met the morning air. The police car motor ran idle outside. The women surrounded the car, still arguing. Probably Randy was strapped in the van. I went the other way. Liona walked by my side for a while but I walked faster, and she was soon panting behind me.

"Liona, come here!" Mrs. Wright called and then Liona left me.

I didn't look back. Not once.

C Chapter 11

Tim Lan

I stormed, past the cop car with its flashing lights, and the van where they hid Randy away. Past the social workers in their stylish dresses and fancy heels and evil schemes. I suspect they knew I left. Maybe not. Their concern was Randy and all the wrongs they accused Mrs. Wright of committing. Maybe she was going to lose the boarding house. I felt bad for her. I felt bad for Randy. What could I do to help? Nothing. So, I kept walking. No one said anything to me, except Liona. She was the only one who cared that I was leaving but what could she do? Nothing. I didn't want anyone chasing me, not even her. I needed to be alone. Far away. I didn't think about where my feet took me. Toward the sea, like a magnet, because the sea was my refuge. The ocean knew me and was my friend. My only friend.

I stumbled down the woodsy trail that led from the house to the road, and which didn't follow the driveway where everyone was congregated. The trail veered north a bit. Hedged with wild rhododendrons, salal, and thimbleberries. Shadowing firs soon cloaked me from all sides until I couldn't see the house. The trail didn't seem like it had been used for a long time, the path was so overgrown. Twigs scratched at my clothes and I had to slow down and wrestle with sticker bushes which caught my clothes and pulled my hair. Thorns dug into my fingers when I freed myself and I had to fight my way through thick clumps of branches to pass.

Once at the bottom of the hill, I stepped out on the road. Thankfully, no cars passed by because I couldn't stand to look another person in the eye, stranger or not. I just wanted to be gone. Gone! I turned left and crossed the street, shuffling along as quietly as I knew how, hoping I was invisible to the world.

Mrs. Wright's boarding home nested in the woods that made up most of Elwood Estates. Not far away, however, were rows of houses lined up along the street. Big fancy houses with fresh paint, manicured gardens and white picket fences. Not a soul stirred in any of the front yards for morning had not yet woken the world. The paper boy had left his trail of newsprint-stuffed-in-plastic bags on everyone's driveways. I hoped no one ventured outside to pick them up because the sight of me might cause neighbors to be suspicious. Who knows if I could pass as a normal man casually taking a jog, instead of a crazy person running away. If I had known how to use my magic to become invisible this would have been the perfect time.

The corner lot which opened to the beach was within view. The beach meant safety. I jogged across the street past a large red house with a chain link fence. A gate hung open. Out of nowhere, and with a terrifying bark, a big black dog charged at me, snarling and growling and carrying on as if I were a thief. He ran along the fence and then raced through the gate, out of the yard and on to the sidewalk. In a flash, he caught up to me, snapping at my heels. I panicked and pulled my backpack off my back and used it as a buffer to keep him from biting me. I tried to run away but he kept at my shoes and my bag, jumping and snapping. He didn't let off until someone from the house called him several times. He ceased his assault, snarled at me, and then raced back to his master.

"Sorry!" the man called out to me as he picked up the newspaper on his steps.

I had no breath left to respond. I turned toward the beach again and ran. I jumped over grassy sand dunes and skipped over driftwood logs until the cool hard and wet sand tingled under my feet. I hadn't thought about where I was going. The only thing I was aware of was my racing heart. I knew if I stopped I'd have an anxiety attack, so I kept running.

When I was sure no one from the boarding home could see me, I eased up and caught my breath. Once I felt the ocean spray on my face my heart slowed, and I calmed down. Once my pulse quieted I could feel the hurt. Losing Annabella was like losing Uncle Jim all over again.

How I wished I could take time back. I'd have tucked my shoe box away in my closet in my room and left it there. I'd have never let anyone see Annabella, or the glowing marble and kept her for myself. Mr. Gravestone would have never touched the box. Randy would have never picked it up off my lap. Annabella would never have flown across the room. I squeezed my eyes shut because I didn't want to see her pieces scattered all over the carpet. It didn't help though because the image was burned into my mind.

Right then I heard the crash of a wave and the cool water that tickled my toes woke me up to where I was. Man, how I missed being here alone, listening to the surf. Not another soul stirred, only me and the gulls and constant heartbeat of the breakers against the shoreline. My legs were tired and my breath hot, so I walked even slower. I didn't need to run anymore. No one followed. No one cared where I was or that my heart was broken. Walking was much easier on my body, but not on my mind because my thoughts drove me to despair. I counted my loses. Uncle Jim. Annabella, and now the social workers were taking my poor friend Randy away from his home and he had no say. Trapped in his body, no one would listen to him.

"I know how it is, Buddy," I said, wishing he was here to hear me. "I know."

My life emptied out right there. I gave it to the sea just like the oysters with their scattered shells broken and ground into sand. Like the empty crab skeletons plucked clean by the seagulls, sandpipers and crows. Sand fleas devouring the remains. Remnants of something that could have been. That was, once.

What had I been?

I stumbled when the shoreline grew rocky. I wanted to cry, but I didn't. I'd keep that kind of feeling inside because I'm not a cry baby. Uncle Jim told me I wasn't. I could fight just about any emotion if I wanted to. So, I did. The fight kept me going. I walked straight toward the buttes that sheltered Windy Point. Homesickness rumbled inside of me just as hard as the breakers crashing against the rocks. Homesickness was one feeling I could overcome, because I could, and would go home. I'd sneak into my old house and stay there. If Aunt Agnes stayed away.

The walk to Windy Point took a long time. The sun sank low in the sky and when I rounded the Point, soft blue twilight welcomed me. The familiar oyster beds stretched out before me in the distance. I thought I'd venture to my house, but I was tired. I couldn't walk any farther and there was still about half a mile to go, so I fell onto the wet sand near a pile of driftwood. I made sure I was far enough away from the sea so as not to wake up wet or washed away if the tide came while I was asleep. I constructed a lean-to from some sun-bleached driftwood logs, a fortress which would keep me sheltered from the wind and any snooping transients that sometimes wander to the beach from town. The logs glowed under the starlit sky. So ominous did my little shelter blaze, it reminded me of an abode on the lost world of Tatooine. I pretended I was Anakin Skywalker come home to save my planet.

This was my first night on my own and I amazed myself for being able to get away without anyone following me. No one would find me here cause once I laid down, I was invisible to the road.

I tucked my pack under my head for a pillow. There were holes in my shelter's roof; long slits of open space where the twists of the logs didn't match up so that I could see the sky. I watched the clouds curl and turn and float above me until they blocked the stars and eventually massed into dark. I must have dozed because the next time I opened my eyes, a cheerful brown face leaned over and peeked in at me through the doorway. His crooked teeth gleamed white like the moon.

"Tim Lan!"

He crawled into my shelter. "Where've you been, Em? Sleeping?" he whispered.

"No. I mean yes." I sat up. "I must have dozed."

"Why are you sleeping here? What happened?"

"Oh man, you don't know!" I said, remembering I had neither told Tim Lan about my uncle, nor had I a chance to say goodbye. I sat up and brushed the sand out of my hair. "I'm sorry. My uncle died. I should have told you."

"Oh, so sorry." He sat down next to me. "So sorry."

"Yeah, me too."

"You live homeless now? How come?"

"Not homeless. This is home," I said. "More than any house I'd been in lately."

"That's not right. Homelessness is not for young people like you. Maybe old men like me, but not you. Too much future."

"Well, I don't think there's a future for me. Other than this."

"No, there's a future for you."

Not sure what future Tim Lan meant. I hadn't seen any future in anything that had happened this last month. I ignored that sickly look of sympathy. "Aunt Agnes is selling Uncle Jim's house."

He let out a long drawn out moan. Then he shook his head. "You should fight in the courts. They're stealing your house. Don't let them do that."

I scowled. "I think what Aunt Agnes is doing is legal and she has her mind made up. Maybe she already sold the house, I don't know. I can't argue with her, though. What's done is done." I had heard Uncle Jim say that a lot and now was a fitting time to repeat his words.

"Why not argue?"

I had no good answer except for the fact that I never argued with her, or any of my other relatives for that matter. Except maybe for when I grabbed the muffin tin from Shirley. I shook my head and looked out at the shifting fog, creeping in closer, masking the sea so that there were only me and Tim Lan under a driftwood roof floating in a cloud.

"What happened?"

"Things got bad." That's all I could muster to say, but Tim Lan had a special knack at pulling my thoughts out of me. "Something broke." I wiped my face with my sleeve. Tim Lan leaned in closer.

"You could make new again with your magic, no?"

I shook my head. The idea had occurred to me, but I buried the notion. "No." I looked him in the eyes because I wanted him to understand. "You can't replace something like that. Annabella is gone. She was grandma's and then she belonged to Uncle Jim. How can I replace her without bringing them back? And I can't do that."

He was silent for a moment after that, having no idea who Annabella was. He touched my shoulder. "I understand," he whispered. "Still. Go back."

I felt sorry for him-trying to convince me of something I knew I couldn't do. "I'm slow. Aunt Agnes thinks I'm not capable of taking care of myself. I guess I don't think fast enough, or right enough."

"Who told you that? You're a smart boy. Maybe naïve, not dumb though."

I shrugged my shoulders and shifted in the sand. "I don't know."

"You just need help."

"My uncle helped me. Now there's no one."

"There's me."

He was serious, I could see the sincerity in his eyes. His smile had straightened, not to a frown, but to a grim sort of expression; the kind Uncle Jim would give me before he included me in on a secret.

"You have a gift. I appreciate your gift. Stay with me," he said.

I searched his eyes for a long moment before I sat up straight, before I sensed hope of something better happening to me than being tossed around like a rag doll by people who didn't care about me, or only new me on the surface, or who wanted something from me. "Really?"

"Look." He took hold of my left hand in both of his and squeezed it. "I've seen the magic, right?"

"Yeah. Sometimes there's magic."

"Sometimes is all we need. Stay with me and I'll take care of you."

I wasn't sure I wanted anyone to take care of me. I wanted to take care of myself. "I just want to be alone, Tim Lan."

"You will be alone, but still have a place to sleep. A bed, food. And all of this." He gestured out to the sea. That's when I realized that Tim Lan knew me. He knew what was inside of me. Maybe because he felt the same way. He kept shaking my hand and nodding, forcing an unsteady smile out of me. "Okay?" he asked.

"Okay," I agreed, still not sure what we were agreeing on. "Where at?"

"My house is not much. A shanty. I made it myself. Reef Hollow. Right on the water. Close to the woods. You come with me to Reef Hollow. Okay?"

I looked around me at the cloud covered beach, the vast, dark shoreline illuminated by the moon. Reef Hollow had to be a long walk from here. I'd been there before. A long time ago. Mom and I used to beach comb down that way. We'd find glass floats, sand dollars, and fancy pieces of driftwood and then take them to the Shoreline Trading Post. She'd sell them for beer money. After that she'd get drunk and I'd run away to the cove if the tide was out. Sometimes I had to run away at night. I swallowed the lump that formed in my throat. I wasn't sure I ever wanted to see that place again.

"Okay?" Tim Lan asked again.

I nodded.

"Let's go then!" He jumped up, but I didn't.

I don't normally argue, but fatigue and doubt glued me to the ground. "Can we wait until morning?"

Tim Lan put his hands on his hips and shook his head. He must have seen how sleepy I was because he fell back down again and lay next to me. "Okay," he said.

Not much time passed before I fell asleep, I was so tired.

Not too tired to dream, though. In my dreams, I heard the ocean crashing, and the fog rolling in like fog always invades the coast. I walked from the corner lot where I used to stop with Randy and watch the seagulls. We weren't watching seagulls in my dream. I pushed him there and he sat alone in his wheelchair and laughed and waved goodbye to me. Then in the mist I saw Liona, that cocky stance, her hair brilliant as a policeman's flashing lights. She tilted her head to the side, waiting for me to change my mind, chewing her gum. In my dream, I considered going back. Maybe I was considering going back in real life too. I wondered if Liona could read my mind while I was dreaming. She kept chewing her gum and held her hand on her hip waiting. I couldn't move one way or the other as hard as I tried.

I woke still struggling to decide. Go with Tim Lan or return to Liona? The waves splashed and rumbled on the beach, creeping closer, bringing in high tide. I took a deep breath when I realized where I was, that I had been dreaming and that I didn't have to decide.

I lay there for a little bit going over the vision in my mind. I thought about Liona and how we were just getting to know each other. How maybe she didn't want me to run away. Maybe I didn't want to go. Then I thought about Mrs. Wright's house, and how the social workers rolled Randy away like a criminal into a strange van by the police, and Annabella all broken up in pieces in front of the fireplace. A sick feeling came over me and I turned on my side and closed my eyes to shut the images out. I missed Annabella. My future wasn't in the boarding home. That part of me was gone, now. Fractured into tiny pieces waiting to be swept away. My future would be with Tim Lan.

C Chapter 12

The Enchantment of Reef Hollow

I woke early with my entire body shivering. All my efforts to keep dry had failed. My clothes were drenched from dew, and from lying in the wet sand. Tim Lan was no longer by my side and that worried me. I thought maybe I'd see him on the beach gathering shellfish, I sat up and peeked out my make-shift entry way.

Windy Point hadn't changed at all. Even though a few weeks had passed since I was dragged away from Uncle Jim's house, nothing had changed. Some of the oyster shells I made pearls from were still laid out in a circle. There were footprints in the dry sand coming from the neighborhood that very well could have been mine. I paused for a moment, taking in the sights of the familiar beach. Windy Point smelled different than the other beaches. Maybe because the road and houses were so near. I could smell breakfast being made in the neighborhood. Bacon. I had half a mind to go visit my old house, turn on the range and cook something scrumptious. I wondered if I could sneak in the back window.

I quickly discarded that idea when I glanced at the cul-de-sac. Aunt Agnes' van was parked in the driveway along with a fancy car I'd never seen before. A sign on the side of the red SUV read Brewer Realty. I guess the reality of the house being gone forever never hit me until now and it hurt. All those years of feeling safe in that little house with Uncle Jim were wasting away. He was the only person

117

who ever really cared for me and that home was the only one I ever really loved. Now it's for sale. Who's going to buy it? Strangers?

I wished even more I hadn't looked that way when I saw a lone figure staggering toward me.

I knew that walk, those gestures, the unkempt hair, the sour grimace, and the verbal abuse that came with them. My insides churned when I saw her, and I thought I was going to throw up.

My mother was not dressed for the windy cool weather. She had no coat and only a sleeveless blouse that blew against her frail body. She had something in her hands. Binoculars? "Dylan!" she called and ran at me.

I jumped up with the intent of fleeing, but I froze instead. I didn't want a confrontation, but my old self, the little boy that had always done what she told me to do, waited for her to catch up.

"Dylan! We've been looking all over for you. What the hell are you doing freaking everyone out?"

"What do you mean?"

"That housekeeper phoned Agnes. She said there was trouble at the boarding house and you ran away. What trouble did you cause, now? Did you steal something?" she pressed.

"No! I didn't cause any trouble. I did nothing!"

She scowled, her voice high pitched and accusing. "Nothing my foot. Then why are you running away? Agnes gave good money to put you in that home and keep you there. You ought to be horsewhipped wasting your family's resources." She moved closer as I slipped my pack on my back, and then she grabbed my arm. Her fingernails scrapped my skin as I dodged away from her. I brushed her hand off my sleeve.

"Don't touch me!" I said, feeling an anxiety attack coming on. I already had a hard time breathing, and my face felt hot.

"Don't get sassy with me. Get in your aunt's car so we can take you back to where you belong. Go on. Get!"

I wanted to shout at her. I'm not a kid. I'm not getting in a car with her. I'm not getting in a car with Aunt Agnes, either. I'm not going back to the boarding house, and I sure don't need a horse whipping. But the friction of her presence raced through me, numbing every inch of my body. I couldn't think. What I wanted to say didn't come out except in a grunt. I pulled away, stronger than her but the cowardly little boy oozed back from the past and I let her drag me over the rocks. I tripped and stubbed my toe.

"I'm not going back to the boarding home," I managed. The fire in me burned. I tried to scream but my throat was closed.

"Then you'll come back to Reef Hollow with me. I've got work for you."

"No!" I shot a hopeful look down the beach. Sure enough, Tim Lan headed our way and the sight of him brought me to my senses. I wasn't the little boy she thought she was talking to. I didn't have to be dragged around and submit to her abuses. I was Dylan the full-grown man with a mind of my own. "No! I'm not going with you," I said as I pulled away, pivoted around and broke into a jog, heading straight for Tim Lan. I heard her feet behind me, but I didn't look back, not until her long skinny arms reached out and grabbed at me. She caught my sleeve, so I jogged faster. Eventually she let go. She was still behind me though.

"Don't tell me no." Her breathing grew heavy. She panted "What're you going to do? Live like a bum on the beach? Not any son of mine. You'll come home with me. Get in the car." She lunged at me and pulled my shirt again from behind. Electricity raced through me at her touch.

I hated the sensation. "Leave me alone!" I roared, and the tone of my voice sent Tim Lan racing. Surprisingly, my mother stopped in her tracks.

"You're awake!" He slowed down just before he reached me, calm and composed. He had a smile on his face when he neared, and he looked into my eyes, as if nothing unusual was happening; as if he didn't see my mom; as if she wasn't even there. "Ready for our hike, now?" he asked me.

"Yes." I said and didn't look back. He slapped me on the back and took my arm to get me to hurry. With my spirit restored, I jogged at his side through the oyster beds together toward Reef Hollow. I looked back once but that was all. She couldn't keep up with us.

We ran all the way to the buttes which formed the familiar coves of Reef Hollow Inlet. We ran until she no longer trailed us.

Tim Lan put his hand on my shoulder when we slowed. His touch felt good, friendly, comforting. I took a deep breath of freedom. That was the first time I ever stood up to my mother. I felt proud of myself after my pulse slowed to normal and I could finally return Tim Lan's smile.

"You okay now?" he asked me. I nodded and took in a deep breath.

"Yes," I answered. I was all right, now. Being so close to nature and not having anyone around I had to answer to excited me. An added strength came from the salty spray. A strength and a surge of power that was magical, like how the wind rolling off the waves seemed to increase the power of the breakers. It doesn't really, but there isn't a good surf without a good wind. The magic was like that now. Not just a tingle in my left arm. The energy came on me when I breathed deeply. It was in the air. I could taste it.

Next thing I know my thoughts carried me over the shoreline, with Tim Lan a short distance ahead because he was more agile than me. High tide crept into the pools, sea stars and anemones swayed back and forth with the coming and going of the current. I shuffled quickly over the rocks and stumbled into the soft dark sand, holding tight to a boulder whenever the salt water came rushing in. My clothes hung against my skin wet, but the warm sun had burned the fog off earlier that day. We cleared the butte just in time and entered the cove at Reef Hollow. Had we arrived any later, we might have been swept out to sea with the rising tide.

We reached the tidepools by midday. The cove brought back vivid memories, almost as if I was there in the past again. As if I were twelve years old again. How painful those memories were! This cove had provided refuge when I was little. It was the place I used to run away to. When I thought of the whippings and all the wrong things I must have done to earn them, the energy in me brewed like a hot tea kettle. There was so much black. Candles flashing in dark rooms. Pain when she'd hit me across the face or with the belt on my back. Sorrow when she accused me of stealing. I swear I never stole anything from her. She'd take me with her when she pawned her valuables, her jewelry which had belonged to my grandma, or her gun, and then buy vodka or beer, and by the time we got home she didn't remember where her money had gone, and she accused me of taking it. When I told her the truth, she'd slap me hard, or put me in my room and seal the door shut. Sometimes I wouldn't go to school because I'd have a bruise she didn't want anyone to see. I remember those times because not until I was twelve years old did strangers step in. That month was horrifying because the social workers would take me in a private room and ask me questions I had a hard time answering. They pretended to care, but I could tell they were angry. Maybe not at me. Maybe at my mom, but they scared me none the same. They didn't do anything right away. I learned later from Uncle Jim that there was too much paperwork for them to act quickly. Mom thought I had reported her. That's when the black power entered me the first time. The night the first group of social workers left. I don't like to remember that day. The black magic was my only defense. Otherwise I think she may have killed me. I had bolted my bedroom door shut with it. The power had shaken my whole body as well as the house and it had scared me for the rest of my life.

Walking in this cove brought the memory back because I used to come here and nurse my wounds when I was lucky enough to escape. I stopped for a moment, the dark of the yester world hovering over me. I waited until the dizziness wore away before I could go on. I sank against a boulder, the salty water in the tidepool stung my toes. Tim Lan moved farther ahead but stopped once he looked over his shoulder.

"Coming, Em?"

His voice kept me from sinking into the past completely. The name "Em" encouraged me. It proved that someone in this world cared. That someone saw me as a friend. I lifted myself to my feet and leaned on the cave wall for a moment. "Yeah. I'm coming."

When we arrived at Reef Hollow my mouth dropped open, for it bore no resemblance to the beach town I knew from my childhood. There were no crowds of people, no beach goers in their bathing suits carrying surfboards, no alluring smells of clam chowder, fish and chips or candied popcorn. The penny arcade, the carousel gone, the cotton candy, the roller coaster all a thing of the past. Weeds covered what had been a parking lot. Sand dunes had either been blown by the wind onto it, or the sea had swallowed the pavement up in a storm, leaving only fractured blocks of cement and a lone pole that leaned into the wind with a weather-beaten sign that read "Handicap Parking Only."

The wharf where the Shoreline Trading Post had reached out over the ocean past the surf now ended abruptly. Lost as a fragmented and battered pier, the failing platform wore damage at both ends. Bleached wooden beams hung carelessly over the sea, the ends bouncing on the surge as the waves rolled to shore. Rotting pilings barely supported the platform which at one time had been buzzing with shops, tourists and fishermen. All those shops had completely disappeared.

The long stretch of beach which I remember strolling many times with my mother lay bare. Deserted, save for a small shack up against the far cliffs, constructed of driftwood and two-by-fours most likely confiscated from the crumbling ghost town. I presumed the shed was Tim Lan's home, for he led me against the wind, in that direction.

C Chapter 13

Island of Paradise

The rickety door of Tim Lan's shed could have fallen off its hinges when he jiggled the wooden handle. It didn't only because he held the door in place when he opened it. Tim Lan bowed low, his cordial greeting added an odd formality to such a scruffy home. I stepped inside.

"You laugh," he said, his grin as wide as mine. "My house is a simple wooden shed, but it is warm and will keep the dew away. Nice, Em?"

"Nice," I answered. Who was I to complain? My clothes hung off me wet and laden with sand. I had already taken my shoes off and carried them laced together on my shoulder, with my socks stuck inside of them. Any dry place would work as a home right now. I wasn't fussy. I was grateful. Maybe I could have used my magic to change my clothes, but I was too tired to try, and I wasn't sure about letting Tim Lan see me use my powers for more than marbles, anyway.

"I can cook for you, Tim Lan. Whatever I can do for you I will be happy to do."

"Yes!" He grinned even wider. "You can pay your way. I have a plan."

"I don't know about paying my way. But I'm a good cook."

"Maybe, if you want to cook, okay. But not for payment. I have a better plan for you to pay me."

I had no idea what he was talking about. "I guess."

"No, Em. No guess. Just say 'I am able, and I will." His eyes locked onto mine hard, to indicate the importance of what he was saying. I swallowed and tried digesting his words, though I doubted I should agree. I think he could tell my uncertainties by the look on my face. "You say what I just said."

I stared at him.

"Say the words after me. I am able."

"I am able."

That made him grin wider. "Say I will."

I hesitated because he was asking me to make a promise. Uncle Jim told me never to make an oath unless I was certain I could keep my word. I didn't even know what I was swearing to. My face heated up and I'm sure had I looked in a mirror I'd be blushing. That didn't seem to faze him.

"You trust me?"

I had no reason not to.

He encouraged me with his nod and moved his lips for me as though his actions would prompt my own. Finally, because he wouldn't stop unless I obeyed, I did. I made the vow. "I will." I cringed afterward.

"Ah! There! You won't regret it." He spun around and led me through his one room shanty into a kitchen area where he offered me a place at his table.

"Where did you get the furniture?" I studied the dark wood which had been etched with dragons and lotus blossoms. Pretty fancy for such a funky old shack.

He chuckled. "The Hungry Lion. You remember?"

"The Chinese restaurant that used to be on the pier?"

Clever Tim Lan, the hermit crab, made use of the ruins of Reef Hollow Amusement Park. I could see now that most of his house was built from scrap wood and furnishings from forgotten businesses of the old tourist center.

"You're pretty clever, Tim Lan. Like a magician!"

He sat across from me with pleasure written all over his face. "And now all that I have is yours too. Don't worry. For this home, you pay only a small price."

This time my smiled disappeared. "I have no money," I said.

"No, not money. Pearls."

"Pearls?"

"Your oyster marbles, yes? You can make me some every day. For living here. That's all I ask."

"Why marbles? I mean, I don't care. Making the marbles is easy, but why would you want marbles?"

"I like them," was all he said, and I took him for his word. I had more questions for him, like how many was I to spin, and for how long. And how long would I get to live in his shanty. I had no time to ask those questions though because he rose.

"Come, follow me." He led me through his rickety shack, explaining all the relics which shaped every corner. Junk, both ragged and falling apart, all nailed together. In the kitchen hung crates which had been reformed into shelves, milk boxes assembled into storage drawers, and a pantry filled with boxes of macaroni and cheese, and readymade dinners. Right away I made a mental note to cook him some genuine healthy fantasy food.

An assortment of mats and driftwood end tables, and an old coat tree by the door made up his living area. Two faded old logs stretched across from each other, flattened and sanded, served as a couch. A rusty oil barrel placed in the center of the room had been made into a stove. A heavy steel pipe reached through the roof to let out the smoke.

He showed me the outhouse behind the shed nestled under the cliffs; concealed with a veil of ivy which draped over the wooden walls, hidden from the adjacent forest.

There was one area blocked off by a delicate room divider decorated with showy paintings that looked like images from a Chinese restaurant. We didn't go behind the screen, but I could see the furnishing as I walked by. A bedroom I suspected, and one not made up for a man. "You sleep there?" I asked.

"No. Not now."

"Who does?" I peeked in at the cherry blossoms painted on the wall, a gilded framed mirror over a chestnut dresser, and a collection of Asian dolls on a shelf. "It's pretty."

The dolls reminded me of Annabella. I wondered if they meant something special to Tim Lan like how my figurine had.

"Not for you to know," he mumbled, and I thought his reply a bit rude. "A special room. That's all." His voice lost luster when he answered me, and the sparkle in his eye dimmed. He guided me away, and we did not say anything more about that area. We came to the far northern corner, dark and unfurnished, and he gestured to the floor. "This space is for you."

"Yes, sir," I said, grateful for having a place to lay down. I slipped my pack off by back and placed it on the sleeping bag that had been laid out for me. There were no windows in that part of the shed. No tables, no chairs, no bed, no blankets, only the sleeping bag and a soft sandy floor. But the room, like the rest of the house, was dry and reasonably warm.

"Now, let's get to business, okay?" Tim Lan took my arm and guided me back outside.

The wind whipped at my face as soon as I stepped out the door and beat my hair around wildly. The tide was out so there was a good body of sand before we reached the Reef Hollow oyster beds. When we came upon the dark crusty layers of oysters, Tim Lan said nothing. He simply bent over and started shucking, dropping the meat in his bucket. After harvesting each oyster, he carefully spread the shells opened-faced on the rocks in a row in front of me. He nodded. "It's a good day to make pearls, you think? Keep your mind busy and off your problems. Off your mother."

I couldn't argue with him. I had a lot of problems and because my hands were shaking, he probably saw how stressed I was. Making pearls had always been therapy for me. Tim Lan must have known. He must have watched me before at Windy Point, and seen how it helped ease my mind, just like Uncle Jim knew I was happier on the beach.

"The tide will be in and the oysters will be under water soon. Don't worry about anything else. Free your mind."

He was right about the tide. Even in the last few minutes the surf curled over a string of seaweed near my feet. I sat down in front of the shells and tried quieting my mind enough to do what he asked of me. I took my eyes off him, and watched the waves in the distance, lifted my face to the salty wind, and absorbed the warm sun on my back. I spun a pearl as I had always done. One twist of my finger pulled the entire iridescent layer into a huge ball, popping it out with a loud snap. I fell off balance at the impact and landed on a jagged rock.

"What happened?" Tim Lan hurried to my side.

"I don't know. I didn't know that was going to happen!" I rubbed the sore on my behind.

He lifted the monster pearl from the oyster shell, a flamboyant chunk covering the palm of his hand. Though glimmering with color, its misshapen structure swanked of splits and cracks and ill-placed lumps. The shell that birthed the pearl had cracked and turned black. "This is odd," he said.

"I've never spun anything like that before."

"Control. You need to control your magic. Take your time. Don't think of anything except calm, Okay?"

I nodded. I knew what I should do. Release all that black energy that had come with the loss of Annabella, and

Randy and when mom touched me. "I'll work on it," I promised.

"Okay, because pearls like this will be too hard to sell."

"Sell?"

He ignored my question, handed me the monster pearl, which I tossed aside, and then he walked away. I jump up and followed. "You're going to sell the pearls?"

"Yes, Em."

He bent over again, breaking more oysters from the jagged shore, popping them open with his knife, and scrapping the meat into his bucket. "You like oyster stew?"

"I make the best oyster stew." I whispered my weak boast, less confident than ever because I had messed up on making a pearl. "Better than anyone. I didn't know you were going to sell these." I added.

He straightened his back and looked me in the eyes. The wind blew his hair, whisking in the air and across his face but he never once flinched. He talked to me like a wise man. Calm and wise. "Everyone needs money sometimes. I'll take care of you. I'm giving you a home. I'll keep you safe. Like your uncle, eh? You're running away, no? Hiding from the boarding home. From your aunt. From your mother. Right, Em?"

"Yes," I admitted, sorry for questioning his motive.

"Is this home not worth it to you? Does it matter what I do with these?" He waved to the oyster shells, the unharvested pearls waiting for my touch. "It's not worth your labor to have me benefit too?"

"No, I mean yes, it's worth it. I'm sorry."

"Be thankful for what you have." He pulled open the rest of his shells and spread them out at my feet. "Always be thankful. Then good things will come to you."

"I am. I only thought…" I began.

"What?"

I wasn't sure what I thought. I had a habit of feeling sorry for myself sometimes so maybe that was my problem. Uncle Jim would remind me not to bellyache, and now that he was gone I had no one to keep me in check. "The world isn't against you," he would say. "The world hardly knows you're here. Ignore those who don't like you and you can do whatever you set out to do, if you have a good attitude."

I believed in those words, too. That is, I believed those words when Uncle Jim said them. Enough to try and have a good attitude. The best thing was he made me believe in myself. Right now, without him here, I wasn't sure I had a friend in the world at all.

"Better not to think at all, then," Tim Lan said when I didn't answer his question. He pointed at the shells. "You have only an hour before the ocean swallows this beach. Then we'll go inside and relax. Talk. Be friends. Or like you said you wanted, you can go off and be alone. No matter. Do whatever you want. First the pearls. Uniform size. Not big like that monster one. About like this," he held his fingers a short distance apart, maybe the size of a large pea, as if there were a pearl in-between them. He patted my shoulder. "Don't worry, Em. You're a good man. We'll get along. Okay?"

I nodded obediently. So what if he sells my pearls? Once I gave them to him, they are his to do whatever he wants. I guess.

I knelt on the beach by the row of shells, and when I did Tim Lan walked back to his gray and dismal shack at the bottom of the cliffs.

"Control," I whispered to myself, and took a deep breath. That had been the first time ever that I hadn't had control of my magic. Maybe I lost control because I hadn't had time to meditate and let the peace come to me, first. Maybe without the stress of him looking over my shoulder I would do better.

I sat quietly, watching the waves, blocking my mind from all the bad things that had happened to me lately. Instead, I let myself open to peace. The kind that being on the beach brings. Then the magic came to me, just like old times. I became fully aware of the growing power inside of me. I knew exactly when to stop beckoning for the magic to come; right before my whole body tingled so that I wouldn't make any more oversized nuggets.

I must have been out of practice. The first pearls I made were lopsided and used up too much of the color in the shell, so I knew I had more concentrating to do. I tucked those pearls in my pocket and tried again. Each time the marbles took on the appearance of the ones before, each one becoming more and more uniform, smooth and lovely. I worked all afternoon until I had thirty-two perfect pearls in all. Then the tide came in and the first ocean wave washed over me and soaked my clothes.

Thirty-two was a good number so I stood, content with what I had done and certain that Tim Lan would be happy. I planned on apologizing for doubting him because I had no right to argue with him. I was wrong, and I'd tell him so. I would pay my rent in pearls and wouldn't ask what he did with them.

I tucked the pearls into my empty pocket and stepped away from the splashing waves.

When I turned to go back to his shack, I saw someone on the beach far off in the distance in the direction of Windy Point. Squinting against the brightness of the beach, I watched, and hoped. Her profile blended into the shadows of the buttes. Once she moved into the sunlight I didn't have to look twice to know who that person was, not after seeing the purple and orange hair.

I stood real quiet, wondering what she was going to do if she was going to walk all the way over to me. I wanted her to. I didn't understand why. I didn't know what this feeling was inside of me that yearned to see her again. I had run away from the boarding house. I hadn't fled from her. I ran from everything that had happened, but I still wanted Liona as a friend.

I already came into a good living situation, me and Tim Lan. Making pearls in trade for rent exceeded anything I had ever done for myself. I was working now. Paying my way. I planned on making a fancy dinner for him, too so I just about had everything I ever wanted. Still, I liked Liona.

I sat down in the wet sand, glancing at her while she walked the long stretch of beach. Surf slapped up against her knees the same way the breakers had crashed up against my knees. She stopped and rolled up her pant legs. She'd already taken off her shoes and slung them, tied together, over her shoulder. I didn't want her to catch me staring, so I put an oyster shell in front of me and started spinning. Not without first noticing how her hair flew wildly in the wind; purple and orange and a natural shade of auburn. I took my eyes off her again and concentrated on the pearl, gathering the colors at the tip of my fingers. This one was an especially pretty marble, lit by the sun, shinning blues and greens. Smooth to the touch. Maybe I'll give it to her.

What are you doing with that oyster?" I'd been so engrossed in making that pearl that I didn't notice her come up to me, and then hover over me.

I cleared my throat and followed her with my eyes as she sat down, glad that she had come. Her presence was like sweet cream and strawberries. "I'm making pearls."

"Why?" she asked.

I'm not fast at thinking and I didn't know how to answer her right away, so I just shrugged my shoulders and said the first thing that came to mind. "Tim Lan told me to."

"Did Tim Lan tell you to come all the way down here to Reef Hollow, too?"

"Sort of."

"And you do everything that Tim Lan tells you?"

The sun caught the color of her eyes so that they shone like glass under her black lashes. She held her head up when she spoke. I wondered why she asked, what she was getting at, what she might say next if I told her the truth. Then I remembered she could read my thoughts faster than I could think them. I choked a little when I replied. I was suddenly ashamed of the answer. "Yes," I said. "Pretty much, anymore."

"What happened to Dylan, who thinks on his own? Who makes his own kind of magic cooking oyster stew and stuffed cabbage?"

"I can still do that."

"Can, but do you?"

"I cook for Tim Lan."

She looked away with a frown.

"Cooking isn't everything you know. I've been doing other stuff."

"I see," she said softly as she gazed at the waves crashing on the shore.

Not sure what else to say to her, I put the pearl in my pocket and watched the ocean too. "What are you doing here?" Those words didn't come out the way I wanted them to. I wanted them to be gentle, but they came out mean. I wanted her to know, without reading my mind, that I was glad she was here. That I liked being around her. That when I was with her not much else mattered. That I was thrilled she came and, so I wanted to know why. "I mean, what brought you all the way over here?"

"I came to see you. To see what you're doing."

"You walked all the way from Elwood Estates just to see what I was doing?"

"No. Not from Elwood Estates. Mrs. Wright let me use her car to go to your old house and see if you were there, so I'm parked at Windy Point. Which is where I walked from."

"You knew where my old house was?"

133

"We had the address, yes."

Immediately questions poured into my head. I wasn't sure which ones to ask, so I just stared at her.

"Everyone is looking for you. Your family is worried about you."

"That's impossible," I mumbled, knowing my family. "I mean, who in my family is worried about me?"

"Your aunt. Your mother."

I shook my head, not believing either Aunt Agnes nor my mother cared enough to worry about me. "Why?"

"They don't think you should be wandering around on the beach by yourself, I guess."

"Oh." I knew my mother probably had other plans for me, plans I wanted no part of. Aunt Agnes wanted me in the boarding home because she paid for it. I doubt Shirley cared one way or the other but Liona hadn't mentioned Shirley.

"Mrs. Wright thought maybe you went home to Windy Point, so I drove to the house myself. To see. Your Aunt and your mother were already there."

I didn't say anything, but I felt a fever rush to my head.

"Your aunt was upset."

"I don't know what to tell Aunt Agnes about her money." I dared not let Liona know I was afraid of Aunt Agnes. Or that my mother already found me and approached me on Windy Point while I was on my way here. Silent thoughts don't stay silent, though, when you're standing in front of a mind reader.

"Your mom talked to you?"

I nodded.

"Where at? What did she say?"

"On the beach in front of the house when I was passing through. She tried to drag me away. I won't stay with her, Liona. Not ever again. I stood up to her."

"What would happen if you lived with her?"

134

"Probably what used to happen before. She's wicked. I told you she does drugs."

"You're right. You shouldn't live with her. Not if she still does drugs. I thought there was a restraining order, still."

"I don't know. Uncle Jim always took care of the legal stuff for me. Are you going to tell them where I'm at?"

"Why would I do that?"

I shrugged, not being able to guess what was going on in her mind.

"What are you going to do now?" She squinted at me, the wind blew sand into our faces.

"Pretend I'm dead, maybe." I couldn't think of any better solution.

She laughed and when she did she relaxed and put her hands in her pockets and looked prettier than I'd ever seen what with the sunlight shining on her smooth skin and her green eyes brilliant. "I think they're smarter than that. Give them a little credit."

I smiled a little because to look at her made me tickle inside. Then my smile turned to a frown when I thought about where she'd been. "What exactly did Aunt Agnes say?"

Liona sighed heavily like she had something deep to talk about. "Dylan, what happened in your childhood?"

Heat rushed to my head. "I can't tell you."

"Oh." She looked away.

"I mean, it's too much to tell you sitting here in the wind. It'd take a long time to tell you everything and some of it I don't even want to remember or talk about."

"I thought so," she whispered. She took my hand and stood, pulling me up with her. We walked toward the water. Slow. Her hand was warm and soft and holding it made my heart jump. "Your Aunt was really nervous when I started asking questions."

135

"What did you ask?"

"I asked them if they were going to visit you. I wasn't going to say anything about you running away. I guess Mrs. Wright had called them after I left and let the news leak that you weren't at the boarding house. It was your Aunt Agnes who told me you had escaped."

"Escaped? Like from jail?" My expression sobered. I didn't like that phrase at all. "So, they had me locked up to keep me out of their hair? And now that I'm gone, I'm an escapee?" I kicked the shells at my feet.

"Their term, not mine. It sounded brutal to me, too. I told them the boarding house wasn't a place to escape from, because no one was forced to live there. I told them that you went for walks sometimes. They called me a liar, so I stopped asking questions. Your mother said she saw you walking this way, but she didn't tell me she had talked with you. I wonder if your aunt knows that you two met."

Liona waited for me to respond, but I had no idea what Aunt Agnes knew.

"In any case, we all agreed Reef Hollow was quite a long distance for a stroll." She stared at me then, as if she wanted me to explain why I came here, but I was tongue-tied. She got her answer when Tim Lan stepped out of his shack.

"This must be Tim Lan?" she whispered after looking over my shoulder.

I glanced at Tim Lan's figure in the distance. "Yes. He's letting me stay at his house in trade for pearls." I turned to watch him mostly to avoid looking at her.

"You won't come back, then?"

I bowed my head instead of answering her.

"Why not?"

"I don't know. Lots of reasons I guess."

"Because of Randy?"

I started walking and she strolled alongside. We brushed arms, our sweatshirts rubbing against one another.

136

When I didn't say anything, she guessed again, speaking softly. "Because of Annabella."

"It's dumb, isn't it?"

She didn't answer.

"I don't want to be around people. I want to be alone."

"I'm sorry, Dylan."

I looked into her eyes and saw that she meant what she had said. Just like when she had apologized the day Annabella crashed into the fireplace and shattered into a million pieces. "It's not your fault."

"No. But that doesn't mean I'm not sorry." She stopped walking and took my hand in hers, squeezing it gently. "Sometimes terrible things happen in our lives. All we can do is let it pass, not dwell on it."

I gazed on her face, wondering where her wisdom came from. "Is that what you did?"

She knew what I was talking about, even though I didn't. I just knew there was something in her past haunting her too. Why else would she get depressed?

"I'm still trying," she said.

"Well let me know if you get lucky, because right now I can't forget. Annabella wasn't just a pretty doll. She was my uncle, in a way."

"I know."

"And Randy, he was my friend. He wanted to stay. You saw what it did to him. He didn't want to break Annabella. He didn't want to hurt me. That's the worse hurt ever, hurting people you care about."

She turned sharply away when I said those words about Randy, as if she didn't want to hear me.

"What?"

"Don't talk about Randy. Just please don't talk about him. Just come home. For me."

Home? I knew she was going to ask me to go back. And now she calls the place home. "It's not my home."

Part of me wanted to go back to Elwood Estates, but only because of Liona. I mostly wanted to stay here because Tim Lan was like Uncle Jim and I needed someone like him. I was free here. I could be alone with no rules and no one to bother me or push me around or criticize me or tell me I should be ashamed. I hoped she could hear my thoughts, so that she could see it in my eyes how confused and hurt I was. And I saw in her eyes that she understood. "Tim Lan is letting me work for a place to stay. I've never done that before. He's nice to me. I should learn to be on my own."

That's when Tim Lan came right up to us. "Is there something I can help you with?" he asked, grinning wide, but his grin seemed forced and the exchange between him and Liona worried me. Liona's eyes darkened too, as if a shadow had passed in front of the sun, but there were no clouds in the sky. Her beautiful smile dimmed to a sneer and her eyes darted back and forth between me and Tim Lan.

"I doubt it," Liona responded. "Just getting my exercise." She turned to me. "Our door is always open to you," she said. "Please don't forget."

"I won't forget," I whispered, saddened that our communication had been suddenly cut off. She nodded, though her nod was more disbelieving than affirmative. Brushing her hair out of her face she turned away from me and began her walk back to Windy Point.

I didn't give her the pearl.

"Why did you do that?" I asked Tim Lan. "Why did you chase her away?"

"Did I chase her away? Or did she leave on her own?"

Tim Lan did not give me enough time to brood. I would have. I would have sulked for the rest of the day because I watched her walk away and when she did, she took a piece of me with her. Before she got halfway to the buttes, he took my arm and guided me toward his house, away from her, droning words I barely heard. "I heard your heart, you know? You want to be alone, to be free, to be with the sea. That's what you told me. Practice making pearls. Become great at this. I don't ask much, but you and I have a partnership, no?"

"I guess so."

"Good. What gems do you have for me?"

I pulled the fruit of my morning labor out of my left pocket. I kept the one I wanted to give her in my right. I placed the thirty-two perfectly formed pearls in his hand. His patted me on the shoulder.

"Thank you, Em!" He kept smiling and nodding. Instead of dropping them in his own pocket, he pulled a small leather pouch strapped to a lace around his neck and let them fall one by one. When they were nested into the pouch he slipped the necklace under his shirt and patted his chest. "This is very good," he said. "Very good."

I soon forgot my sorrow for having traded Liona's friendship for Tim Lan's pride in my work. I can't remember the last time I had pleased someone the same way I used to please Uncle Jim. Something right had happened because of my decision to stay at Reef Hollow. Life was good.

C Chapter 14

Riding the Wake

Tim Lan and I made a routine of pearl-making every day after that. Early morning, we worked the oyster beds. With the pearls, I paid him my daily rent, and then he'd go to town, or dig for clams, or work on his house. There was still debris laying under the pier from the ruins on the wharf. Somedays he would drag the timber, or boxes, or relics up the beach to his shanty. I think Tim Lan had plans to remake the entire remains of the once bustling dock into a mansion for himself. Once he even dived under water and retrieved a glass case full of sand. After cleaning the case, he used it for a shelf in his secret room. I never saw what he displayed, as I was never allowed in there, but I imagined the case was being used for something special.

Occasionally, if he had something heavy to carry I would help him, but he never asked me to work on his house. That was not our agreement. I had the day to myself and I spent my time combing the beach for my favorite findings, like sand dollars or sea glass or cork floats which I rarely found. Occasionally I would visit the tidepools. Mostly, though, I would let my mind wander, sometimes dreaming up what sort of banquet to prepare for me and Tim Lan that night. Or I would just sit and listen to the sounds on the beach. That's what I liked the most about being free.

I felt creative the evening Tim Lan found the glass case, so I cooked him a beautiful Asian meal that night. I set the table when he was still outside wiping the case clean, using my magic to spread out a red tablecloth with golden dragons embroidered on the edges. I used simple napkins, and chopsticks. Tim Lan still didn't know how I acquired these special items for our dinners, but because there wasn't any other explanation, I think he suspected a supernatural answer.

"Your magic has the power to create tangible things." Tim Lan spoke frankly after I had made him a meal of pho hoi soup, egg rolls with sweet and sour sauce, jasmine rice and vegetables sautéed in peanut sauce. "Where did you get the ingredients for all of this?"

"I know a grocer in town," I lied. Tim Lan never questioned my lies.

He bit into his egg roll and nodded approval. "I have never seen this kind of magic before."

Startled, I looked up at him. Did he know my cooking was magic?

"Illusions, yes. Slight of hands, of course. But this with the pearls?" he shook his head. "You are a good cook, Em. Maybe we should open a restaurant."

I laughed at the thought but when he nodded as if he was serious, I shook my head rapidly. "No. No way, Tim Lan. I like to cook, but I don't think I could handle a restaurant. When I was younger that's what I wanted but not now. Now I just want to be alone. On the beach."

"Why not? You'll make money. Live in a nice house."

"A nice house? Where?"

"I don't know. Maybe in a ritzy neighborhood."

The more I thought about owning a business, the less his suggestion made any sense. I was not that sharp a thinker, so I worried about this. "Is that what you would want to do?" I asked him, because he had once said his heart was the same as mine.

"No," he admitted and dipped the tip of his eggroll into the sweet and sour sauce, shoved the roll into his mouth, and licked his fingers. When he finished chewing he nodded. "Just testing you."

"Why?" When he didn't answer, I let the conversation stay at that. The prospect of being a famous chef had been something I wanted ever since I conjured up my first bologna sandwich years ago. I practiced improving my skills ever since. However, I wouldn't enjoy being bogged down in one place all the time, never being able to leave the kitchen. That would take the fun out of what I do. I still remember Uncle Jim's words that day he gave me Annabella. He told me to find what I want in life, and that didn't mean what I do in life. I was to find love and acceptance, he said. Tim Lan accepted me just like Uncle Jim had. I think that was good enough.

When we finished eating, and had cleaned the dishes, I stepped outside to get a breath of fresh air. The stars were out, the sky a deep blue. The breakers whispered in the distance and nearby I heard frogs which were probably croaking the creek in the forest. Everything was quiet except for movement down by the ocean. Curious, I stepped a little way past the shack where I could see the beach better.

There were people moving around in the oyster beds. No one ever came to these beds that I knew of, so I was a little bit annoyed with the invasion. I'd always thought we were in a secluded area down here by the old wharf. Tim Lan should know about any trespassers, so I quickly returned to the shack.

"Tim Lan, come see this," I whispered and waved him to the door.

He hurried to me and peeked over my shoulder. By now the invaders were close enough that we could see them from the shed. He let go a low whistle.

Four people moved about on the beach. Three men and a woman. The woman carried a bucket, swinging the empty container back and forth carelessly. One of the men placed a cooler down and then sat on it. Another held what appeared to be a guinea sack. He knelt low to the ground, but I couldn't tell if he was just sitting there or what. After a while, the man who was seated stood up, lifted the cooler lid and took out a can. I heard the pop all the way where I was at and watched him take a drink.

"Give me one of those."

Their voices were loud and carried all the way up the beach so that we could hear them no problem, though I couldn't understand everything they said.

"Who are they?" I whispered to Tim Lan.

"Don't know," he answered quietly.

"Are they digging for clams?" I asked, because I saw one of them with a shovel. Soon everyone joined the man on his knees. A flashlight was lit and beamed all over, on the ground, the beach, the water.

"No," Tim Lan answered. "They're not far enough out. They're digging up the oyster beds."

Tim Lan was right. They were in the beds, not the sand. And from the laughter, and occasional pop of a can, they were drinking.

"Digging oysters with a shovel?" I could only imagine what kind of damage they would do.

"A difficult task," he answered. "I don't think they'll have good luck."

At the sound of another pop of a can, I was ready for war. "They need to go," I rolled up my sleeves and prepared to charge out there like a madman, but Tim Lan held onto my arm.

"What are you going to do once you get there?"

"Stop them!"

"How? There are four of them. We're only two."

"But they're destroying the beds."

"We can fix the beds. Think of what they would do to us if they get mad, eh, Em? Too many for us if they want to fight. They're drinking. Men without minds make for

143

trouble." He patted me on the shoulder and eased me back inside. "Come away before they see us."

Tim Lan snuffed out the lantern, watched for only a moment longer, and then went to bed. I lingered by the door, half in and half out, studying them.

The woman looked familiar. I couldn't see anything but their forms because of the night, and the figures were only dark profiles against a starry sky. Her movements were familiar though, her unkempt hair, the way she tossed back her head and puffed on a cigarette, and the off balance of her walk. I didn't want to wake him up and say anything to Tim Lan. Why would I? But, though I hoped not, she looked very much like my mother. I stood guard until I couldn't keep my eyes open any more. They didn't leave before I went to bed.

I woke early, and I think Tim Lan had the same idea I did because he was already dressed. The sun had not even risen yet when we stepped outside. Tim Lan had a bucket in his hand and together we made a bee-line for the beds to see what sort of damage the invaders had done. A mess! There were cigarette butts and tobacco pouches and beer cans and plastic wrappers, and even a broken vodka bottle in among the oysters. I cut my finger picking out the glass from in-between pebbles and shells and had to suck on the wound to stop the bleeding. Tim Lan shook his head in disgust whenever he found another piece of trash.

He put the garbage in a bag and took it to his house. I figured he would take it to town when he took our garbage. I stayed on the beach nursing my finger and watching the sea gulls that swooped near shore. When he came back, he went right to shucking as though nothing foul had ever happened. He tossed me the shells and I lined them up in a circle. By that time the bleeding had stopped, the peace had returned to me, and tingling magic entered my body.

I held my healed finger over the shiny colors of the shell and started spinning. When the first pearl appeared a foul smell and a raspy voice broke my concentration. I looked up and there was my mother. I about puked.

"I thought I'd find you here." Her voice smacked of anger.

I was quick with rolling the pearl into my fist and dropping the gem into my pocket as I stood.

"What...?" was all I could manage--her presence had shocked me so.

"You and your conniving, sneaky conspiracy ruined my life."

"What? What are you talking about? What did I do?"

"You think I don't know about this? Gathering pearls on the beach?"

"What pearls?"

She leaned over and looked at my shells, drool from her toothless mouth dribbled into them. "Pearls."

"Those aren't pearl oysters," I said. That was no lie. They weren't, at least not the kind that make real pearls by themselves.

"They're around here somewhere."

"No, mother. I don't think so."

"No? That's a lie and you know it. You know how I know?"

She pounded her finger on my chest.

"Because I ran into that China man yesterday. He was at the trading post with his shiny little baubles. Selling them." She leaned into me, expecting a reaction. I stood stiff as a brick. "He had pearls, Dylan. This is your friend we're talking about. And they were worth so much more than what I had, that I couldn't sell my shells. Do you know why I couldn't sell my shells.?"

I remained speechless, still in shock from seeing her, and wishing she'd go away.

"Because they spent all their money buying pearls from your friend. They snubbed me. I don't like being snubbed." She pushed her pointed nose into my face, reeking of vodka breath, probably vodka from the broken bottle I cut my finger on. "So now I find you, my only son, in cahoots with the China man."

"I don't know what you're talking about."

"Yes, you do. I've seen you with him before. You used to hang out with him at your uncles. Lots of times. Jim even knew him. You don't fool me. Your lies don't fool me. I got friends that tell me the China man hangs out on this beach. Right here, as a matter of fact. And would you look where I find you."

"He's not Chinese, he's Vietnamese."

"I don't care what he is. He's a crook and you are too. Always knew you were a good for nothing, just like your father."

"My friend is no crook."

She spat at my feet and jabbed her finger into my chest, pushing me off balance so that I staggered backward. "Give me some of that money, Dylan. Pay me back what you owe me. Help your mom."

Steam had to have been rolling out of my ears I was so angry. I didn't owe her a thing, but I didn't say so because that cowardly little boy from my past crept into me like a ghost hovering over a graveyard.

"Give me some money, Dylan."

"I don't have any money."

Her eyes widened. Foam dribbled from her mouth. "You lie."

"I'm not lying."

She wiped her face with her arm. She was loaded with something; drugs, beer, I don't know what, but her eyes couldn't focus on me. "Bull! You always lied to me, always did. Lied and robbed. Good for nothing thief. Take after that bum dad of yours."

"I swear I don't have any money."

She studied me for a moment, blinking. Maybe she believed me because she stepped back and gave me a once over from head to toe. "Then you're a damn fool."

I caught my balance again and stepped away from her. The friction of our relationship quaked, like how the earth trembles when a train rumbles on the tracks. My fists were white from clenching them.

"If you're broke, then you're letting that old man take you for a dupe. Do you know how much he's selling those pearls for, Dylan? Did he tell you?"

I shook my head.

"Thousands. I saw the bills myself. Thousands of dollars. And here you are hanging out with him in rags. Can't even afford to wash your clothes or…" She leaned forward and yanked at my hair. I reached up to pry her fingers off. "Or get a haircut. Look at you. Dreadlocks, is that you're style now? Gonna be a pirate, are you? You look like crap. When's the last time you had a bath? Your shoes are full of holes. Can't afford shoes, Dylan? And the China man is letting you hang out. What? Is he your friend? Say it. Is he your friend? What's he doing for you, Dylan?"

I would have answered her, but I didn't want her to know I was living with him. I didn't want her to know anything even though she thought she knew all about me. She pulled on my shirt. I brushed her hand away. She gasped in surprised that I would do such a thing, and then mocked me. "Don't you dare recoil from me, boy!"

I eyed the beach, the cliffs in the distance, wondering how far she'd follow if I ran. That's when I saw Tim Lan. I moved toward him, and she pulled on my shirt again.

"Leave me alone," I growled.

"Don't sass me, Dylan. I'm still your mother."

"Stop!" I said louder, partly to vent the steam, and partly to get Tim Lan to move faster. "Leave me alone!" I

pulled away from her and jogged toward Tim Lan. She
made tracks right behind me, just like she did last time she
stalked me on the beach. I could hear her breathing heavy.
She stopped when I met up with Tim Lan.

"You!" she said to Tim Lan when they came face to
face with each other.

He smiled at her, his friendly Asian smile, and
bowed cordially. "Good morning."

"Not really," my mother retorted. "Not without
breakfast or dinner or facing the day poor again."

Tim Lan's smiled disappeared. He glanced at me.

"You should know what I'm talking about. I saw
you yesterday at the trading post. That's my bread and
butter, the wares I sell. But you! You had to go in there and
sell your precious pearls and now they won't even talk to
me about my stuff."

"So sorry," he said.

"No, you're not because you'll go in there again and
again. And now I find out you've got my boy and you're
letting him starve. You with all that money. Look at him!"
she pulled my arm and maneuvered me in front of her,
between Tim Lan and her. I couldn't stand to face Tim Lan
like that, so I turned away. "You call yourself a friend?
Who let's their friends down like this? He can't even afford
a haircut."

"Mom," I interrupted and loosed myself from her
grip. She caught me again.

"You're both a couple of scam artists. Probably
steal those pearls is what you do."

Tim Lan said nothing. I pushed my mother's hands
off my shirt sleeve and stumbled away from her. Tim Lan
put his hands in his pockets and bowed again. "Good day,"
was all he said before he walked away. Not toward his
shed. He was smart and didn't bring attention to his little
home. Instead he headed toward the beach, south. He was

not happy, and I think she had just ruined my chance of continuing to live with him.

"Go away!" I said to her.

She lifted her fist and shook it in my face. "You'll pay. You'll both pay."

"Is that all?" I asked, giving her my dirtiest glare that I could, and then I tramped away from her. Fortunately, she didn't follow me. I needed to catch up to Tim Lan and apologize.

C Chapter 15

Riptide

I ran along the beach to catch Tim Lan, out of sight from my mother, beyond the buttes of the far shore where huge flat rocks played stepping stones with the sea. A perfect habitat of tide pools and miniature caves and flat stones that held the sun's rays so that when you lay on them they warmed your back and made you feel like a fat sea lion basking on the reefs. Tim Lan had already chosen a boulder and sat meditating by the time I reached him. I climbed on another rock below his, exhaling relief that I had dodged the Accuser and saved my soul.

"I'm sorry," I said, not knowing how else to express the regret that ate at me.

"For what your mother says?" he asked. "You're not responsible."

I didn't respond. I felt that I was. She was my mother. It was my fault she was even here on the beach, or that she approached Tim Lan. Or that she had accused him of treating me ill.

"She doesn't treat you well."

"No." I admitted. "She didn't treat you well either."

"No matter."

The waves crashed and splashed at us, agitating the sand and pebbles below before they slid away.

"What was she so angry about?"

I looked up at him for an indication as to whether my mother's claims had been true. A calm smile on his face, his shirt unbuttoned exposing his chest to the morning sun, the lack of care about what had just happened, kept me questioning.

"I'm not sure," I said. As much as I hated my mother, the words she threw out at me could have held some truth in them. Tim Lan could be selling those pearls for a lot of money, and hiding it from me, though I didn't think that what he got for the pearls was any of my business. Still, he could be generous and offer a bonus occasionally. I could use new shoes. "Did you see her yesterday? At the Trading Post?" I asked.

He was quiet for a moment. "What trading post?"

I didn't answer.

"No. I don't think so."

I lay back down again. His reply should have made me feel better, but I remained uneasy. Maybe I would have been happier if he had told me he had seen her; that he did sell pearls in front of her, and that he did sell them for thousands of dollars. At least I would know they were both telling the truth. Now I had to guess.

"Why?" he asked.

"She said she saw you."

"Maybe she had me mixed up with someone else." His answer was quick and under any other circumstance, could have made sense, if I hadn't been suspicious.

"Probably," I said. Not trusting him made me feel dirty, like I was to blame for not believing him, and I wasn't a good friend, or a loyal friend because I didn't trust him. I didn't like feeling dirty, so I slid from the rock I was on and took off my raggedy shirt, spreading it out in the sun so it would be warm when I dressed again. I slipped out of my worn shoes which were already unlaced and placed them next to my shirt.

"What are you doing?" he asked.

"I need to bathe," I mumbled and jogged away from the cliff and tidepools toward the breakers. Once I hit the cold salty water, I let out a holler. The shock of the temperature woke me up. I screamed loud and hard and strong. With each shriek, I moved past a row of thundering surf until I was in water up to my chest. The tide lifted me and gently brought me down, rolling to shore, splashing on the beach behind me. Larger waves came and each one swelled and ebbed taking me farther away from land to where I couldn't touch bottom. I treaded water then and waited for the one wave that would submerge me, bathe me clean from all my bad thoughts. Wash my body and my mind in one grand sweep. The rising wave trundled toward me, swirling higher and higher, blocking my view of the horizon, caps of white fingers spitting out at the cloudless sky above. In a split second the wet mass plummeted on top of me, then churned my body like butter, pressing me into its liquid shelf. I held my breath, scrubbed my face, as I rolled in its embrace. This powerful force sloshed me around in salt as if agitating me in a washing machine. Just when I could no longer hold my breath, I gushed to the surface, left in foam and coarse sand, which raced away back down the beach, yanking at my body, throwing me off balance, pulling me back to sea.

I struggled to my feet and pushed my soaking hair out of my eyes. The air breathed cold against my wet skin. I walked back to where Tim Lan lay watching me. Grabbing my warm shirt, I dried my eyes, shook sand and kelp out of my hair, and blew the salt out of my nose. Refreshed, I dressed again, but without the shoes.

"Feel better?" he asked.

"Yeah," I answered. "Kind of."

Tim Lan slid off his boulder, and without looking at me, without inviting me to join him, walked away in the direction of his shanty. I wondered if that confrontation with my mother would have a lasting effect on him. If so, I may be more homeless than I thought.

C Chapter 16

Stormy Day

Very early the next morning, before dark gave way to dawn, I stepped outside to get a breath of fresh air and listen to the sea. Even though I had bathed the day before, the thoughts of Tim Lan's deceit still haunted me, and I had barely slept. I needed the solace that the constant song of the ocean gave, so I walked away from the house to hear the sea better. Unlike the pleasant weather the day before, the ground was wet from evening rain, and the clouds spit out a misty shower. I pulled the hood to my sweatshirt over my head, thinking maybe I'd go back inside and wait for a drier moment. That's when headlights near the old torn up parking lot shone on me. I froze, the beams glared into my eyes. The rain came down harder and so heavy I couldn't hear the motor, yet I knew the car was still running. The headlamps dimmed, a car door slammed, and though I couldn't make out who got out of the car because of the light shining in my eyes, I could tell it was a woman. My heart jumped when I heard her voice.

"Dylan!"

Holy cow, that was Liona! At 5:30 in the morning? I didn't move because with those lights in my eyes I couldn't see anything, but I didn't have to see to tell it was her. She came running my way, tripping over rocks and cement blocks and debris that cluttered the path to where I stood. "Liona?"

"Dylan, I'm so glad you're up. I need your help."

"At five thirty-six in the morning."

"I should have been here earlier."

"Why?" I couldn't imagine why she would need me, nor need me so early in the morning. Still, her needing me at all made me happy.

"I didn't know where else to go."

She stumbled into me and grabbed my coat to catch her balance. I held her steady. "What happened? Are you in trouble?"

"I will be if I don't get home soon. Mrs. Wright is in the ER. She had a stroke, I think."

The clouds opened on us with a downpour right then, and we were both soaked within seconds. Liona had no rain coat or anything, so I tried to pull her toward the house, but she resisted. "Let's talk inside," I urged.

"I can't. Not now. Let's talk in the car. Come to the house with me and help me. I'm the only one to take care of the tenants and I can't possibly manage all there is to do by myself."

I'm not good at making quick decisions, so I stood there like an idiot, dumbfounded. She kept tugging at me.

"I have to cook breakfast, get Mrs. Benson up, help them all take their meds, feed them. Please Dylan. I need your help."

"Wait. Let me think a minute." I had planned on going to Elwood Estates anyway this weekend. Tim Lan was gone into town, and there wasn't anything holding me back from seeing Liona, except for the promise I had made Tim Lan. "I'm the only one here and Tim Lan wanted me to watch the place."

"Oh, good god, Dylan, is that more important to you?"

I wasn't sure. My word was important. But so was helping Liona, especially since this was an emergency. I had little time to process the options. "No, but don't want to have anything happen to Tim Lan's things. I made him a promise. How can I leave with no one here?"

155

She took a deep breath and turned to Tim Lan's shanty. "What is your commitment? Just to watch the house? Make sure no one breaks in?"

"Yes."

"Then let me take care of that." She stepped away from me and held her hands in front of her, tapping her fingers together quicker and quicker until they rattled against each other so rapidly that her fingers glowed. "Sinju," she said, her voice hissed like a snake. Then, with a sweeping stroke of both of her hands she sent a great lightning bolt which reached well over Tim Lan's shack. Light from the flash reflected for a split second and then an invisible dome floated gracefully over his house, which I only saw because of the reflections. "There."

I gawked. "You have that kind of magic? I mean besides reading minds?"

"A little. Will you help me now?"

I had no excuses anymore, and frankly I didn't want to make one up. "Okay." In a flash, her excitement became mine. I ran to the car with her and jumped in the passenger seat. Out of breath I looked at her anxiously. "If you have that much magic, why can't you just use it on everyone at the boarding house?"

"Because that's not the way I work." She glanced at me with a smug smile on her face. "Besides, if I did that I wouldn't need you. And I want to need you."

"You do?"

She didn't answer, and the confidence I had seen in her before was not there. "Yes," she whispered. "I missed you."

That made my heart sing. "Okay. So, what's next?"

"Fasten your seatbelt."

She said it in such a way I thought we'd be taking off like a rocket ship, so I quickly snapped the seatbelt and leaned back against the seat. Rain splattered on the windshield, but it was cozy in the car, just her and I. I hadn't known Liona to be weak or emotionally upset about much except the day when Randy hadn't taken his medicine. Today, as she was backing up the Dodge station wagon, I saw tears in her eyes, and her hands shook.

"How is she? Is Mrs. Wright going to be okay?" I asked, hoping this wasn't going to be another scene like Uncle Jim, where the boarding mom doesn't come back and then the house gets sold, and the tenants are pawned off to someplace else, like I had been.

"I don't know, Dylan. She fell over this morning while I was in the kitchen. I found her lying on the floor in the living room mumbling words I couldn't understand. I helped her sit up, but she wouldn't come out of it. The ambulance came and took her away. That's all I know. I took a big chance driving here. Everyone was still asleep at the house when I left. We need to hurry and get back before they start waking up. Thanks for coming. I was freaking out. I can't do this alone. I just can't."

"It's okay, Liona. I'll help you. You don't have to get upset. I'll help." If panic was catching, I caught hers. My chest started hurting and my stomach felt oozy. Sweat formed on my brow. "Are you sweating too?" I asked.

She nodded but waited until we came to a stop sign to glance my way. "Dylan, I know when depression comes on. I know when I'm about to feel suicidal. I've had enough counseling to recognize the signs."

I hadn't ever seen this Liona before. Pale, frightened, unsure of herself, and now talking about her symptoms like they were happening right now.

"I don't want to die. Not by doing something stupid."

"Don't do anything stupid." That didn't come out quite the way I meant it to.

"Believe me if I can prevent myself from acting rashly I will. Mrs. Wright had left Mrs. Benson's sleeping pills on the kitchen table. I had them in my hand, Dylan.

This morning. As soon as the ambulance left. I was just going to end it all. I didn't think I could handle the responsibility. Too much stress. I thought about popping the whole friggin' bottle of pills."

My mouth hung open, and drool slipped out, so I wiped my lips with my sleeve. I barely understood what she said but I knew it was scary. "I don't get it. You wanted to take Mrs. Benson's drugs?"

"Not just drugs, Dylan. I was thinking about killing myself. If you take too many sleeping pills you can die. I was ready to chug the whole bunch of them."

"No! Don't! Liona you can't die." What could I say to her? The thought was terrifying. "Like Uncle Jim died? You can't die, Liona. No!" I twisted in my seat, loosening the seat belt to face her. "Please don't do anything like that!"

"Well I don't want to."

"I'm stopping you. Right now. I won't let you."

She shot me a quick smile, as if I had anything to say about what she does with her life. "Fasten your seatbelt back up."

I clicked it back in place and faced forward. "Too many people need you." That didn't sound right even though it was true. It sounded selfish, but I don't think I was being selfish. I hated the thought of something like that happening to beautiful Liona. "Everyone at Mrs. Wright's needs you."

The car started rolling again. She made a noise with her tongue when she sighed and glimpsed out the window. "Right."

"I mean, I need you."

She was quiet for a moment as she drove. "You do?" It was a meek response, and sent a tickle through me, as if she was happy to hear that I needed her. I nodded so hard my neck kinked for a second and then I remembered she was watching the road, so she didn't see me nod. "Not like a sick kind of need either. More like just needing to be around you. Because I like you. Not because I want you to do anything for me. I don't. I just want to be near you. Maybe for a long time. Maybe for life." I surprised myself saying that. It came from deep inside.

"Really? For life?" She wiped her nose. "Then why are you staying with Tim Lan?"

I thought about it for a minute, how to tell her. I didn't want to hurt her feelings. "It's quiet. I need quiet, Liona. Otherwise I get, I don't know, depressed. Like you."

"Oh."

"There are lots of people at the boarding home. Some not so nice. Social workers come around, too. You saw what they did to Randy."

"Yeah, I saw."

"Besides, I'm on my own with Tim Lan. I pay rent. I pay my own rent."

She looked at me with wide eyes. "With the pearls?"

"That's right. I can support myself now."

"Using magic?"

I nodded, glad that she could understand. "He sells them and lets me stay at his house."

"Oh." She didn't seem too impressed that I earned my own keep.

"That's not all." I started, and then recanted.

"What else?"

"I don't know." The time didn't seem right to talk about every reason I needed to stay on the beach with Tim Lan. Maybe the time to talk would never come. I'd have trouble telling her all my fears. Like how afraid I am that my mother would come for me at the boarding house and embarrass me or convince Mrs. Wright to release me to her. Or that I didn't like crowds and people and having to mind rules that took me a long time to understand.

"I see," she said, letting me know she read my mind.

"Well, and what will happen now? I mean with Mrs. Wright being gone?"

"I don't know. The social workers might send another caretaker. I don't expect the responsibility of taking care of everyone will be on my shoulders for very long. But I think you may be right. This may not be the best time for you to come back."

"No, not for good. But today I'll come back and help you."

We sped on to the boarding house after that and didn't say anything more. After she parked the car, she slammed the door and ran up the stairs to the house, me at her heels. Our haste was unnecessary though, as the lights were out, and no one was awake.

"Start making breakfast," she whispered to me, and took my hand. "But please don't use magic."

"Why not?"

"Just don't."

She raced down the hall to check on the tenants.

The thought of using magic hadn't even occurred to me so I wasn't sure why she said that. I washed my hands and found the apron. The kitchen wasn't in order. Liona must have been cooking when Mrs. Wright fell over with a stroke, because potatoes were in the sink, and one was half sliced on the cutting board. A towel had been thrown on the counter and a cup of coffee spilled. I cleaned the mess up first and then got to work. Soon the fresh aroma of food cooking started filling up the house. I heard people moving, a wheel chair rolling. Mr. Gravestone hacked like he usually does in the morning when he gets up. A toilet flushed. I peeked out the door and saw that Liona had moved Mrs. Benson into the dining room. Mr. Bromheimer peeked into the kitchen at me.

"Welcome back, Dylan."

I hesitated to greet him because by all rights I wasn't back. Not for good. I was just helping Liona, but I wasn't going to tell him that. I didn't want to hurt anyone's feelings. "Good morning, Mr. Bromheimer," I said. He smiled wide, that bright handsome old man smile that is always on him. I had forgotten how cheerful he was and how he can make my own day brighten. He sat down at the table. I served the food, placing a serving of potatoes and eggs on everyone's dish. After returning the skillet to the kitchen, I took my seat where I used to, across from Mr. Gravestone, and next to an empty chair where Randy used to sit. I paused for a moment, looking at the table where his food should have gone.

"I hear Randy is doing well at Forest Ridge nursing home, Dylan. I think he likes living there. He can have visitors." Liona suggested. "You could go see him."

I glanced up at her. "Maybe sometime. I would like that." She winked at me and smiled. I had never thought about visiting Randy.

"Where is Mrs. Wright?" Mr. Gravestone asked. His question bolted through the silence. "That's what's more important, now."

"Shopping most likely, Mr. Gravestone," Mr. Bromheimer offered and then he turned to me. "Your cooking just gets better and better, Dylan," he said.

"Mrs. Wright is in the hospital," Liona said matter-of-factly keeping all uncertainty out of her voice.

Mr. Gravestone huffed. "Probably Dylan's cooking is what made her sick."

I set my fork down. It'd been a little while since I took an insult from the old man.

"Nonsense," Liona defended me. "She went to the hospital this morning and then I drove over to Dylan's to ask for his help. He's been very kind offering his services this morning."

"Thank you, Dylan," Mr. Bromheimer smiled at me.

"Besides, you've always loved his cooking, Mr. Gravestone."

Mr. Gravestone grunted but he kept eating until every bite on his plate was gone. Liona glanced up at me, and then gave Mrs. Benson another bite of food.

"Are you going to be staying with us?" Mr. Bromheimer asked.

I flushed. I mean my head grew way hot right then with the look Liona gave me. I don't know why. She probably read my thoughts. She always does. She knows I don't mean to stay. "I'm just here for the weekend."

She then wiped Mrs. Benson's face with a napkin, pushed the plate out of the woman's way, and took off to the kitchen. I followed her with my eyes, thinking she was mad, or hurt, or something. Things started slamming in there.

"Excuse me," I said to the others. The men could feed themselves, so I assumed I could leave them.

Liona had the water running into the sink full blast, soap suds building up.

"Liona," I began. She didn't respond, so I kept talking. I hated seeing her like this. I hated when people got mad, especially when they were mad at me. She threw silverware into the water, shut the faucet off forcefully, and began scrubbing the skillet. "Liona, I can't stay here. We talked about this in the car on the way here!"

She didn't respond. She didn't even look at me.

"I have to go back. I want you to come with me."

"Where? Tim Lan's shanty?"

"No. I think I can build us a place."

She rolled her eyes and spun around. "Dylan, you can't just go building a shack on the beach like Tim Lan did. You can't just build a house anywhere you want and then move into it. There are laws. Building codes. Property rights."

"How does Tim Lan do it?"

"Luck maybe, I don't know. Maybe he owns that part of the beach. If not, he's fortunate he's gotten away with it for so long. But the time will come he'll have to leave. Then what will you do?" She turned her back to me again. I stood there stunned because I didn't know about building codes.

"Then I'll find something else to do."

Her purple locks rustled when she shook her head, an orange highlight fell over her eyes and she brushed it away with a sudsy hand. "No, Dylan."

I took her arm. I don't usually touch people. I had held her hand the other day but that was because she wanted me to. Right now, she didn't want me to touch her and flinched when I did, but I didn't let that stop me and I surprised myself. "Liona." I pulled her around to face me. "I really want to be with you. Just the two of us. Not all these people, here. Just you. With me."

She had a smile for a moment, but the longer we looked deep into each other's eyes, the more her lips straightened, until she relaxed, and her mouth opened just slightly, showing her beautiful teeth. I couldn't help myself. I leaned over and kissed her.

I have never in my whole life kissed anyone. I only knew about kissing from movies and never understood how people could do something so gross like touching their lips together. Here I was kissing Liona and didn't have any bad thoughts like that at all. I enjoyed kissing her. When she caressed my neck, and pulled my head tighter against hers, my heart raced. I couldn't breathe but I didn't care. I wrapped my arms around her. My whole body pulsated. I didn't know what was happening, but it felt good.

She pulled away and we looked at each other again. Her dazed eyes came back to reality and stiffened into a scowl. "I have to do the dishes. I have responsibilities, Dylan. Running away with you sounds like a dream, but I don't live in a dream world. Maybe you do. I don't. I have tenants to take care of. Someone must do the dirty work, and in this case, I'm the one since I'm the only one here who knows how."

I know she was talking about for the moment. But I think she was talking about for the rest of her life, too. She was telling me 'no' in way too many words. She should have just said 'no', not given me all that other spiel about responsibilities. Not after asking me to leave my duty to watch Tim Lan's house. I licked the sweet taste of her kiss off my lips and grabbed a towel. She handed me the skillet to dry.

"Maybe you can come with me to the beach today?" I said, my voice cracking from all the feelings I had inside of me. I don't know what they were, just that they were there. I know they were the same kind of feelings whenever I got rejected, only this time the pain was greater. Before, I didn't really care before. Most of the people who rejected me were my relatives and I learned how to overcome those feelings, thanks to Uncle Jim. I cared a little, but not much. Liona rejecting me hit in the gut. Hard!

"Okay."

We didn't say anything else after that. I stayed at the house for the full day. In the afternoon, we took everyone for a walk. I pushed Mrs. Benson's wheelchair, and stopped at the corner where I used to stop with Randy. But Mrs. Benson wasn't impressed with seagulls catching clams. And she was cold, so I wrapped her blanket tighter around her and gave her my jacket and then we kept on to the corner and back.

There were social workers at the house when we returned. I didn't want to continue up the driveway.

"Come on, Dylan they aren't here for you," she said and took my arm. We both pushed Mrs. Benson up the hill and Mr. Gravestone and Mr. Bromheimer followed us with their walkers. Once in the house, I sat down on the couch right away. The social workers followed us inside. They had an older woman with them. She was tall and wore a cotton dress, but she wasn't fancy enough to be a social worker.

"Liona, this is Mrs. Healy. She's here to caretake the house during Mrs. Wright's stay in the hospital." Liona nodded a greeting. She had put on her suspicious look like the one she had when we first met. I hoped she didn't have any plans of tripping the woman. Mrs. Healy was very cordial and smiled sweetly.

"Here are the tenants," Liona said nodding at the two men who were still wheeling their walkers into the house. Mrs. Healy shook Mr. Bromheimer's hand, but Mr. Gravestone only grumbled at her.

"Mrs. Benson has dementia," Liona said.

"Pleased to meet you, Mrs. Benson."

Mrs. Benson nodded.

Liona came around to introduce me. I stood and offered my hand in welcome, not sure what Liona was going to say. I was still supposed to be a tenant. My escape from the boarding house could have been compromised right at this very moment.

"And this is Brian. My boyfriend," Liona said. I dared not look into her eyes or the caretaker's eyes either. I shook the lady's hand and sat back down. Liona shouldn't have lied, but she did. And I did nothing to stop her. What she said, though, thrilled me inside. She called me her boyfriend. Life couldn't get much better than that.

C Chapter 17

Turmoil

I waited on the couch while Liona showed Mrs. Healy around the house. I thought they'd only be a moment, and then the two of us could go for a walk on the beach, but the moment turned into longer than that. Liona took Mrs. Healy upstairs after she showed her the kitchen and the dining room, and all the bedrooms downstairs.

I tuned on the TV for Mr. Gravestone and Mr. Bromheimer, so they wouldn't be restless. The two men soon got bored with the talk show, however, and pulled out their chess set. The afternoon seemed to be fading and I lost hope that Liona and I would ever get to go on a walk by ourselves that afternoon. I also worried that maybe Mrs. Healy would discover who I really was. Mr. Gravestone shot me an evil eye and immediately I felt guilty.

When Liona led Mrs. Healy back downstairs, she held up her finger to tell me she'd only be a minute. I hoped she was right, but Mrs. Healy kept asking her questions and they disappeared down the hall toward Mr. Gravestone's room again. I sighed and slumped on the couch, unable to focus on the TV.

While Liona was in the back room, there was a knock at the door. The shades were drawn so I couldn't tell who our visitors were. Mrs. Healy came out of the hallway to answer. When Liona and I heard the voices of our visitors, we both shot each other a wide-eyed glance. I recognized both their voices.

"We're here to visit Dylan," Aunt Agnes said.

I jumped off the couch and bee-lined for the stairs, stumbling over my own feet to get out of eyesight. Liona flew into the living room and stood next to Mrs. Healy.

"Where is my son?"

I was hidden from whomever was in the living room. I watched at the top of the stairs and moaned silently when I heard my mother. I could tell she was mad by the sound of her voice.

"Dylan? There's no Dylan here. I'm sorry, ma'am, who is your son?" Mrs. Healy asked. I felt sorry for the new caretaker. She had no idea what was going on.

"He's not here anymore, Mrs. van Pelen." Liona saved the day.

"Bull!" my mom cursed and pushed her way into the house. She had better clothes on than the last time I saw her on the beach. They probably belonged to Aunt Agnes, who followed her inside. Mom's face closed in on Mrs. Healy's. Aunt Agnes' snoopy eyes scanned the room, and the stairwell. I slipped farther back against the wall.

"The old China man on the beach said he saw Dylan get in a car with you." She spun around and pointed at Liona. "Purple and orange hair. No identity mistake with that description, is there?"

Liona popped her gum and stared back at my mom.

"Five o'clock this morning. Early bird catches the worm, didn't she? What did you do with him?"

"Emma, calm down," Aunt Agnes interrupted. She walked further into the living room. Mr. Gravestone sneered at her and I held my breath certain he'd fink and tell her where I was.

"Your son's not a worm," Liona said. "And I did pick him up this morning." Liona's response was so smooth I felt pride that she was protecting me. "And I dropped him off at the store in Reef Hollow."

"Why are you lying for him? No one goes to a store that early?"

"He was applying for a job." Liona blew a very large bubble. So big I thought the gum was going to pop on my mother's nose. It didn't, but almost. My mom jumped back as Liona gathered the gum off her lips with her teeth and started chewing again. She stopped long enough to address my aunt. "Agnes, if I remember correctly, you said there is still a restraining order keeping this woman away from Dylan? You're not allowed to see him even if he were here, ma'am."

My mother answered before Aunt Agnes could respond. "I changed all that. I got the order lifted, went to court and everything. So, that makes you a liar!"

Mrs. Healy interjected right away.

"Look, ma'am, I don't have any idea who you are, but this is a private residence. We have restrictions about who is allowed on the premises. I'll need to see some identification before you start asking about any of our tenants. And if there was a restraining order preventing you from seeing anyone here, I need proof that it's been lifted."

Aunt Agnes pulled out her purse and rummaged through the contents while my mom got all huffy and puffed out her chest like she was someone important. "Hogwash," she said, but that was all the response she had. Most likely she didn't have any I.D. "I shouldn't have to show I.D. to talk with my own flesh and blood."

"Here is my driver's license," Aunt Agnes held up her wallet to show Mrs. Healy. "Emma here doesn't drive so she doesn't have one. We just want to see Dylan. If he's run away, I'd like to have my money back, and Emma would like him to move in with her. I believe she did get the order lifted."

"She needs to identify herself. And any information concerning our tenants is classified, ma'am."

Right away, I liked Mrs. Healy.

"Furthermore, I find this confrontation rather invasive, so I'm asking you to leave the premises. If you don't I will be calling the police to remove you."

My mom spat out a bad word at Mrs. Healy. Liona raced for the phone.

"I'll remember you, you bitch," my mom said to Liona. That made me mad, but I didn't dare risk going down there to tell her so. Both my mother and Aunt Agnes left after that. I don't think my mom wanted to see the police.

Once they were out the door. Liona yanked back the curtain. Everyone in the room watched their car pull away. Finally, I could breathe again and, so I stepped quietly down the stairs. I hadn't expected everyone to stare at me. Mr. Gravestone pointed at me and Mr. Bromheimer pushed Mr. Gravestone's arm down, but it bounced right back up again, long knobby fingers playing the devil at me. Mrs. Healy with her back against the door, her face red with fire, glared right into my eyes. Liona looked out the window and fidgeted with a strand of purple hair.

"I need some answers," Mrs. Healy announced when I reached the bottom step. I was tongue tied, I had no idea what to tell her. A lump swelled in my throat, a cold sweat formed on my brow. My stomach turned inside out, and I about choked for air. Still I tried not to let anyone know how afraid I was just then. I avoided looking at Liona because I didn't want her to get in trouble. This was all my fault for running away in the first place.

"Crazy old woman, is all," Liona blurted, still looking out the window. Mrs. Healy quickly responded to that.

"I am ashamed that you would lie to me young lady. I had been given the most flattering referral about you from Mrs. Wright. How upstanding you were, honest and capable. She had nothing but praise for you. What lies did you tell her? What shenanigans did you play behind her

169

back? I was almost ready to hire you instead of charging the State for your room and board. And now this! Aiding and abetting a runaway? How dare you play a trick like this on me. Shame on you!"

Liona's mouth hung open. I couldn't stand it. Not the shame. Mrs. Healy's words stabbed me in my heart as if they were daggers directed at me instead of Liona. I wished they had been.

"No!" I blurted right away, before she said anything else bad about my girlfriend. "Stop accusing Liona! This isn't her fault. She was protecting me. I'm not Brian. I'm Dylan van Pelen. That woman who came here is my mother but she's evil. Look what she's done to everyone here! She's turned you all against each other." Liona was near tears. It broke my heart. "Look what my mother has done! This is all my fault. It's my fault she's my mother!" I barged toward the door. No one was going to stop me there was so much force inside of me. "I am a liar and a runaway, and I won't cause any of you any more trouble. I'm not staying here because I'm a jinx to you all. Call your police if you want to. Lock me up in jail. Just don't talk about Liona like that." I was shaking by the time I opened the door. "She's everything that Mrs. Wright said she was. She works harder than anyone. Anyone! She's not the bad one. I'm the bad one. Not Liona." I stormed outside without bothering to close the door. Uncle Jim taught me never to slam doors. Instead I used that fire in me to run.

C *Chapter 18*

Despair

I didn't see any sea gulls in the sky or on the beach. If there were any, they'd have flown away in terror because I charged at the shoreline like a crazy man. Sandpipers raced across the glistening sand, the surf so far in the distance it seemed like miles away. I could see the cliffs to the left and knew that just beyond them were the oyster beds, the cul-de-sac, and Uncle Jim's house. So homesick for Uncle Jim, my heart ached for the simple little world we used to live in. Homesick for peace and quiet like we used to know. A world without strangers. A world without confusion.

"What are you doing, Dylan?" I couldn't believe Liona had caught up to me. Her gaze had followed mine, surveying the beach, eyeing the buttes that marked Windy Point. Our eyes met, and I pretended I wasn't upset, or thinking about running away again. I didn't answer her. I didn't know what I'd do. "Can't run forever, you know," she said.

"Yes, I can." I could, and I would. Whatever it takes to be free of the shame that people wanted to throw at me.

"Why?"

"I don't know why. I don't fit in at your boarding home. I don't fit with your people. Didn't you just see what happened in there? I got you in trouble."

"No, you didn't."

"Yes, I did. You had a good thing going with Mrs. Wright, and that lady was going to hire you until I came along. Now she thinks you're…." I didn't want to say it. I couldn't. "She thinks you're bad."

"I don't give a crap what she thinks of me. I covered for you on my own. You didn't ask me to. I did it because I like you. I care what happens to you. I'm tired of seeing you running away all the time."

Our eyes locked on to each other. Inside of me swelled with as much emotion as Randy had, and like Randy, I didn't know what to do with it. I hated Liona getting in trouble because of me, because I have a rotten mother. "It's not fair," I said. "Not to you."

"No. Nothing about life is fair. Life is what it is. Period. You got to take life as it comes. That's all."

I faced the sea and wiped the mist off my face with my sleeve. I kicked off my shoes and started walking. She kept pace with me like a shadow, not letting me disappear. I tried to relax and take in the quiet of the morning, the salty smell, the mist. I tried.

"Yeah." I mumbled, just to say something in response to her wisdom, because accepting life as it comes wasn't my forte. "What's worse is Tim Lan snitched on me too. On you, too. I thought he was a friend."

"So, stay and all of this will be over."

"I can't stay."

"Why not? Why do you want to leave?"

"Why do you care?" I managed to ask. The more I felt the ocean beckoning, the more I wanted to answer the call. I didn't see a future anymore, not living with old people who hung onto life by a thread, locked up in a house, living by rules and regulations and having to sneak out if they wanted to see the ocean. Not in a boarding home that keeps tabs on me like I'm a prisoner. And not with an old Vietnamese man that lies to me, either.

"Cause," was her answer and I didn't mind if she didn't say anything else. I didn't want her to care, anyway. If she cared, then I might care.

172

"Did Mrs. Healy send you out here to talk me in to coming back?"

"Dylan," she protested.

"So, they can keep Aunt Agnes' money?"

"Stop that!" she pulled at my arm, but I brushed her away. "Where did that come from? I stood up for you back there," she insisted.

I wasn't being nice. I knew what I said wasn't true. But saying what might have happened gave me an out. I didn't want to trust anyone anymore. Not even Tim Lan. Not even Liona. Saying those things made it easier to leave.

We left tracks in the sand in the direction of the sea. The breakers rolled and rumbled toward us but never came any closer, tossing and trundling in constant motion. I stopped then, mesmerized by the white foam which broke into splatters of fog against the gray sky. Sparkles of sunlight glistened on the water beyond the waves, and in the puddles on the beach, the nebulous shape of a cargo ship far out to sea as the sky brightened with the rising sun; the monotonous rumble of surf hitting the shore. The salty air tasted good. This was home. This was the peace I'd been dragged away from, and to which I desperately yearned to return.

"Try to find a balance again, Dylan. Try to find peace again. You had it once. You can have it again. Nothing ever stays the same," Liona whispered, her face lifted to the breeze, her eyes closed. Sea spray landed on her lashes. She looked calm and I resented that she was content, and that she knew so much about life, or about people and that she knew how to be kind and caring, and I didn't. I walked away from her. I didn't care if my shoes got wet. Why should I care? Nothing seemed to matter anymore. Why would anything matter? I didn't matter much to anyone. Only Uncle Jim and he was gone.

I walked all the way past the sandpipers as they scattered away from me on long spindly legs. I walked to the pools which glimmered like mirrors in space. I didn't care if the cuffs on my pants acted like a sponge and soaked up the sea. The surf met me and reached out to pull me deeper. I kept walking and now the arms of the ocean rushed over my knees and sucked me further away from the city, away from the boarding house I never wanted to live in, away from the shack on ocean front property that once was my home. Closer to Uncle Jim.

"Dylan," Liona called after me. "You're going too far into the water!"

Why did she care? I didn't want to stop, but the alarm in her voice caused me to spin around. "Stay out of my head." I roared back, the sound of my voice resounded over the crashing surf.

"You stop right now, Dylan van Pelen!" She ran toward me.

"No!" I barked like a sea lion when she got near. "Why are you and everyone else always trying to control me?"

She stopped and stared at me, her eyes wide like she hadn't expected me to lash out. But I was mad. I was tired, and I was mad. Why were people always telling me what to do and what not to do? Where to live, how to act, what to wear. "You don't control me!" I said, and she flinched. The sea spray beat against my face as the waves pushed my knees and made me stumble. The breeze blew sand in my eyes and drove hair into my mouth. I pulled the strands away from my lips and then I felt bad because I didn't really want to yell at Liona. I was mostly mad at Aunt Agnes and Shirley for making me move out of my house, and at Uncle Jim for dying. My voice softened. "I mean, how am I supposed to live with everyone pulling me this way and that way?"

She opened her mouth, but she didn't say anything, so I asked her again.

"How am I supposed to…" I looked at the ocean glistening in the morning light looking almost as though the sun had already drifted below the horizon. The ocean was my friend; right now, my only friend. "…live? How am I supposed to live?"

"You are living. You're alive. Stay that way!" She reached out and took my arm. I didn't fight her. All the fight was out of me, if I had any. I considered her eyes, which were like green bullets that pierced into my mind. She dug at my thoughts and purged them from my body. "Give yourself some more time, Dylan. You've got to try harder. This is only a fraction of your life. You have a future. Please don't despair."

I looked away. The waves broke around our knees and I staggered.

"Damn Dylan you lost people in your life and so did I. I don't want to lose anyone else."

I didn't know what she was talking about. She had anger in her eyes, though.

"Yeah. I lost my brother. You think I didn't feel like you are right now? I survived, though. As much as it was my fault, I kept on living. I knew it was wrong to end my life even though…" She stopped and swallowed her words. Then her voice soften only enough that I could hear her over the surf. "I worked too hard to get where I am now to watch someone I care about get washed away into that same hell hole. Don't ever think about giving up on yourself. No matter how hard life is, there's still something to live for and you'll find that something. I know you will."

The waves rushed in around the both of us again, splashing on my shirt now. I lost my balance a little when the surf receded. She pulled me back to the beach. Once on drier ground, drenched clothes hanging off me, my body shivering, she slapped my arm. "Don't be an idiot." She had a smirk on her face when I looked up. I rubbed the bruise.

"Get ahold of yourself," she whispered, picked up my shoes and tucked them under her arm.
"Come on."

I trailed behind her back to the boarding home.

C Chapter 19

Mud

When we returned to the house, Mrs. Healy called her into her personal den and the two of them had a private conversation behind closed doors. They were in there for a long time. After Liona came out of the den, she bagged the clothes that I had left in room eight into a duffle and turned to me,

"Get a shower," she ordered. I paused for a minute, not knowing what would happen to me. She tossed me a towel.

No one said a word to me after that, so when I had dry clothes on, and I was clean, I sat outside on the porch on the swing with a sandwich Mrs. Healy brought me. I ate and watched the sun set and the rain come down. The air was chilly, but the ground smelled sweet from being damp. Around eight o'clock at night, Liona stepped outside. She jingled the keys in her hand and walked to Mrs. Wright's car.

"Coming?" she asked. I scrambled to catch up to her.

We didn't talk all the way to Reef Hollow and neither had the rain stopped. Potholes in the gravel road filled with water and streams trickled along the gutters. The station wagon bounced and swerved around them. Liona, who had little experience driving, ended up bottoming the car out. The left front wheel dug further into the mud while the other three burned holes into the ground when she stepped on the gas. After several tries, she shut the engine down, slapped the steering wheel and buried her head in her hands. I sat next to her speechless having no experience at all with motor vehicles and even less with trying to say something comforting to a girl stuck in the mud.

I hated seeing her cry though. Depression could set in and the thought that she might take sleeping pills worried me. We'd already been fogged in as we sat in the car, so I couldn't see outside very well. It was dark though. Dark, damp and cold.

"Liona?" I spoke over the beat of raindrops on the windshield. "Why don't we just leave the car here for a little bit and walk to Tim Lan's house? It's dry in the house. We could make a little fire and talk. I could make us some cocoa. We aren't far."

She didn't move, nor did she answer.

"Maybe the rain will stop a little bit later, and we can figure out how to get the car out of this hole, then. Or maybe I can conjure up some…"

"No!" she interrupted me and finally raised her head. "You can't just keep depending on magic to solve all your problems."

"But…" I wanted to argue that we didn't really have any other solution now. We were stuck. She opened her door and got out before I had a chance to speak.

She was already drenched by the time I got to her side of the car, so I shook my left hand, pleased with how quickly magic came for the small tricks, and popped an umbrella open. No sooner had I lifted it to hover over her then she gave a sharp nod of her head. The umbrella disappeared. She moved to the back of the car and inspected the hole Mrs. Wright's car had sunk in.

"Stuck, stuck, stuck!" she groaned and kicked the tire.

Thinking there had been some mistake with my magic, I made another umbrella and again she scowled at me, nodded her head, and made this one disappear, too.

"Why are you doing that?" I shouted over the sound of the rain.

"Because I'm sick of your magic," she answered as she stood up again. She pulled her foot out of a puddle and trudged through the mud to the other side of the car.

"You're using magic too and you don't seem to be sick of that!"

"I don't use my magic to keep me away from people I care about."

"That's what you think I'm doing?" I raced as quickly as I could to catch up to her.

"I don't think that's what you're doing. I see that's what you're doing. Why else aren't you living at the boarding house?"

"I can't live there anymore. Mrs. Healy doesn't want me there anymore."

"You don't know that. Maybe if you didn't keep coming back here to Reef Hollow you could stay with us. There'd be a chance if you weren't hanging out with Tim Lan using your magic to make him rich."

"He appreciates the special things that I can do with my magic. And what I'm doing is earning my keep. That's a lot more than I do at your boarding house, at least."

"Making pearls? So, he can sell them? He's using you, and you're worth more than that. Have some self-pride, why don't you?"

"I bet I could use magic to get your car out of this hole. I bet you would appreciate that!"

"Don't. I'd appreciate you more if you pushed my car out of the hole, like a normal person."

"I'm not normal."

She sloshed through the mud back to the driver's side, got in the car and started the engine. I barely had enough time to get to the rear before the wheels started spinning. Mud flew everywhere. I leaned my weight against the trunk of the car and pushed with all my might,

179

slipping and sliding until the rear tire grabbed hold of the ground. The car moved slowly, and finally jumped out of the hole, leaving me a muddy mess. She did a three-point turn around, slowed alongside of me and rolled down her window. "Doesn't that feel a whole lot better than using supernatural powers to solve your problems?"

I wasn't sure how to answer her. Wet, muddy, and exhausted, and with a blank stare I took too long to respond, so she rolled up her window and stepped on the gas, red tail lights being the last I saw of her that night.

C Chapter 20

Black magic

When I stepped into Tim Lan's shack, a lantern light greeted me. Tim Lan sat at his kitchen table, his bag of pearls spewed out in front of him. I wasn't sure what to say as he didn't look very happy with me.

"Hello," I mumbled.

"I asked you to watch my house," he said, glancing at me briefly. "I am disappointed."

"I'm sorry." All this time I had trusted that Liona's magical shield had kept the shanty safe. "Did something happen?"

The golden light of the lantern glowed on his face when he looked at me. Shadows danced under his eyes. I could smell the burnt kerosene.

"The door was opened," he said.

"I swear I closed it." At least I thought I had. Then I realized he had his pearls out because maybe he was counting them. "Is anything missing?"

"I came home just in time. I saw them run away. No. Nothing is missing."

"Did you see who they were?"

"No."

"I'm sorry," I said again, but I knew that wasn't enough. "I should never have gone. I'm sorry." I pulled my wet sweatshirt up over my head and dried my hair with it once it was off. I draped it over the bench, then went to my corner and crawled into my sleeping bag. Tim Lan dropped his pearls into the leather pouch, snuffed out the lantern and slipped into his bed.

Guilt riddled me after that. I had returned to my routine, making more pearls a day than I had before, hoping to get on Tim Lan's good side again. He wasn't mad at me, but something seemed to be missing. Trust maybe.

Not only was I upset about having disappointed Tim Lan, but I also couldn't get my mind off Liona, especially since she had been angry when she left Reef Hollow. Seemed like maybe I'd never see her again. Between my worries about her, and the silence between Tim Lan and I, my heart wasn't into making pearls.

"Why so sad?" Tim Lan asked me one morning after I dropped nine of my marbles into his palm. I hesitated before I let go of the rest and instead took time studying his anxious eyes.

"It's not what it used to be," I said.

"No. It's not," he admitted. "Are you done?"

I shrugged and glanced at his shack, and then at the ocean, and then up the way toward Windy Point. "I don't know."

"What's the matter? Is it the girl?"

I didn't answer. I didn't want to tell him it was because it would hurt his feelings, maybe.

"She was the reason you left, wasn't she?"

"She needed help. Why did you tell on me?"

He gave me a questioning glance. Maybe he didn't understand what I meant.

"Why did you tell my mother I was with Liona?"

Tim Lan shook his head.

"You didn't tell her?"

"I didn't see your mother."

So, she lied. Or he was lying. He picked up a shell and played with it, then tossed it toward the water. "You have a place to stay. With me." He squinted up at me, the lines in his face revealing hope and discontent both at the same time. "What do you want? To stay?"

182

"What do you want me to do?" Silence took over as I played with the remaining pearls, rotating them on the palm of my hand with my fingers. Silky smooth to the touch, their colors sparkled in the sunlight. Tim Lan studied them, too.

"No. I am not going to decide for you," he said in almost a whisper. "That is your decision."

"You're not happy with me."

"You bring people here that are disruptive."

"My mom? I didn't bring her here."

"I think it was your mother that ran off in the dark."

"She broke into your house?"

"I think so." He brushed his hair back with his hand. I hadn't noticed before, but he seemed tired. Weary and spent as if he'd been losing sleep over something and I wasn't helping his life to be any less stressful.

"That's not my fault, if it was her," I said.

"If you weren't here, she wouldn't have come. I know who digs up our beach. I recognized her too. They came again. That's why I think they broke into my house. She complained to the trading post, and now I must go farther into the city to sell my pearls. I wanted you to watch my house, to keep it safe."

"I'm sorry about your house. I don't want her interfering with us, either."

"Tell her."

"I can't."

"Then perhaps our deal is off. Perhaps you need a new place to live."

I shut my fist over the remaining thirteen pearls. "Perhaps." I said.

He eyed my hand. I sensed anger stirring in him because his face grew red and he trembled. "You have become rebellious. I can't trust you anymore, Em. What happened?"

"No, I haven't."

"Irresponsible then, and that girl is to blame for that."

"You have no reason to say that."

"No? She had you leave your obligation. Jeopardizing my home."

He moved closer to me. "Don't let your feelings blind you, Em. Keep your senses. We need each other right now. Unless you want to go back to where you came from. Do you?"

"No. I don't. But Liona has been nothing but kind to me. She likes me."

"When was the last time you saw her?"

I thought for a moment. He knew. I knew too, but I didn't want to admit how long it had been.

"Two weeks ago?" I wasn't sure when she had dropped me off that rainy night.

"A month." he corrected.

Had it really been a month? No wonder I felt bad. I looked away.

"Look what's happening. It's over or she would have been here. Time now to grow up." He held out his hand. "What did your uncle say to you. Come on, you told me once."

Was he telling me that my time with Liona had ended? Was he saying that she was not one of the persons I needed around me? She was gone. If she cared for me she wouldn't have dumped me in the middle of the night. She wouldn't have asked me to abandon Tim Lan's house so that thieves would break in. She wouldn't have stayed away for a whole month.

We stared at each other for a long time, but I knew he would win. I had no fight in me. I dropped the last thirteen pearls into the palm of his hand. He slipped the pearls into his pocket and gave me a nod before he wandered down the beach toward Windy Point.

Drained, my excitement for life, for Liona, and for magic seemed to have fizzled.

And then there was my mother who was still ruining my life even though I was grown. What was she doing breaking into Tim Lan's house?

C Chapter 21

The Plea

For weeks I struggled with making up my mind about where I wanted to live, even though I thought I already knew. Uncle Jim's question kept popping up like a neon sign in my brain. I wasn't sure if making pearls for Tim Lan was as fulfilling as I thought it might be. My stay at Reef Hollow had lost all purpose. Earning rent was not enough for me anymore. I missed Liona terribly. I just wished she needed me like I needed her. She made me feel important. Normal, like other people. Like I wasn't someone' pet to be taken care of, like Aunt Agnes always made me feel.

I had so many sleepless nights that the day came when I decided to leave Tim Lan for good. I decided to end our agreement. I hoped he had enough money for whatever he was buying, but I was not going to make any more pearls for him. I had to make sure, though, that Liona would take me back before I said anything to him.

I had enough reason to leave Tim Lan. Despite all the talks we had, he never explained why he needed so much money. He never let on what he was doing all day when he went into town and had me watch the house. Sometimes he was moody and acted nervous and anxious when he came home. Sometimes he didn't even talk to me. I don't know if he was getting tired of me being there, or if he was afraid my mom would come back, or what. Something wasn't right, that I knew. Maybe he had been lying to me all along. I wasn't going to play his game any longer.

Anyway, if my idea that I'd been dreaming up worked, maybe I could get my own place if my pearls were worth all that much money. Maybe Liona and I could live together. Alone!

I woke up at sunrise as I always had. I sat on the beach and watched the sea, the gulls, the pipers. Doing so used to give me peace, but not anymore, and I blamed Tim Lan for that. All the energy inside of me; all the magic wanted a release. I needed a long walk. Instead of going to the oyster beds, or instead of making pearls, I walked up the beach toward Windy Point.

I should have felt guilty for going back on my word with Tim Lan. I would have before, but this morning I didn't. I felt strong. I think it was because I made up my mind to leave. The magic I used to make pearls didn't tingle on the left side of me today. Instead, I felt a tingling all over my body, as if my blood had absorbed the magic and was carrying the power through my veins, to my heart. I breathed easier. I felt like the wind, traveling on air. Floating in the sky like a sea gull. I was free. I wasn't running away from anyone with no destination and a lot of doubt like I had before. Instead, my feet were taking me somewhere that I wanted to go.

Mornings were always foggy along the coast, so I could never tell if the clouds would bring rain that day, or if the fog would lift and the sun would shine. I didn't care much. The tide rose, but there was still plenty of beach to maneuver around the cliffs. The coves were the most beautiful part of the coast. White foam would shoot up into the sky as the breakers hit the rocks, and turquoise tidepools further inland housed all sorts of interesting creatures. I took a little time exploring them and then moved on.

The sun was at its zenith when I came to Windy Point. I peeked up the beach toward the cul-de-sac to see how my real house was; to see if Aunt Agnes was there with a real estate agent again. Maybe I could sneak a look in the windows and reminiscence.

I scoped out the neighborhood I knew so well and had to stop in my tracks because even standing still, I didn't see the house. I saw a bull dozer and an empty lot where our house should have been. At first my mind went blank. I blinked and looked beyond the corner, to the sidewalks and the streetlights, and the other houses thinking maybe I was somewhere else. I wasn't. Everything at Windy Point appeared as it always had. Except Uncle Jim's house wasn't there anymore. My heart sunk, and I got a lump in my throat. They had buried Uncle Jim all over again. I didn't want to cry, or yell, or scream because I didn't want to make a fool of myself. There were neighbors that could see me. Dogs would bark. Maybe a kid would point at me. So, I kept on walking.

My hope to ever go back home was gone.

The tears leaked out silently. I tried to stop them. The wind picked up about that time, and I lifted my head to it so that the tears would dry. Still, they kept coming. And then my nose started dripping and I had to wipe my eyes and my nose with my sleeve.

My feet moved quicker than they ever did before because with my house bull dozed over, I had no ties to Windy Point. I ran and didn't watch where I was going. Of course, I tripped, but that was natural for me. Maybe my feet were too big, or I was naturally clumsy. I fell over the rocks and grazed my knee, but picked myself up, remembering how Uncle Jim told me to always get up after I fall, no matter if I fall on the ground, or fail in something I try to do in life. I needed that advice right now because I felt I had failed in making good decisions. Nothing had worked for me. I wasn't happy. I wasn't around people that loved me. I wasn't finding what I wanted in life.

The day passed, the sand, the rocks the oyster beds, they all passed. The tide came in and splashed on my shoes.

By the time I got to Elwood Estates, the sun was sinking into the horizon and I was wet. Drenched, just like the day I ran away. Nothing changed, I guess.

My shoes squeaked as I stepped onto the sidewalk. Cars went by, their headlamps low as twilight colored the streets a foggy blue. I found the driveway still hedged in by rhododendrons and ivy and other prolific growing plants. The porch light was on, and a light flashing colors in the window told me the TV was going. According to my watch, the tenants had just finished dinner. I wrung my hands together, nervous about whether Liona was even there. I wanted her to be, but dread came over me thinking maybe she had moved away. Maybe she left with no forwarding address. Maybe she found another guy to call boyfriend and he treats her better than I ever could. Maybe he was a normal guy. A month had passed since I'd seen her. Maybe she had tried to contact me in Reef Hollow when I was on a walk. Maybe Tim Lan lied about her never showing up. Maybe not. What if she didn't want to see me anymore?

I had to find out if Liona still liked me if I was going to leave Tim Lan. I stepped up on the porch and took a deep breath. I had a difficult time knocking. I had scared myself with all my negative thinking, and now I considered turning around and running away again. Uncle Jim would have scolded me if I did, so I tapped on the door. I could hear voices inside but no footsteps. Maybe they didn't hear me, so I knocked again and then for sure I heard someone walking around to the door, a latch unbolted, and the door creaked open just a little. And stayed that way.

"Liona?"

She opened the door wider and stepped outside. I didn't know what to say after that. I hadn't even rehearsed anything. She chewed her gum and stared at me. I knew about her gum chewing. She chewed when she's nervous, or upset, or maybe when she wasn't sure what to say.

"I…I missed you." Probably the stupidest thing to say but I did miss her, and Uncle Jim always told me to be honest. She switched positions, crossed her arms over her chest and popped a bubble. I kept talking since she didn't say anything. "I've been lonely, all alone. And all."

"I bet!" she said, still chewing her gum.

"I came here to see you."

We stared at each other for a little bit, and then I broke the silence again. "How are things here?"

She popped another bubble, gave me an awkward look which I couldn't read at all, and then came outside, brushed by me and sat on the porch swing. I sat next to her, not waiting for an invitation.

"Life's been pretty quiet here without Randy. I still visit Mrs. Wright in the hospital. She's recovering slowly, getting better little by little but having a stroke and getting well again is a long process."

"Oh. Sorry. I mean that's good that things are quiet, and not too busy for you. Sorry about Mrs. Wright."

"Stuff happens."

She pushed the swing a little, enough to rock us and make a gentle breeze. I twisted the corner of my hoodie into a knot and then, after realizing what I had done, I ironed out the wrinkles with my hand.

"We're a lot alike, Dylan," she said, still looking out over the yard.

"We are?"

"All my life I'd been hiding, ashamed of things that I'd done." She glimpsed at me quickly and then returned her gaze to the flowerbed. "I think you kind of do that, too. Hide, I mean."

"I hide?"

"That's what I call it."

Maybe that's what I was doing. I never thought of it like that.

"You haven't done anything to be ashamed of."

190

"Sometimes I'm just ashamed of who I am, not what I've done." I said. "So maybe, yeah. Maybe I am hiding. I can see how you think so. But I never thought of you hiding."

"I do."

Maybe I should ask her why, and then I thought not. And then I remembered it didn't matter if I asked, because she could read my thoughts anyway.

"Special powers can be destructive. You should remember that. My magic. Your magic. They can hurt people. Bad."

"I just make pearls is all. I cook sometimes. I don't think I hurt anyone with my magic."

"People can take advantage of our magic." She eyed me, and I knew who she was talking about. "You know I can read people, don't you?"

"Of course. You read me all the time."

"Well am I right in what I see?"

"Yes."

"I read Tim Lan. He's got something up his sleeve, Dylan. He's not being honest with you."

"I know."

"That's why I'm scared for you. I wonder how much control he has over you. What kind of dark thoughts he's left you with? You know?"

I knew her eyes were digging into my mind looking for the kind of stuff she was talking about, the blackness. My first instinct was to plead innocence, but I didn't know if I was or not, so I just sat there and let her search me until she turned away.

"Well?" I asked.

"I don't know. Seems like you're too naïve to latch onto anything really evil."

"Then you want to come to Reef Hollow and spend some time with me?"

She laughed. Not a happy laugh, a cynical laugh, kind of like how Shirley used to laugh at me. "Reef Hollow? You want me to hang out around Tim Lan? No!"

"I was thinking of something else. Not with Tim Lan. Maybe if my pearls are worth a lot of money I could sell them for myself. Maybe I could sell enough pearls to get a real house. Like Uncle Jim's. Then you and I could get married and live in it. Maybe have a family."

Her laughter stung a little because I thought it was a good idea. I also thought I made a mistake saying thing like that and was ready to apologize.

"What? Rely on your magic? To make a living?" She shook her head.

"Why not?"

Our eyes locked, mine hopeful, hers critical, until the hurt sunk deep. I guessed this was my last rejection because it's a long walk and I didn't plan on coming back just to be told no again. I think I surprised her when I stood. The swing rocked, and she had to stop it with her feet.

"What are you going to do?" She looked up at me

"I'm not sure. Go back." I said. I couldn't stand to look into those pretty eyes anymore, so I focused on the tree tops and noticed how the wind bent the branches back, and how a group of birds took flight in formation like dancers leaping out on stage when the music starts. I wondered what music there could be today. A lament most likely.

"Are you coming back here?"

"What? To a boarding home? It's like prison."

"Mrs. Healy isn't all that bad. She's even nicer than Mrs. Wright. We had a long talk and now she understands what happened. She trusts me now. She's paying me for my work. I'm not a tenant anymore. I'm not a patient. She sees me as an employee. I bet she'd see you like that too. I'd put in a word for you."

I couldn't grasp the idea of coming to this dark hole that I'd been forced to live in. Tim Lan's shanty wasn't all that great, but at least Aunt Agnes wasn't paying for me to live there. At least I had some control over my life. "No." I said it softly, not all that sure of myself. "Besides, Mrs. Healy doesn't trust me."

"You two could work that out."

"I don't belong here."

"No? I guess Tim Lan does have a hold on you. What a shame."

"No, he doesn't!" My eyes narrowed when I turned to face her. "He doesn't have a hold on me. I didn't even see him this morning. I don't like him anymore."

She snickered. "Just because you don't like him doesn't take his hold off you. Do you know what he does with your pearls?"

"He sells them."

"What does he do with the money?"

"I don't know."

Liona rolled her eyes and shook her head. "Dylan, Dylan," she said, sort of in a condescending way like I should know better. I had heard that voice in too many people before. "How many pearls do you make for him?"

"Fifteen some days. Thirty-two on better days. Whatever time I have to make them before the tide comes in, that's what he gets."

"That's a lot. Do you know how much he gets for them?"

I was silent for a while because I knew how much he got for them, or at least if what my mother had said was true. I also knew Liona would flip out if I told her. I waited for a moment before I answered.

"How much?" she asked.

"Thousands. That's what my mother said."

"Each?"

"I don't know."

"Did you ever ask him what he spends the money on?"

"No. He gets mad when I ask him questions. I don't think he'd answer me truthfully if I did. I think he wants it to be a secret."

"I wonder why. Don't you?"

"In a way."

"Does he have nice things? Nice clothes? Anything in the house new?"

"No. He makes his house out of scraps and remnants from the old pier. He lives like a poor man."

"Sounds like drugs then."

I scowled at her because the thought of Tim Lan doing drugs bothered me. "He doesn't act like my mother." I didn't need any more questions from Liona. The conversation had not turned the way I wanted it to. I flipped my hood over my head and put my hands in my pockets. "I guess that's it then."

"What?"

"You and me. I guess that's it."

She pushed the swing with her feet and looked out past me, into the yard. "Doesn't have to be that way Dylan. We both like each other. Nothing needs to end. We just don't know how to work things out but maybe we'll find a way. You won't get me near Tim Lan, though. He doesn't want me there and he has enough influence over you to keep me away. If you and I are together, he might make things even harder for you. I don't want that to happen. I care too much for you."

A lump swelled in my throat when she said she cared for me. Here I was fixing to leave her for good and she says she cares for me. I swallowed quick. "Maybe I can explain things to him."

"What can you explain? You don't even know what's up."

"I can explain that you are an inspiration to me. That you don't mean any harm to anyone."

"No, Dylan. Besides, even if we did like each other, I'm not living in his shack. And I'm sure not living someplace that you rent with magical pearls. I'm trying to make sense of my life, not walk out on a limb. Just stay out of it. How Tim Lan feels about me is not your fight"

"It's my fight, if I love you." I surprised myself telling her I loved her, but it was true, and those words had been burning inside of me ever since we first kissed. I'm just slow.

Our eyes froze on to each other, and I think she got a lump in her throat too. She moved off the swing slowly and walked up to me. There was that fragrance again, her sweetness. She tucked her arms around me and the warmth of her body swept through me like a wooly blanket Uncle Jim used to tuck over me on a rainy day. Her lips came near my face. She pulled me closer to her. I leaned over and then we kissed, long and hard. I closed my eyes, took my hands out of my pockets, and then pulled her tighter to me, never wanting to let her go. Never. Why did I want a stupid house at Reef Hollow? Or to live on my own, or to practice magic? I just wanted her.

When we were finished kissing, she stepped away and touched my cheek, her eyes so gentle, and my body so heated that I melted. "Make a decision, Dylan."

"I will."

"We can't live like this—you walking back and forth from Reef Hollow to here just to talk to me."

"I know. That's a long walk."

"And you have to decide if you want to keep using your magic for Tim Lan's mysterious bank account."

I knew that too, but I sealed my lips.

"You know?" she pressed me for a reply.

"I'm not just making pearls for him. I'm making them for me, so that I have a place to stay."

"You have a place. Here."

I shifted my weight, glanced at the door to the boarding house, turned and looked at the yard, the driveway, the swing. "Liona, my Aunt Agnes paid for this. I don't..." I choked up some. "I don't want Aunt Agnes to pay for my home. She'll control me. I'm tired of being controlled by her. I'm tired of Aunt Agnes and my mom thinking they own me."

Liona fidgeted with the zipper on my sweatshirt. "I can't promise you, but I will ask Mrs. Healy if she'd hire you."

I had little hope Mrs. Healy would even want me in the house, much less hire me. I didn't say that to Liona, though. I didn't want to be negative. Uncle Jim said never to discourage other people.

"Would you try that arrangement?" She read my thoughts. Again.

"Try?"

She nodded, a tear welled in her right eye and I quickly wiped it with my thumb, gently touching her so as not to mess up her make up. "You think she'd let me work here?"

"She plans on getting more tenants. She's going to need the help."

"I ran off pretty wicked like."

"She understands, Dylan. That's why she let me drive you back to Reef Hollow that night. She sympathizes with you. She was horrified by your mother."

"She was? I mean, she does?"

"Let's give it a try."

"I don't know." I suppose with all that was happening with Tim Lan now, I could break away easy enough. "Maybe. Maybe I can try. But I would have to tell Tim Lan. I can't just break my word with him. I don't know what he spends his money on, but he needs to know he won't have any more pearls. He won't have any more money." I laughed a little because the thought that I supported Tim Lan was funny.

"Wait here." Liona slipped back inside the house and I could see her through the window.

I saw Mrs. Benson too, and I waved at her. She waved back like she remembered me, but I knew she'd just call me Eddy if I went inside. Liona came back out and tucked a cell phone in my pocket. "It's got lots of minutes. I want you to call me. Let me know if you need a ride back. Stay in touch."

I took the phone and played with the buttons a little bit. "Where's the numbers?" I asked, and she showed me.

"Just look for my name in your contact list. Here."

That was easy enough. I stuck the phone in my pocket. "I'll call you every day."

"Whenever you need to."

"Whenever I want to." We hit an awkward moment, just staring at each other expecting something but not knowing what. "I supposed I should go. I guess."

"I'll drive you home."

C Chapter 22

Island

Once I got back to Reef Hollow I didn't want to watch Liona drive away, so I didn't look back until I reached the beach. By then her taillights were disappearing into the dark. She hadn't parked or anything, she just stopped the car and I got out, and then we waved goodbye. I don't think she wanted to leave but what else could we do? I had to work things out with Tim Lan.

The hour was late, so I snuck into the house quietly. I didn't see Tim Lan, or hear him snoring, so I tiptoed to his corner of the shed to see if he was even in the house. His bed was empty and still made, so he hadn't come home from town. His leather pouch and a few pearls were spread out on the table in the kitchen, as if he left in a hurry. I didn't touch them. Maybe I should have put them away; however, I didn't like touching Tim Lan's personal things, so I left them where they were. I strode over to my corner, curled up into my sleeping bag, and closed my eyes.

The walk that day had worn me out. I should have fallen asleep right away, but I had a hard time quieting my mind. I kept thinking about Liona, our kiss and how good I felt when she put her arms around me. There was no way that I could live without her, especially since she felt the same about me. I was sorry that she wouldn't let me get my own place with my magic. Still, I had made up my mind that I would move in with her, even if I had to live in the boarding home. The only thing to do now was to talk to Tim Lan and let him know my decision. I had to tell him that I wasn't going to make any more pearls for him. Then I would ask him what I wanted to know, like why did he hate Liona when she was such a nice person, and what did he use the pearl money for?

I tossed and turned in my bed with those thoughts racing through my mind. Finally, I faced the wall and closed my eyes, hoping for sleep. I started to doze when I heard the door creak open. I just lay quiet as I wasn't ready to talk to Tim Lan yet, so I played possum. He stepped over to the table, but he didn't turn the light on. I kept my eyes shut until I heard a crash. I figured he might have hurt himself in the dark, so I sat up quick.

Tim Lan wasn't in the room. My mother was. A chair in the living room had fallen over and she stood next to it, an astounded look on her face.

I jumped out of the sleeping bag. I think I startled her as much as she startled me. She sprang back. "You!"

"What are you doing here?" I asked, sensing black magic pouring into my veins from the shock.

"You rotten little devil. It's true! You're living with him."

"You're trespassing."

"What? By visiting my son?" She snickered and shook her hair out of her face, shining the flashlight around the room. First in my eyes, then the walls and then the beam landed on Tim Lan's pouch on the table.

"Oh no you don't!" I said and made a bee line for it.

She intercepted me, shining her light in my eyes. The brilliance blinded me. I lunged at her and grabbed the flashlight. She pulled back. We struggled right there in the middle of the room, knocking over the other chair. We skid across the floor and fell on the ground. She pulled my hair and bit me. Her fingernails dug into my arm. I threw my elbow into her face, hitting her nose. She snorted and growled, her hair flying wildly into my eyes. I got a hold of the flashlight with both hands and yanked it away from her. We both got up off the floor and before I could catch her she dove for the table, and the pouch of pearls. I couldn't let her have them, but she was faster than I was. Several more pearls fell out of the bag as she jumped away from me, pouch in hand.

"Those aren't yours."

"You owe them to me." She dove for the fallen pearls.

"They aren't mine, either," I said. Anger soared through me like venom. It rattled through my left arm as I watched her scramble on the floor chasing the marbles as they rolled. I pointed at her, the electricity in me burning to be released. "Stop it!" I commanded barely able to contain the magic.

"Get to hell with you," she retorted and stood, the pearls clattering in the palm of her hand. "You'll make me a rich woman yet, despite your insolence." She tossed her hair over her shoulders, sweat dripped down her neck. She smelled of alcohol. "All your life you tried to keep me down, just like your father. All the suffering I did because of your pity parties, calling CPS on me, rallying your friends against me, you'll pay for it all Dylan." Her spit hit my face when she talked, her eyes squinty like an old bat. "Hiding behind your crippled uncle's wheel chair, collecting his money, living off him when he could barely afford you. You killed him, you know? You know that, don't you? You killed your uncle and now look what it's got you."

"I didn't kill him. I loved Uncle Jim."

"He was in bad shape, and you made it worse for him."

"No! That's not true! It couldn't be true. Uncle Jim loved me. He would have told me if it was too much for him."

"No, he wouldn't. He'd have suffered and not told anyone. Your uncle was a nice guy. Unlike his nephew." She stepped closer to me. Her mouth contorted, saliva smeared across her face. I could see the malice spew from her lips. "You made him die, Dylan. You made him die! How do you feel now?"

"Stop it!" I couldn't take it anymore. Her words dug too deep, her hate bore a hole in my heart. I stepped back away from her, away from the spray of her foul mouth, far enough that I could stretch out my arm. The power had swelled. I was a dam bursting and I couldn't hold the bitterness inside any longer.

I released it. All of it. The black energy spun out from my fingertips onto each of the pearls in her hand, illuminating them. They glowed. Her eyes widened at the sight. The radiance lit up her face. And then she screamed as the pearls turned red hot and scorched her. I smelled her flesh burn. She dropped them and screamed again, holding her wrist, doubling over. Nothing inside of me wanted to stop the outpouring. I burned her hair as she fell to the ground. Her pain felt good to me. Evil, but good.

Not until Tim Lan came running inside did I let up.

"Stop it!" His voice traveled high over my mother's cries. I pulled my arm back and hid my hand in my pocket. Suddenly a light came on inside of me and I saw what I had done. My mother weeping on the floor in pain.

"What is going on here?" Tim Lan asked.

"She broke into your home. I caught her taking your pearls." My voice trembled. I was looking at the scene from somewhere else, somewhere outside of my body. My hands shook, sweat dripped from my forehead.

"That's a lie!" my mother cried out, still groaning in agony. "He let me in the house, told me to take the pearls and sell them. Said he wouldn't tell. He wanted to meet me later to split the bounty."

Tim Lan turned to me sharply. My mouth hung open

"Get out. Both of you."

201

"It's not true!" I pleaded but Tim Lan had already grabbed the pouch and pearls from my mother's burnt hands.

"Get your mother to a hospital," he ordered me.

He helped her up and nodded toward the door. "Now! And don't come back."

I was livid and speechless and about to wretch whatever was in my stomach. My jaw clamped shut but it didn't matter because no way would Tim Lan believe a word I had to say. I pulled on my hoody and stormed across the room. Grabbing my mother by her elbow I pulled her out the door. Tim Lan threw my backpack outside on the ground, and then slammed the door hard behind us.

The night was amazingly still. Stars and the milky way crowded the midnight sky. A misty chill hit me in the face and steam seeped from my mouth.

My mother wrenched her arm away from me. "Get your hands off me, you filthy warlock." She stumbled toward the old parking lot and I followed. Even though I hated her, and wished her evil, I knew I had to get her to a hospital. I pulled out the phone that Liona had given me and clicked on the "emergency call" button.

"What's your emergency?"

I froze at the sound of the stranger's voice. They asked again.

"A burn," I finally whispered.

"Location?"

"The beach by Reef Hollow." I hung up after that. With my mother furrowed against an old oak tree in the gravel, holding her wrist up, and crying, I moved away from her. I had done everything I could do for her. To her. Everything. I turned and ran down the beach not sure which way I should go, or if I should call Liona, or if I should just die.

Ó Chapter 23

Torment

The ocean was as dark as the night. Even the breakers melted into the ominous seascape. I could hear the pounding of the waves, the steady drumbeat of water making sand. I felt the foam at my feet. I ran in the direction of Elwood Estates, but part of me didn't want to get there. I needed to see Liona, but I was ashamed of what I had done.

I looked back and saw red and blue blinking lights in the distance where I had left my mother.

She wasn't going to die.

Breathless, I fell in the sand before I reached the rockpiles that sheltered Windy Point. I wiped the sea spray, tears and sweat that had formed on my face. My nose ran. My hands shook. I took the phone from my pocket and dialed Liona's number and then hung up before it rang. I hid my face in my sleeve and moaned. Louder, until the sound came from places inside of me I didn't know were there. My cries harmonized with the growl of the ocean.

I called out to the midnight abyss repeatedly, bellowing strange and uncanny sounds that came from my gut. In that way, I drained everything inside of me. My hate, my grief, my shame for having attacked my mother. I cried out until there was nothing left. No energy, no grief. Only emptiness. Then I wiped my eyes and fixed my gaze on the heavens, mesmerized by the stars. How much time passed, I didn't know nor cared. My hollow body bore no thoughts, nor any feelings.

The sound of a sea gull brought me back. I pulled out my phone again and dialed Liona's number. This time I let it ring. I almost hung up after the third tone but then her voice came through, clear and strong.

"Hello."

"Liona," I stuttered. I sounded like Randy. I sniveled and choked on my slobber and wiped my face again. I coughed because the mucus had collected in my throat, and then I spat.

"Dylan? It's so late. Why are you calling? What's wrong."

"I need to talk to you."

There was silence for a moment and I feared maybe she hung up on me.

"Now?"

Oh god I didn't want her to refuse me. What would I do? I didn't answer.

"Where are you?"

"Windy Point. I mean I'm almost there. Maybe ten minutes. Please, Liona. I really need to talk to you."

"I'll meet you there."

She ended the call. I stood, a little stronger knowing that I had Liona to talk to. She would understand. I made my way around the cliffs, stumbling in murky tidepools and scrapping my hands on the mussel-coated boulders. I was pretty scratched up by the time I reach the beach at Windy Point. My pants were soaked. I had forgotten to take off my shoes, so the sand seeped through to my toes where the seams came apart. I stumbled across the oyster beds and when I reached a loamy dune, I collapsed face down into the ground.

I fell asleep.

When I awoke, the fog was thick, and the temperature had dropped. I shivered. My head hurt, my energy drained. I opened my eyes. Through the mist a glow of headlights beamed in the street near where my old house used to stand. I assumed Liona had arrived, as not many people would be driving in that cul de sac this time of night. I closed my eyes again. Part of me sighed with relief for a moment, but then I tensed up. Telling her what happened would not be easy. I struggled trying to think of what I was going to say, opening my eyes once. She trudged through the sand and stumbled through the oysters to get to me.

"Dylan, what's going on? What are you doing laying here in the wet?"

She knelt next to me. The concern in her eyes tore my insides. I sat up, dazed.

"Tell me," she spoke softly and took my hands in her. "What happened, Dylan?"

It took a while to put words together. I stuttered once and groaned shaking the sand out of my hair.

"What, Dylan? Are you hurt?"

"No."

"What then?"

"You warned me. You know? I'm a fool."

She nested next to me. "What did I warn you about?"

"Using magic." I swallowed because I could barely talk. "What do you do when you've been the devil? Where do you go? How can things ever be right again?"

"What are you talking about?" She frowned and searched my eyes.

I saw fear in hers. She was right to fear. She should fear. I'm afraid of me. I don't trust myself. "I did the blackest thing anyone could have ever done."

"What did you do?"

"I burned my mother."

She pulled back to study me, as if she wasn't sure I was the person she knew. I wasn't.

"With magic?"

I nodded.

"What happened?"

"She said I killed Uncle Jim." The tears welled, and I wiped them away quick. "I swear if I had known Uncle Jim was dying because of me I'd have left. I swear it."

"Stop it, Dylan." She touched my cheek, her hand soft and warm. Gentle. "You didn't kill your uncle. He had a kidney failure. That's what your aunt told me. What your mom said is not true. Don't let yourself believe those lies. You didn't kill your uncle."

"You don't know that. My mom knew her brother. She's probably right. She said I killed him and I hated her for telling me. The magic was in me, Liona. Dark. Mad! Rage, that's what it was. I didn't mean to hurt her like that."

Liona brought my hand to her lips and kissed it, which stopped my tears. "Is she okay?"

I shrugged. "I called the emergency number on your phone and they took her away."

"Was she breathing when you left?"

"She was crying. Her hand was blistering. It looked bad."

Liona relaxed. "She'll live."

"Maybe. I left before they came. I hate myself Liona. I hate myself." I gasped for air because my heart started beating hard. "I hate myself."

She sighed long and hard while I wheezed. The panic set in. I saw myself sitting on the beach with Liona, but I couldn't control myself. Maybe I was having a seizure, I don't know. I shook. I grunted. I slobbered. I was a mess. Liona watched me and I hated that she saw me like this, but I couldn't stop. Finally, I buried my head in my hands and sobbed.

"Settle down, Dylan." She put her hand on my head, knelt, and kissed me on the forehead. When her cool hands touched me, I got my breath back.

"Settle down."

206

I wiped my eyes and took some deep breaths like Uncle Jim had taught me. She moved closer.

"Take it easy. Don't hate yourself. You'll get through this."

"I'm not sure I want to. I need to punish myself for being so bad."

"Stop that."

"No one does things like I do. I could have killed her."

"Okay, look." She scooted away, and her voice lost its gentleness.

Not by much, but enough to pull me out of my self-hatred because I didn't want her to leave. I needed her.

"I know what you're feeling. I know the darkness." Even though Liona had a stern look on her face, her voice was more than sympathetic. Deeper than that.

"How could you know what I'm feeling? You've never even hurt a fly. Except maybe when you tripped me and that didn't even hurt. My pride maybe?"

"Don't kid yourself. I was in the same place you are. Only worse."

"Hurting someone?" I wiped my face with my sleeve and spat in the sand.

She nodded. The moon rose east of us just then. A big full moon that peeked over the rooftops of the houses in the neighborhood. The light made Liona's face glow. "I'm ashamed of what I did. So ashamed I never told anyone. But I know how you feel."

She had my attention. I wiped the last tear, rubbed my hands clean on my pants, and then clasped her hands tight.

"I'm trusting you," she whispered. "With my secret."

"I won't tell anyone." And then I questioned if I could be that loyal because I betrayed Tim Lan's trust. If I did it once, I might betray Liona. "I mean, not if I can help it I won't ever tell anyone."

"It's hard."

"I know," I whispered. Gosh did I know.

"I had a younger brother. He wasn't a healthy boy, but he was a beautiful boy. I loved him so much. He was much like Randy - stuck in a wheel chair most of the time. No one knew if he'd ever be able to walk. My parents had been talking about getting braces for him, but it took a long time. Years."

"That's hard."

"Yes, well I was young and foolish back then. I thought for sure, having magic, I could help him. Cure him even. I tried to help him walk. Every day I'd get him up and walk with him."

"That's good."

"Good. Yeah," she snickered. "Remember what happened when you used your magic on Randy?"

I wrapped my arms over my chest, feeling the pain. How could I forget? "Did that happen to you?"

"Not the same as it did you. I didn't get any pain from Tommy. My magic didn't work like that."

"Oh." I sensed she was going to tell me something awful. Something dark. She read my mind.

"Yeah. It was black as the sky is tonight. We were alone that night, upstairs in his room. I coached him to take some steps. We practiced like that often. Tommy got out of his wheel chair, holding my hand of course, and took a few steps. We were both delighted. Then I got arrogant. I sent some magic his way. First time I'd ever done that with him." she sighed and squeezed her eyes shut and moaned a little. "I'm sorry Dylan. This hurt."

I didn't know what to say so I just sat there and gaped at her. She buried her head in her hands. She didn't cry. She was quiet for a long time. When she took her hands away her eyes met mine. "I've never told anyone and now I can see it all over again."

I bit my lip, trying not to interrupt. I put my arm around her shoulders because she started trembling.

"You don't have to tell me."

"Yes, I do. For your sake. For mine too."

She composed herself and then went on.

"He walked on his own once the energy was in him. It was beautiful He followed me out of the room. The magic traveled through us both. It made him laugh. What a handsome smile he had. I turned to lead him back to the bedroom." She shuddered and stared at the moon. "I thought I had healed him, but…" She breathed in deeply and swabbed a tear from the corner of her eye. "He didn't follow me. Instead he went to the stairway and called my name. 'Look!' he said. He was going to show me how he could walk down the stairs. Before I got to them he fell. His little legs just weren't strong enough. He rolled to the bottom of the stairwell and hit his head on the wall. There was no blood. No broken bones. He lay there unconscious with a small gash on his head." She stared at the ocean, I stared at her. I don't think I had a pulse right then, waiting for her to finish. "He slipped into a coma. Never came out of it." She glanced at me. I never thought a smile could show so much remorse. "He died."

"Oh." I said, sickened by the thought. Saddened for Tommy, and for Liona having to carry that guilt. "I'm so sorry."

"I loved little Tommy. I never meant to harm him."

Neither of us spoke again for a long while. We didn't cry anymore. The fog settled in around us, covered the moonlight, and then we couldn't see the ocean at all. We snuggled together, our bodies exchanging heat, shivering and then comforting each other.

"I didn't tell you everything," I said.

"You don't have to if you don't want to."

"I want to. You should know. My mother broke into Tim Lan's house. She took his pearls. I couldn't let her do that. I set the pearls on fire in her hand. I wasn't sorry about it either."

"That's scary, but I can understand that."

"Tim Lan thinks I invited her. She told him I helped her steal from him."

"Oh, Dylan."

"So, he kicked me out."

"Oh god."

"Yeah." I breathed in deeply. "I hate her sometimes. But I feel bad that I hurt her. How can that be?"

"Because you're a good person, Dylan."

"The magic was black. Evil."

"It's gone now, isn't it?"

I shuddered at the thought of what had happened. "I never want to experience that kind of power again. I never want to. I'm sorry for you, and your brother Tommy. I'm sorry for using that power."

C Chapter 24

Refuge

Liona snuck me into my old room that night. Room 8. She locked the door and made it seem like I wasn't around. Being there felt odd, like nothing had happened in between the time Shirley had dropped me off months ago, and tonight. But it had, and I couldn't forget my mother's words, her spite toward me, or the smell of her burning flesh. I tried.

The bed was comfortable and the house warm. Liona let me take a shower after everyone went to bed which helped me sleep. Early in the morning I heard the tenants downstairs, people moving around, and I smelled bacon cooking. I wished I wasn't hidden away like a robber, but Liona didn't know how Mrs. Healy would take to me coming back. She wanted to break it to her gently, I guess. Not that I planned on staying. I didn't. I wanted to go back to Tim Lan and apologize.

I jumped out of bed when someone tapped on the door. "Dylan," Liona whispered. "Open up." She handed me a tray of food and a glass of orange juice. "I promised Mrs. Wright I would visit her in the hospital today. You must come with me. I can't leave you here."

"Okay."

She handed me a car key. "When you're done with breakfast, take the back stairs and exit out the side door and wait for me in the car."

"Okay."

"I just need to do dishes. By that time, you'll be done eating. Make the bed like no one's been here and bring everything you have with you. Don't leave a trace that you were here."

"What about these?" I nodded at the tray I had in my hands.

"Bring them too."

She slipped out the door, shutting it quietly. I heard her footsteps as she ran back down the stairs. Thankful for the hot meal, I probably ate faster than I should have. When I was finished eating everything, the bacon, the eggs, the toast, everything, I wiped the plate with the napkin she gave me and stuck the tray, glass and dish in my pack. I made the bed tight and then prepared my escape out the back.

The car had a musty smell to it. I kept my head low in case someone looked in the window, but no one did. Soon Liona appeared on the porch waving to whomever was inside. I didn't relax though until we were headed down the driveway.

"Did you ask Mrs. Healy about me coming back?"

"No. There's been some changes."

"What changes?"

"Your Aunt threatened to quit paying your rent."

That stunned me for a moment. I wasn't sure how to handle the news. "How do you know? Did you ask?"

"Not exactly. Mrs. Healy was discussing finances over the phone with the social workers and I overheard her mention your name."

"So, I'm out?"

She shrugged her shoulders. "We could go talk to your aunt if you wanted."

"No!" I snapped.

"What then? You have to live somewhere."

The old car rumbled as it picked up speed. Liona drove much safer than Shirley, but I held onto the edge of my seat anyway, not being used to high speeds; not being used to cars at all, for that matter. We didn't go far on the

Interstate before she took an exit and coasted into Elwood Medical District. A large wooden sign with fancy lettering welcomed us. I forgot my train of thought and the question she had asked, lost to the glass buildings that towered over us, the hundreds of parked cars along the street, the ambulance that pulled away from the hospital with its lights flashing. I cringed because those were the same lights that flashed in the distance when I abandoned my mother under a tree at Reef Hollow.

"Do you think my mother is in this hospital?" Dread took over and I bit my lip.

"Not likely. They probably took her to Urgent Care in Reef Hollow."

"Not here?"

"Don't worry, Dylan. Chances of you seeing your mother today are slim."

Even so, I didn't like hospitals. I never did. They reminded me of when I was a kid. I'd been taken in a few times after my Mom punished me. And then there was the time I had to wait in the waiting room with social workers when my mom was sick from the drugs she took. I never liked the smell, or all the machines they hooked me or my mom up to. Or the needles and tubes in my arms. And when Uncle Jim left to go to a hospital he never came home. No, I didn't like hospitals. Still, maybe this visit would be different because I was with Liona, and I had no ill feelings toward Mrs. Wright. I kind of liked her.

We drove around the parking lot a few times before we found a place to pull in, all the while I gazed at the huge building. Thirteen stories high, I counted. Windows and brick, the place looked like a prison I had seen in a TV show. Once we parked I had trouble getting out of the car. My heart beat hard and my body froze up. I'd never been in a building that intimidating before. Enormous! Much larger than the hospital at Reef Hollow, where I was taken when I was young. So large and unfriendly I didn't want to go inside.

"Come on, Dylan, let's go." Liona hurried to my side of the car and opened my door. She held out her hand. I couldn't help but take it, but I didn't really want to get out. "Don't be so afraid. And don't worry, this is just a hospital and they aren't going to kidnap you. I'll be with you. We're just going to visit Mrs. Wright, not remove your appendix!" She laughed and when she did my head got hot.

Feeling like a fool for being scared, I got out of the car and trailed her inside. The large glass doors opened automatically for us, more welcome than I expected, or wanted. The interior—vast, open, and sterile—did nothing to comfort me. Cold, unfriendly, with smells that brought me back to unhappy and painful days. I loitered behind Liona when she went to the desk. She asked which room Mrs. Wright was in. The lady typed something in her computer and then looked up at us, eyeing me with a frown. I turned away.

"Room 405," was the answer.

We took the elevator to the fourth floor, stopping once to let a nurse with a cart in. I bit my lip and grasped the railing when we moved again, motion sickness turned my stomach.

"Hang in there, Dylan," Liona whispered after the nurse got off on the third floor. "We're here to make Mrs. Wright happy. That's all. It's a good thing."

The idea that I was helping Mrs. Wright feel better made the trip less daunting. When we reached the fourth floor, I wandered behind Liona through a maze of cream colored walls—passing people in blue suits with white masks over their faces—until we came to the nurse's station.

"I'm looking for Mrs. Wright." Liona told the nurse. They pointed down the hall and soon we found room 405. Liona tapped quietly on the door.

"Come in," Mrs. Wright said. Her voice was soft and raspy. She sat upright in her bed in a hospital gown and had a tray over her lap with her lunch half eaten. There was little light in the room. Machines surrounded her, and a gloomy sound beeped monotonously. She gave us a surprised smile when we entered.

"Liona! Dylan!"

Seeing her in bed like she was, I was taken over with remorse. I barely recognized her. She wasn't the jolly lady I knew from the boarding house. Her skin fit loosely on her form, dark age spots were more pronounced than I remembered, her arms were bruised like Mrs. Benson's, and her hair thin. Tubes were implanted in her arm and hooked up to machines so that she could barely move or sit up any more than she was. Her smile disappeared as quickly as it had come, as though there was too much pain to move her lips.

"I'm so happy you came to see me!" She offered her hand out and I noticed then that part of her face didn't move when she talked. "And you brought Dylan. What a wonderful surprise! Thank goodness you've been found. So good to see you. How are you? Where have you been? My, I have so many questions for you, but I won't bother you with all of them. I'm so glad to see you're well."

"Thanks. I'm happy to see you too," I mumbled taken aback with some of her comments.

"I was afraid for you when you ran away."

"I was fine."

"That was a terrible day. Just terrible."

"Yeah," I agreed and glanced at Liona. I didn't really want to think about that day. I still missed Annabella.

"I thought maybe you'd just gone back to your old house, but your auntie said she hadn't seen you."

"No. I didn't go back."

"Where were you?"

I shrugged not really wanting to answer. "The beach."

"Oh dear, Dylan! Why didn't you just come back? You must have been cold out there on the beach by yourself? You could have gone to your mom's if you didn't want to be with your Aunt Agnes."

"No!" The answer came out a bit rough, but I could barely say anything about my mother without feeling rough inside. I wished people would forget that I even had a mother.

"Well I won't ask you the particulars if you don't want to tell me." She waited. I didn't say anything. "Did I make you feel unwelcome at the boarding house?"

"No! I...it wasn't you," I stuttered over my words. I hadn't expected to be confronted about my disappearance. If I'd known she was going to ask me so many questions, I may not have gotten out of the car. "I'm sorry." I kept staring at her, troubled.

"A lot of things happened that day, Mrs. Wright. If you remember." Liona saved me from having to answer.

"I don't remember much, Liona. Not since I fell ill, I've lost some of my short-term memory. I do remember what a sweet boy Dylan is, though." She smiled at me and I felt the blood rush to my head. Not many people have called me sweet. Maybe a teacher or two in elementary school. "I missed you both. I know that." She must have felt self-conscious with me staring as she touched the left side of her face with her hand. "Looks bad, doesn't it?" she asked. "Half my face is paralyzed. Strokes will do that to you."

"We're thankful you survived, Mrs. Wright." Liona nudged me, and I looked away.

"I'm sorry for staring. I didn't mean to make you feel bad." I said.

216

"Physical therapy will help you," Liona said.

"So, is that's all that's wrong?" I asked, wondering Mrs. Wright couldn't go back to the boarding house.

"My face is not the only part of me that was affected, Dylan. I can't move my entire left side. I'll probably be in a wheel chair for a long while. Maybe for the rest of my life." She let out a long sigh. "You'll be going back to the boarding home?" she asked.

"We don't know." Liona responded quickly. I was glad she spoke up, because I wasn't sure what to say. "There are some things we need to take care of. But don't you worry about Dylan. He's got people helping him." She winked at me. "Just get better."

I took Mrs. Wright's hand and squeezed it gently. "I'm sorry you're in the hospital." I was. She didn't deserve to be lying in bed with tubes in her arms and machines beeping all over the place. The thought came to me just then that my mom was also in a room like this and it was my fault. Sorry was the only thing I knew to say. Sorry for a lot more than Mrs. Wright would ever know.

"The nurses are taking good care of me Dylan, so don't be sorry and don't you worry! This is the best place for me right now."

I stepped back away from her and walked to the window not really seeing what was outside, the parking lot, the fountain or the big hospital building. No, my mind slipped away from reality right then because I hadn't gotten over the night before. I could still see my mom's hair burning, her bent over body, her burnt hand, her weeping, and me running away. Mrs. Wright asked Liona about the other tenants, and the new caretaker, and how things were at the boarding house. The small talk made me nervous. I didn't need Mrs. Wright to ask me any more questions about what I was going to do with my life. I didn't know where I was going to live, or anything. I excused myself and eventually wandered out of the room with the excuse of getting a drink of water, and to get a whiff of the coffee at the nurse's station.

That was when my heart stopped. I saw Tim Lan at the nurses' desk. I took a second look because he was dressed in a clean white shirt and had black slacks on. His hair was combed. He was not Tim Lan the beach comber, but Tim Lan all the same. I wasn't mistaken.

What was he doing here? He didn't know Mrs. Wright, so he couldn't be here to visit her. Maybe he was sick, but he wasn't in a hospital robe. I approached him. He didn't see me. When he finished talking to the nurses, he spun away down the hall.

"Tim Lan!" I called out. The nurses gave me a dirty look and one of them shushed me, so I jogged down the hall to catch up with him. He must not have heard me, or else he ignored me. I followed him determined to have a conversation with him. I needed to apologize and convince him I didn't steal his pearls, nor did I tell my mother to steal them. I didn't want him to dislike me so much. We'd been friends, and friendships were important. I cared about him.

I nearly caught up to him when he disappeared into a room and shut the door. I wasn't sure what to do. I didn't feel right barging inside because I didn't know who else was in the hospital room. Someone sick, most likely. However, I didn't want to miss my chance and have him slip away before I got to talk to him. This would be a perfect place to settle everything because then I could go home with Liona and have at least one burden off my chest, as Uncle Jim used to say. I waited at the door, hoping he'd come out soon. I made note of the room number. Room 411.

I paced back and forth from Room 411 to Mrs. Wright's room so if Liona came out looking for me she'd see me and not leave without me. Soon a young nurse headed straight for Room 411. I skipped in front of the door as she squirted some soap from the wall dispenser onto her fingers. She rubbed the sanitizer onto her hands and smiled at me. "Can I help you?" she asked.

"I just need to talk to the man that went in there." I tapped on the door.

"Oh. Wren Lan's husband? Who may I say is waiting? I'll let him know you're here."

"Dylan."

"Last name?"

"Just Dylan. He'll know me."

"Dylan it is!" She smiled sweetly again and slipped inside.

Tim Lan had never mentioned a Wren Lan. Not that I could remember. If he was married to her, maybe all those pretty things back at his shed belonged to her. I waited a couple of minutes and then Tim Lan came out. He had an angry face and scowled at me. His voice was rough, like a snake's hiss. "What are you doing here? What do you want?"

His coarseness made me step back, but I mustered up my courage. "I want to apologize for the other night. I also wanted to tell you I didn't take your pearls and I never told my mother to steal them, either."

He crossed his arms over his chest and stood up straight. "How did your mother's hand get burned?"

I bowed my head and looked at my scruffy shoes, holey and falling apart at the toes. Ashamed. But then I met his gaze again because Uncle Jim's voice was clear in my head. He had said, "Admit your mistakes, and then move on and try your best not to make the same ones again."

"I used black magic. I needed to stop her from stealing your pearls. Please believe me? It's true."

For a second, I thought he was going to just pat me on the shoulder like he used to, but he went cold, and his voice got rough again. "Go away. Why did you follow me here?"

"I didn't follow you. I came to see Mrs. Wright, the caretaker of the boarding home. Then I saw you. I feel bad that we aren't friends anymore. I wanted to talk to you."

"There is nothing to discuss." Tim Lan had his hand on the door to Room 411, and he was about to go back into the room without talking to me. His anger was written all over his face.

I stood stunned. I told him the truth and, yet he rejected me. I was tired of being treated like that. I was about to argue but we were interrupted.

"Mr. Lan," a voice from down the hall called. Tim Lan's attention switched from me to a doctor walking briskly toward us. He wore a white cotton robe and had a stethoscope dangling from his neck. He had dark rimmed glasses on. "Mr. Lan may I have moment of your time?" he asked and then gave me a friendly nod. I nodded a greeting back.

Tim Lan glared at me, and then met the doctor only a few feet away so I could hear what they were saying. "What's the diagnosis?" Tim Lan's voice shook when he asked.

"I have good news," the doctor answered and nodded at me again as if I wanted to hear the good news too. I stepped closer. "The scan came out negative. I know paying for this operation created a hardship for you, but believe me, you made an excellent choice, Mr. Lan. If our team hadn't caught the tumor in time, the chances of your wife dying within weeks would have greatly increased. Now that the operation is over, Mrs. Lan is going to be fine. I don't know how you managed to come up with the money without insurance, but the staff and I are certainly glad you did."

Tim Lan's muscles relaxed, the color returned to him, his face contorted to a pout and then tears rolled down his cheeks. The doctor patted him on the back and after a short while of Tim Lan sobbing, the doctor turned to me. "Are you his son?"

I didn't have time to answer because he sort of moved us together and the next thing I knew I was holding Tim Lan and letting him cry on my shoulder. I patted him on the back. The nurse ushered us back into Room 411, and so I guided Tim Lan into the room with his wife. I sat him in the chair by her side, so he could take her hand. By this time my eyes were a little weepy too, and I choked on the tears a bit. Wren Lan smiled at me. She was in much better spirits than her husband.

"You are Tim Lan's apprentice?" she asked. I shrugged. I didn't know he called me an apprentice.

"I guess," I said. Even if Tim Lan never wanted to see me again, I still had worked with him. I had been his friend.

"Dylan? He has talked highly of you."

"He has?" That surprised me because Tim Lan hated my guts. She nodded.

"Not lately, I suppose," I mumbled.

She frowned. "We owe much to you." She looked at the door and then lowered her voice. "He told me how you make the pearls. I'm impressed. They're lovely."

I felt the blood rush to my head. "He did?"

"Wren!" Tim Lan shuffled in his seat but kept his back to me.

"Look!" She fidgeted with her collar and then pulled a leather lacing out from under her hospital robe. In the center hung one of the pearls I had made. Surprisingly the pearl had a slight glow to it much like the one I had given Randy. "He didn't sell them all. He saved the prettiest one for me." She smiled. Seeing the pearl, I had made hang delicately around her neck delighted me. Wren Lan had some age to her, but she was attractive, her hair still dark, not white like Mrs. Wright's. She looked a lot like the women in the pictures Uncle Jim had shown me

221

from one of his tours in Vietnam. Her smile made me feel loved. "The others he got such a nice price for. It's how he paid for the operation."

"Oh." I didn't know what to say. "You mean, me making pearls helped save your life?"

Tim Lan coughed just then. She gave her husband the box of tissue that was on her tray, so he could blow his nose and wipe his eyes.

"Yes. Your pearls saved my life. You are a generous young man. We are much indebted to you."

"I am not so generous. Tim Lan let me live in his house in trade."

"I know. But still what you did was worth much more than a few days rent. We are indebted to you."

I looked at Tim Lan's back, bent over. I guess he had nothing to say to me, or maybe he didn't know how to say anything. I could relate. Lots of times I had no words, just emotions.

"I'm glad I was of help." I spoke softly. I was more than glad but I was also ashamed of what I had done. I'd been wrong to begrudge Tim Lan the pearls I'd been making, or of suspecting him of doing something illegal. Or of not being a true friend. Or bringing my mother around to steal from him. "I didn't know. I mean, he never told me that's what he was doing with the money. If I had known they were to help save your life, I would have made more. I would have made pearls all day long. For you."

She laughed a little and shook her head. "He had no need for more. What you gave was just enough."

Still, if I had known they were to save his wife's life, I never would have complained. I didn't tell her that though. "Tim Lan," I said, my voice cracking and barely making any noise at all. "I am sorry for a lot of things."

I was talking to the backside of him. Wren Lan closed her eyes. I could tell by the face that she made she was listening and concentrating on my words.

"I didn't let my mother into your house. I was asleep. She woke me up. She came in to steal your pearls and I tried to stop her."

He bowed his head and brushed his hair back with his hand. He didn't say anything to me. That was fine. I wanted him to know what was in my heart. "You've been like Uncle Jim to me. I would never do anything to hurt you. Maybe I left your house when I was supposed to be watching it, but I didn't mean any harm by it."

He nodded, his back hunched over still. "Why did you resort to violence? That was your mother," he whispered. Wren Lan opened her eyes. They weren't smiling anymore. Instead she studied me, waiting for my answer.

"It was wrong," I said.

"Why did you do it?" he asked me.

"She," I choked then because the reason why still burned me inside. "She accused me of killing Uncle Jim." I bit my lip trying to hold back the flood inside of me. "She said I was a burden to him and made him die. What I did was wrong. I shouldn't have been evil like she was. I'm sorry."

After a long moment and me standing there like a dummy, looking at Tim Lan's back, he lifted his head and looked over his shoulder at me. "You're a good boy, Dylan. I knew your uncle. He loved you. You didn't kill him. On the contrary, you gave him something to live for." He stood then and offered his hand. At first, I didn't think I was worthy enough, but then he nodded, and his smile came back. We shook hands. "You should go visit your mother."

I couldn't tell him I didn't want to. Maybe he was right. Maybe I should see her but that would take a lot of strength. I didn't feel strong right now, so I nodded to let him know that I would. Someday. Wren Lan smiled and winked at me. Such a pretty smile I couldn't help but return it.

Tim Lan sat back down and took his wife's hand, and by the way he looked at her I knew they wanted to be alone.

"Thank you," I whispered and stepped out of the room. I wiped my eyes with my sleeve.

"Where have you been, Dylan?" Liona raced down the hallway toward me from Mrs. Wright's room. "I've been looking all over for you."

I couldn't talk, I was all choked up and wiped another row of tears from my eyes.

"What's wrong with you?"

"I'm sorry. I just…" The words came so hard for me. I shrugged and pointed to Room 411 and then took her hand. A ray of sunlight seeped through the entry way, the door slightly ajar.

She peeked in. "Oh! Excuse me."

I don't know what she saw, or what she thought, but after a moment she took my arm. "Let's go."

We hurried down the elevator and out of the hospital without saying anything to each other. We got to the car and we both strapped ourselves into our seats. Before she started the engine, she turned to me.

"Do you want to explain?"

"I want to." I said and took a deep breath, determined to find the right words. Liona had to know. "The pearls, the magic? You know? They paid for Tim Lan's wife's operation. The doctor said she would have died."

We didn't say anything else to each other but when I looked at her as we drove away from the hospital, I saw tears in her eyes too.

"What now?" she asked, quietly.

"I want to go home." I took no time answering her. "To Windy Pont."

I wanted to be alone by the sea where I used to live, where Uncle Jim would watch me gather oysters. Where I met Tim Lan. I wanted to think things over.

.

C Chapter 25

Death of an Ancient

I barely said goodbye to Liona when she parked. I doubt she knew what to do because I got out of the car and started walking. I didn't mean to be rude, but my mind spun. Too much had happened to understand. I hadn't had time to process my emotions, label them, and figure out why I felt the way I did. All I knew is that I was very sad. Upset, and sad.

I didn't have any desire to go back to Reef Hollow. Not ever again. Tim Lan's house was built out of the remnants of times past, old things that were meant to have been washed away. I don't think he even wanted them anymore. I think all he really wanted was his wife. I think the two of them would be home no matter where their walls were.

I wanted to be home, too, and the only home I had ever known, besides Uncle Jim's house, was the sea. Now times had changed. I had too much remorse to stay at Reef Hollow and I was certain I would be with Liona when I felt better. Right now, I was sad because I had been meaning to Tim Lan when all he was trying to do was save his wife from dying. I should not have mistrusted him. I should have been a better friend to him. He never told me that his wife needed surgery, or that the surgery would have cost a lot of money and he had no way to pay for it, or that he was selling the pearls to save her life. That made me sad, because if I had been any kind of a friend, he would have confided in me.

I took my shoes off when I got to the beach and threw them aside. They were ruined anyway. Why did I need them? The cool sand trickled through my toes as my feet sank deep. The sand was comforting. The sand was my floor; my carpet; shells and stones worn by the sea, beat by the wind, until they became granules piled upon each other for thousands of years. My life was very much a granule like the sand. So was everyone else's. Me. Liona, Uncle Jim, Tim Lan's, even my mom's.

Clouds floated across the sky; not low like fog, but gray just the same. A mild breeze blew, enough to make me zip my sweatshirt and put my hoodie over my head. I stuck my hands in my pockets and walked past the oyster beds, pushing the sand along as I moved my feet. I headed for the ocean, that big vast body of rocking water that never turned away, never faltered and only changed its mood when a storm rolled in. I think that's why I liked the sea. It was faithful. I could always trust it to rumble and roar, foam and spray. I sat down where the dry met the wet. Where the tide had reached its height and now receded to the other side of the world. I watched the gulls like I used to and remembered telling Randy how they broke the clam shells open. I got teary eyed thinking about him, about Randy. He never hurt anyone, but he was so full of hurt. And yet he loved to laugh. He even made me laugh. I missed Randy.

"He didn't mean to break your Annabella, you know."

"I know."

Liona hadn't driven away after all. She had waited in her car and when she saw me stroll along the beach, she had followed. She sat down next to me and took my hand. She took my troubles when she did. Or rather we shared them.

227

"Sometimes stuff happens, Dylan. Simply got to deal with life as it comes."

"Got to have a better attitude when it comes, too," I said, speaking of myself because I was disappointed at the way I had handled things. Or rather didn't handle them.

"Don't beat up on yourself, Dylan."

Silence met us there, silence except for the surf. I breathed in the fresh salty air.

"I wish I could think better. Faster. I wish I was smarter so that I didn't make mistakes like I do. I shouldn't have hurt my mom so bad. I shouldn't have hurt Tim Lan either. I wish I was normal." Being slow probably meant I experienced a lot more heartache than other people. Worse, being slow caused a lot more heartache for other people too. "I give everyone such a hard time because of who I am."

We watched the waves crash for what seemed like half a day but was only a few minutes. "You're no different than anyone else, Dylan."

I peered at her, stunned by that statement. "What did you say?"

"I said, you're no different than anyone else."

That came from out of nowhere and I couldn't believe what I heard. Her words hit me as hard as the waves crashing on the beach. No one ever told me that before. Not ever. I was always told I was different. Peculiar. Less of a person than everyone else because I couldn't think right. Someone that had to be taken care of or watched over. Someone who couldn't live alone because they might hurt themselves or do something stupid like burn the house down. I could have easily argued with Liona over that statement. "Right," I scoffed.

"You're no different than me, or Mrs. Wright, or Tim Lan or even your Uncle Jim. We all have hopes and fears. We all make mistakes. We all doubt ourselves. You're no different."

228

I wasn't sure what to say after that, so I just sat quiet for a long time.

"You had no way of knowing what Tim Lan was doing with that money."

"Why didn't he trust me with the truth?"

A seagull flew overhead, screeching to another further out over the ocean. We watched him as he dove close to the breakers and finally landed on the beach, his downy body reflected in the wet sand.

"Sometimes people are ashamed of things, Dylan."

"What would he be ashamed of?"

"I don't know. Maybe he was ashamed that he couldn't afford his wife's operation. Maybe he was ashamed that she got sick. Or maybe he had some other reason he didn't tell you." She shivered and zipped her hoodie, rubbing her arms to keep warm. I scooted closer to her and put my arms around her so that our body heat would take the chill away. We enjoyed each other like that for a little while, and then I stood up and brushed the wet sand off my pants and gave her a hand up. She let me pull her to her feet. I guided her back up the beach.

My problem wasn't Tim Lan and his ailing wife, nor was my problem Liona, or Aunt Agnes, or Uncle Jim or Randy. Not even my mom. No, my problem was me thinking I needed to be someone other than who I was. That would change. Today. "Tim Lan doesn't need me anymore. His wife will get better. He doesn't need my help anymore."

"I know."

"I'm free." I laughed a little at those words. "All this time I thought I was free being with Tim Lan, and now, come to find out, leaving is what will make me free."

"Where will you go?" She brushed her purple hair out of her eyes.

"Your hair's getting long," I ignored her question. I had no answer anyway.

"I know. It's a pain keeping it short. And dyed."

"What will you do?" I asked her, smiling because the wind blew her hair around faster than she could contain it.

"Simple. I'll let it be free, like it wants to be. Blow in the wind, collect sand, sparkle in the sunlight."

"Perfect," I said soaking up in the green of her eyes.

"And you?"

"Maybe I can watch your hair grow out. Watch you be free, doing what you want to do."

"Maybe you could. You'd have to live somewhere besides here though, because I'm not driving here every day."

I took another look at the ocean. There were more seagulls congregating on the beach than just that one. They stood quiet, soaking the sun. "Think there'd be a room at the boarding house you live in?"

Her grin grew brilliant. Her purple hair danced in the wind. I touched it gently.

"I know of one empty room," she said.

Chapter 26

Renewal

Much to my dismay, Aunt Agnes was sitting on the living room couch when we arrived at the boarding house. She and Mrs. Healy were having tea together. Mr. Gravestone and Mr. Bromheimer had a checker board spread out on a table in front of them, and Mrs. Benson was asleep in her wheelchair. Liona walked in the door first, and when I saw Aunt Agnes, I hesitated to even walk into the house.

Neither Mrs. Healy nor Aunt Agnes acknowledged us at first. They were deep in conversation and had papers on the coffee table in front of them.

"Yes, Mrs. Barber, I'm going to write you a reimbursement right now." Mrs. Healy had a checkbook on her lap, and a pen in her hand, writing as she spoke.

"I really thank you for your understanding. I know you didn't have to refund any of my money…" Aunt Agnes stopped talking when she saw Mrs. Healy glance up at us. Both of their mouths flew open.

"My word!" Mrs. Healy whispered. Liona stepped aside so that Mrs. Healy and I had no choice but to stare at each other.

"Dylan!" Aunt Agnes bolted to her feet. "I thought you were gone. Your mother told me you ran away."

All eyes were on me. It'd be impossible to escape like I wanted to. I visualized the trail outside, how close it was and directly behind me, all I had to do was leap over the porch rail. "I did," I said. "I ran away."

The check that Mrs. Healy had in her hand swiftly disappeared into her pocket. Rage showed itself by the red in Aunt Agnes' face. She stuttered, unable to let any words fly from her lips. I had no question as to what she was thinking. She wished I would disappear. She was glad I ran away and now seeing me again ruined her hopes of getting her money back.

Liona read her mind, I could tell by the scowl on her face.

"Mrs. Healy!" I addressed the caretaker without looking at my Aunt again. "I want to apologize for being rude to you the other day."

Mrs. Healy rose to her feet. A stately lady, dressed as neatly as she had been the first day she moved in. She held herself upright and lifted her chin. "I understand, Dylan. You don't need to apologize. You were under duress."

Even Mr. Gravestone and Mr. Bromheimer were looking at me. Mrs. Benson slept soundly or else I'm sure she would have been worried about her Eddy.

"I was upset, yes, and embarrassed because of my mother." I glanced at Aunt Agnes.

"Dylan, your mother..." she started.

"I know. She's in the hospital." I said to her, a bit more vocally than I should have. "I don't want to hear about her right now. Maybe later, but not now."

"Dylan, listen," Liona interrupted me. Our eyes met, and instantly I knew she had read something on Aunt Agnes' mind.

"Dylan, your mother was in bad shape when she went to the hospital." Aunt Agnes blurted.

My heart raced at that moment because I thought she was going to tell me she was dead, that I had killed her. I braced myself for the worse.

"She was delirious when they picked her up. Who knows what drugs she was on, telling the medics she was attacked by a warlock. Carrying on about black magic and witches. I'm surprised they didn't put her in a strait jacket before they lifted her into the ambulance."

Liona and I glanced at each other.

"She was so drugged on pills and alcohol that the hospital put her in detox. I spoke with a counselor this morning and they recommended we intervene and get her in rehab immediately."

That took a moment to process, so I stared at Aunt Agnes. Flustered, she held up the papers in her hand. "I'm sorry, Dylan. That's why I came to get a refund from the boarding house. I don't have the money to pay for your rent here and for your mother's rehabilitation at the same time, especially if you're in and out of here on a whim every other day."

The silence hung thick as dough. My stay at the boarding house was no longer a given "My mother's going to rehab?" The words choked their way out.

"Oh, my word yes! She was sober probably for the first time in thirty years. Detox at a hospital will do that to you, I hear. Shirley and I convinced her to sign the consent form and now that's where she's going. I'm sorry this puts you out on the street, but I don't have a choice. Maybe after the estate is settled we can get you fixed up somewhere. Right now, I suppose I could get you..." Aunt Agnes looked me up and down. "some proper clothing and do something with your hair. Why aren't you wearing your shoes?"

I dropped my shoes that had been hanging over my back and they fell on the ground. Old, battered, the soles torn apart from their seams. Sand scattered on the floor in front of us. Aunt Agnes grimaced at them.

"As a matter of fact, we came back to give Dylan a haircut," Liona said. I shot her a look, surprised. She winked ever so slightly at me.

"Hurrah!" Mr. Gravestone clapped his hands.

"Mrs. Healy," I addressed the caretaker again, shutting out the others. "Don't worry about me. I'm not here to stay. Please return my aunt's money. We just came back so that Liona can cut my hair."

Mrs. Healy nodded and retrieved the check from her pocket. "All right, Dylan." Mrs. Healy said as Aunt Agnes turned to take the check. "I believe we're even now, Mrs. Barber. I wish your sister the best of luck with her rehabilitation. It's a long road ahead of her, but I'm glad that this is the course your family is taking."

I moved out of the way for her as Aunt Agnes headed out the door. She stopped in front of me. I don't think we've ever looked that hard at each other. Ever. I saw Uncle Jim in her gray eyes.

"Dylan, all we ever wanted was the best for you," she whispered. "I'm not your enemy."

"Okay," I returned as quietly.

She touched my cheek and ran her fingers through my knotted hair. "Try and take care of yourself."

"He will," Liona said, and slipped her arm through mine.

"I don't know where you're going to live. What you're going to do?" Her face was so full of sympathy I about gagged.

"I'll figure something out. I'm not totally stupid, Aunt Agnes. Not completely."

"Jim was always saying that too. You're a good boy, Dylan." She patted my arm, nodded to Mrs. Healy, and then walked out the door.

Liona sighed heavily once we saw the tail lights to Aunt Agnes' Buick disappear down the driveway. She stroked my arm and pulled me gently away from the door. "Mrs. Healy, you have haircutters somewhere?"

"In the upstairs bathroom," she answered. "Before you two disappear again, I need to talk to you Liona, and

Dylan might as well sit in on the conversation, since it concerns him too."

"Oh?"

We exchanged glances and Mrs. Healy smiled. "Yes. We're getting new tenants in the next few weeks, the first will arrive tomorrow. Since Liona will be assisting me with their medications, bathing, feeding, I'm in desperate need of kitchen help…" she looked at me. "I need a cook. I can't pay more than minimum wage, but I have an empty room."

Epilogue

One more flip of the omelet pan, and food would be ready. The eggs were already golden-brown sizzling in butter. Only another moment for the cheese to melt and they'd be fit for the platter. I peeked around the corner and smiled as Liona pushed Mrs. Benson's wheelchair to the breakfast table.

"Remember, Dylan," she said to me, and when she had my attention she mouthed the words "No magic!"

"Only a little," I assured her with a raised finger. I promised her every morning that I would be careful with my powers. "A touch of paprika, and sprig of Italian parsley. Perhaps a pansy or two as garnish to make the meal more attractive. After that, no magic."

She rolled her eyes, but good naturedly, as she watched me grab a dash of spice from thin air with a flick of my fingers, and then pluck a touch of parsley from my shirt pocket. She laughed. "Keep the magic down to a bare minimum, please."

"For your eyes, only," I smiled back at her. "I made a vow."

"I know you did."

"I keep my word." I had vowed to see that all the tenants get a menu to their individual tastes, with as much flair and elegance as I could conjure.

"You do. You've really taken your new job seriously." She leaned against the door frame to the kitchen, crossed her arms, and popped her gum, while watching me slide the omelet out of the pan onto a plate.

"That's because I'm grateful, Liona," I locked eyes with her for a split second. "To be here cooking for everyone. When Uncle Jim asked me what I wanted in life,

I told him to be a cook. But he made me see that I needed more than that. He made me see I needed to be around people that loved me." I looked up at her. She had stopped chewing her gum. I think if I hadn't been holding a hot pan and a clumsy oven glove on my hand, I would have kissed her. There would be time for that. We had our whole lives ahead of us now and we were going to share it with each other.

"I know you're grateful."

"I missed them, even when I didn't know it. Even Mr. Gravestone." I took off the glove and handed her two of the plates and went back for the others. "They're all special. Family. I didn't realize how important you all were to me when I was here before. I'm slow to catch on."

"Not slow," Liona corrected. "Cautious. Careful, Contemplative."

Her words made me feel strong. That's why I liked Liona so much. She made me feel important, kind of the way Uncle Jim did. We carried the dishes to the table and placed them in front of each tenant.

"Good morning, Eddie," Mrs. Benson nodded at me and gave me a big grin. Mrs. Benson would never know me as anyone else but Eddie, so I accepted the role.

"Good morning, Mum," I said. After I set her porridge in front of her, closer to Liona's seat so Liona could feed her, I wrapped her shawl over her shoulders and gave her a hug. Next to the oatmeal I then put a small bowl of peeled and cooked apples spiced with cinnamon, and a dollop of yogurt which was a product of my magic.

"You are so sweet," Mrs. Benson patted my hand. "Always thinking of your dear old mum."

I gave her a kiss on the cheek.

I returned to the kitchen and brought back Mr. Gravestone's breakfast. His were the more difficult dishes. Scrambled eggs with a touch of chives, toast, and he couldn't decide on sausage or bacon so to avoid an

237

argument with himself, I cooked up both and put them on separate plates, a magical garnish of parsley. No special thanks from him, but I understood.

Mr. Bromheimer was happy with the omelet Liona served him, toast, and hash browns.

"Thank you, Dylan. Fine meal, as always."

"Thank you, Mr., Bromheimer," I said.

He took my hand as I brushed by and drew me closer to him. "Do me a favor after breakfast," he whispered in my ear.

"What's that?"

"Give me a neck massage while I'm playing chess with the old geezer." He winked. I peered at Mr. Gravestone. "He's been winning way too many games. It's getting to his head!"

"I will give you a neck massage, Mr. Bromheimer. However, I can't guarantee the outcome of your game." Liona smiled at me. She knew what we were talking about. "Maybe though."

"Good boy," he said.

I patted him on the back.

I made Mrs. Healy breakfast too. Of course, our new tenant ate like a queen, we were so lucky to have her home again.

"Coffee, Mrs. Wright?" I asked. She held out her cup and winked at me with her left eye.

After I had poured Mrs. Wright's coffee, I slipped back into the kitchen and fixed a large cup of hot cocoa in the biggest mug I could find. I pulled out the whipped cream and carefully formed a heart in the center, and sprinkled cinnamon on top.

I reached in my pocket. Among the fragments of seashells and sand I found the pearl I had made on the beach that day, the one I was going to give Liona. I set the pearl on the saucer atop three perfectly formed mint leaves that I have mustered from magic.

I brought the cup to the table and set my gift in front of Liona.

She caught my eye, hers twinkled and she smiled, mouthing the words, "Love you," to me.

Chills traveled up my spine. I nodded and then sat at the table across from Mr. Gravestone, satisfied that I had found what I really wanted in life, just like Uncle Jim wanted me to.

Acknowledgments

Thank you to the many people who helped bring this story about including my editors ManuFixed i.e. Samantha Bohrman and Cristina Pippa. Thank you to Kitsap Transit for allowing me to serve the wonderful disabled folks of our community and to learn about them. Thank you to my critique partners Patricia Stricklin, Carol Caldwell and Penny Percenti for your insight, suggestions and encouragement! And thank you my husband Stephen Gardner who supports me through all my projects.

About the Author

D.L. Gardner artist, author and screenwriter writes primarily fantasy novels including all sub genres. Her latest book is historical romance. She's a lover of the classics, both visual and literary and believes a story should be good enough to hand down from one generation to the next.
Winner of Book Excellence Award, Best Urban fantasy at Imaginarium Convention, and a host of screenings and trophies for the historical fiction screenplay Cassandra's Castle

Visit her website http://gardnersart.com for more information about her books, audio books, artwork and more
Other works by D.L. Gardner
Ian's Realm Saga * Diary of a Conjurer
Cassandra's Castle * Lost in Taikus
Pouraka * Altered
Thread of a Spider
Where the Yellow Violets Grow

www.ingramcontent.com/pod-product-compliance
Lightning Source LLC
Chambersburg PA
CBHW020559030726
47497CB00007B/2016